Warrior Betrayed

"An action-packed and emotionally charged good time."
—The Romance Dish

"Will delight paranormal romance lovers ... Fox weaves mythology and romance into a fun-filled adventure."
—*Romantic Times*

Warrior Avenged

"Sexy immortal warriors ... powerful love stories."
—Risqué Reviews

Warrior Ascended

"Fox debuts with a strong start to the Sons of the Zodiac series ... [a] powerful romance."
—*Publishers Weekly*

"This new series puts a delightful twist [on] the Greek gods and the myths surrounding them. Each character has [his or her] own depth and talents that will keep you turning the pages and begging for more. A great start to a promising paranormal series!"
—Fresh Fiction

"This book was a blast to read; combining paranormal romance, enjoyable heroes and heroines, and globe-traveling intrigue kept me turning the pages."
—Errant Dreams Reviews

"Promise[s] plenty of action, treachery, and romance!"
—*Romantic Times*

Also by Addison Fox

Baby It's Cold Outside

An Alaskan Nights Novel

Addison Fox

A SIGNET ECLIPSE BOOK

SIGNET ECLIPSE
Published by New American Library, a division of
Penguin Group (USA) Inc., 375 Hudson Street,
New York, New York 10014, USA
Penguin Group (Canada), 90 Eglinton Avenue East, Suite 700, Toronto,
Ontario M4P 2Y3, Canada (a division of Pearson Penguin Canada Inc.)
Penguin Books Ltd., 80 Strand, London WC2R 0RL, England
Penguin Ireland, 25 St. Stephen's Green, Dublin 2,
Ireland (a division of Penguin Books Ltd.)
Penguin Group (Australia), 250 Camberwell Road, Camberwell, Victoria 3124,
Australia (a division of Pearson Australia Group Pty. Ltd.)
Penguin Books India Pvt. Ltd., 11 Community Centre, Panchsheel Park,
New Delhi - 110 017, India
Penguin Group (NZ), 67 Apollo Drive, Rosedale, Auckland 0632,
New Zealand (a division of Pearson New Zealand Ltd.)
Penguin Books (South Africa) (Pty.) Ltd., 24 Sturdee Avenue,
Rosebank, Johannesburg 2196, South Africa

Penguin Books Ltd., Registered Offices:
80 Strand, London WC2R 0RL, England

First published by Signet Eclipse, an imprint of New American Library,
a division of Penguin Group (USA) Inc.

First Printing, November 2011
10 9 8 7 6 5 4 3 2

For Kerry Donovan

I only thought I was excited to work on this book—
and then I was lucky enough to work on it with you.

Chapter One

New York City
The Sunday after Thanksgiving

*J*ane Austen had it wrong, Sloan McKinley thought miserably as the black Lincoln Town Car drove her ever closer to the bright lights of the George Washington Bridge and the Manhattan streets she called home. A man in possession of a good fortune only wanted to get laid.

Of course, she thought reflectively, that made rich men really no different from the poor ones.

Despite the fact that dear old Jane was being cheeky in her pronouncements on the proclivities of wealthy young bachelors, Sloan knew her point was valid all the same.

What she didn't know was why her mother thought an endless parade of Scarsdale's finest was going to be the answer to her daughter's walk down the aisle.

She'd known these men since birth—had played Little League soccer with them, dissected frogs in science class as lab partners and attended the prom together. She knew who had been a bad loser, who had stuffed frog parts inside the principal's tote bag and who had puked outside their limo after the prom.

Sadly, she *knew* these guys. None of them had developed any mind-blowing, irresistible qualities as they matured. Sloan hadn't wanted any of them at fifteen and not much had changed.

Case in point: one Trevor Stuart Kincaid the Fourth—Trent to all who knew and loved him. If the asshole stuck his hand on her knee and allowed his pinky finger to creep up her inner thigh one more time, she was likely to go all Terminator on his Armani-covered ass.

And to think she had actually been looking forward to seeing him.

"I'm glad your mother suggested this. It's a far more enjoyable drive back to the city with company."

"She's full of ideas." Sloan shifted yet again, firmly pushing his fingers away as his other hand inched closer on the backseat. "So tell me about what you've been working on. That hotel you designed in Seattle is absolutely magnificent."

"The Dahlia?" His bloodshot eyes sparkled for a moment under the reflected lights of the streetlamps and a surge of hope filled her. She'd visited the hotel shortly after it had opened and had been impressed that it was designed by someone she'd known since childhood.

It had been that spark—that innate belief that who you were at fifteen *didn't* dictate who you were forever—that she'd been desperately searching for since Trent had arrived at her parents' for dinner.

"It's a sweet gig. They're paying me to design a sister hotel in Malaysia, so I can't complain. Speaking of sweet gigs"—he let the words hang there for a moment before leaning closer—"why haven't we ever gone out, you and me?"

Perhaps because Mitzi Goodby shared with our entire class at our fifteen-year reunion just how shitty you were in bed, how you enjoy the occasional cocaine bender and that you are a bad tipper. But Sloan said none of that and instead opted for, "I think we've likely just been in different places in our lives."

"It looks like we're in the same place now."

"We're probably not as close as you think."

"We can easily fix that."

Sloan caught the driver's raised eyebrows in the rearview mirror and shot him a glare. While she knew she wasn't in any danger—Trent was a world-class jerk with opportunistic hands, but that was about it—she also knew most people saw only what they wanted to see when they looked at her. Blond hair, all-American blue eyes and a slender five-foot-eight-inch frame had a way of doing that to a person.

The gangly, ugly duckling Trent must remember from high school—which was one of the many reasons they never *had* been in the same place—had been replaced on the surface by a swan.

But it was the duckling that Sloan couldn't seem to shake loose.

People thought they were so discreet, but Sloan knew how she was discussed in her family's social circle. The only daughter of Forrest and Winifred McKinley had been *saved*, according to the wealthy matrons of Westchester, by the overpowering influence of genetics. The gawky teenager had long ago been replaced by a grown woman with poise, intelligence and flawless skin, a fact for which her mother would be forever grateful.

What Winnie wasn't grateful for, however, was the fact that her only daughter was still unmarried at the oh-so-advanced age of thirty-three.

Oh, the *horror*.

So whatever fears her mother had harbored when Sloan was a teenager—that she'd never catch a husband, have children and take Winnie's place as one of the movers and shakers of Scarsdale—were still firmly in place. And—Sloan couldn't help but dwell on it—she'd become the town charity case to boot, based upon an overheard conversation between her mother's best friends—Betsy and Mary Jo—just before everyone sat down to Thanksgiving dessert.

The memory of that whispered conversation still rang in her ears, no matter how hard Sloan tried to fight it.

"You know Winnie's just been sick over this. I mean, can you imagine? She went to her reunion alone."

"Oh, Mary Jo, it's just so sad. Sara told me when she brought the twins over the other day that Sloan was the only one in their entire class who didn't have a date."

"It's not natural. What's wrong with that girl?"

"You know she's always been independent."

"Independent is having a cocktail by yourself at the Plaza before your lunch date arrives. Not going to your high school reunion alone."

Sloan unclenched the tight fists that had formed at the memory, as the bite of her nails digging into her skin finally registered.

The fact she'd given the overheard comments more than a few minutes of her time was growing tiresome and Sloan was hard-pressed to understand why she couldn't let them roll off her back. She knew she had more to offer the world than her uterus. And despite the fact she fervently hoped to put it to good use someday, it wasn't the only body part she had that worked.

"So what are you doing this week? I've got Coldplay tickets for the Garden on Wednesday night." Trent's invitation pulled her back from her maudlin holiday memories.

What would be the harm in going on a date? Sloan wondered. *Except for the bad tipping and the drugs,* she amended as a quick reminder.

Still—some good music, a nice evening out. A quick glance at Trent's clueless face and overheated gaze and she knew what the harm would be.

She wasn't interested—in Trent or the myriad ways he spent his time—and she'd long ago stopped trying to fake it.

Sloan was prevented from having to craft a polite refusal by a buzzing from her coat pocket. She pulled out her cell phone and quickly forgot Trevor Stuart Kincaid the Fourth as she read the message from her best friend, Grier.

SOS. DESPERATE FOR HELP. ANY CHANCE YOU CAN COME TO ALASKA AND SAVE ME? THIS WHOLE INHERITANCE MESS HAS GONE OFF THE RAILS.

Trent gazed at the phone, a mixture of irritation and jealousy filling his features. Sloan hit reply and tossed a brief apology at the problem. "A friend of mine. Her father passed away and she's dealing with his estate."

"Oh. That's too bad." His tone was flat with irritation, but she'd managed to stamp out the jealousy.

"It is a shame. It was very unexpected. Sorry. Just give me a minute." Sloan tapped out a quick text of her own.

WHAT'S GOING ON? I THOUGHT THE LAWYER SAID THINGS WERE MOVING ALONG FINE. P.S. MOM'S STRUCK AGAIN. YOU'LL NEVER GUESS WHO I'M SHARING A CAR BACK TO THE CITY WITH.

Sloan hit SEND and turned her attention back to Trent. Her exit was coming up soon and now was the time to firmly extricate herself from whatever ideas her mother had put in Trent's head. "Thanks for sharing the car with me."

"So you never answered me on the Coldplay tickets. You up for it?"

"I'm sorry, Trent. It's a full week workwise, so I should pass."

"I'm sure you can get out on the town for one night. The concert doesn't even start until eight."

"Yeah, but I really shouldn't."

The chiseled features that had been distantly annoyed veered straight toward pissed off, evidenced by the narrowed eyes and tightly drawn lips. "Seriously?"

"I'm sorry?"

"I really don't get it. Your mom makes this huge fuss about coming over to dinner. We take a car back to the city together. What the hell am I supposed to think?"

"Um. That two people who've known each other since they were five shared a ride home?"

Trent ran a hand through his perfect hair. "What a fucking joke. You come on to me all night and don't follow through?"

A slow burn started low in her stomach, her rising anger the culmination of a long weekend full of subtle clues saying she was a failure in the only area her family chose to place value. "Again, all that happened is we shared a car. If you thought that was a come-on it's not my fault."

"High-society bitches. It figures."

Sloan abstractly heard the ringing bell of her phone, letting her know another text message had come in, but she ignored it.

How dare he?

When it was roaming hands hoping to get lucky and a few suggestive comments, she could handle it. But *this*? To borrow his phrase—*seriously*?

"Look. Whatever impression my mother gave you isn't my fault. I know *I* wasn't the one giving off vibes I was interested."

The car had come to a stop outside her building and she could hear the driver opening the trunk for her luggage. Trent's face was a cold mask of irritation and indifference. "Whatever. Your mother wonders why you're not married. You can't even go on a date you're so fucking repressed. We've arrived at your castle. Have a nice life, Princess."

The door opened and she knew the prudent thing to do was to ignore the barb, get out of the car and go home.

Fuck prudence, her subconscious taunted as she slipped out of the car.

"Oh, Trent," she crooned as she leaned over and stuck her head back in. "There are about three thousand reasons why I'm not asking you up for a drink this evening. But there's one reason—above all the others—that you should know."

"What reason is that, Princess?" he sneered as he kept his gaze on his cell phone.

"It's your penis."

That got his attention as his eyes snapped from his phone to her. "Excuse me?"

"Aside from its less-than-impressive size, the way I hear it, all that cocaine's ruining your ability to wield it. Maybe you should think about that next time you start shoving a thousand dollars' worth of powder up your nose. Ta-ta, darling."

She slammed the door on her own, before the driver could take care of it. Sloan didn't miss his broad smile before she slipped him an extra twenty on top of the tip already sitting on her mother's credit card.

"Sloan, he's a slimy bastard. He's just pissed you didn't want to have sex with his sorry ass."

The tears had stopped over an hour ago, leaving behind the fatigue of a good crying jag, coupled with raw, angry frustration. Even now, Sloan wondered why she'd let him say those things.

And why she was even bothering to give Trevor Stuart Kincaid the Fourth another second of her time.

"Yeah, well, we can thank my mother for whatever expectations she put in his head. Hell, she's so desperate at this point she probably implied I haven't had sex in five years."

"It's not any of her business anyway, even if it were five days." Thank God for Grier. Her champion, no matter what the subject.

It had only been two years, Sloan thought defensively, not five.

Well, shit.

Had it really been two years?

A quick mental tally indicated her math was correct. And the knowledge only added to the uprising of gloom Trent had managed to unleash. Firmly tamping down on the rampaging self-pity, she turned her focus to her friend.

"So what, exactly, is going on up there?"

"Where do I start?" Grier quickly got her up to speed on the rapidly deteriorating inheritance battle she was waging in her father's adopted hometown of Indigo, Alaska. "So there you have it. A contested will, barricaded from entering his home and the cold shoulder from every single person I've met in this damn town."

"What does the lawyer say about it? Shouldn't this be more straightforward? It's an inheritance, for Pete's sake." Sloan hesitated for a moment, but decided since it was Grier she'd keep on going. "I mean, do you think he's qualified to handle this? He *is* practicing in the middle of nowhere."

"No, he really has been wonderful. And he seems as puzzled as I am by the town's reaction."

"What have they taken sides about? It's nobody's business but yours and your father's."

"Well, there is this other thing."

"What other thing?" Sloan recognized that tone in Grier's voice—a mix of panic and nervous laughter—as exhaustion and it all fell into place.

Things were far worse than her friend had been letting on.

"I have a sister."

"You what?"

"I have a half sister named Kate."

Sloan almost dropped the phone. "You have a sister and it took you this long to tell me?"

"She's the holdup. She claims I don't have a right to my father's estate."

"Um, isn't it called a will for a reason? He willed it to you."

"Well, the will was changed relatively recently and she's making a fuss."

"And your lawyer can't do anything? You can't even get in to see your father's things?"

"Nope. While it's moving through the legal system, neither of us can touch anything. That's why I'm still at the hotel."

Sloan refrained from pushing harder on the lawyer angle, trusting her friend's judgment on that front. "So tell me about this sister of yours."

"From what I can tell, she's about as warm as a python, and instead of the term 'sister,' I think 'bitch' would be far more appropriate."

"Are you sure it's not just her grief talking? I mean, she presumably knew the man."

"I wish," Grier snorted, her disgust more than evident despite the three thousand miles separating them. "That I could understand. I could even sympathize if it made her prickly, but the attitude I'm getting is just way off the charts. She's actively waging a campaign to alienate me."

"Have you tried talking to her?"

Grier never had any problems winning anyone over, her effervescent personality drawing people to her like a lodestone. Sloan knew grief drove some strange behavior, but the idea that Grier's sister was purposefully shutting her out was hard to understand. If she was mourning the loss of a father, shouldn't she try to accept a new-found relative?

"Oh, Sloan, I've tried everything on the rare occasions I can even get her to look at me. Friendship. An appeal to sisterhood. Hell, I've even tried to boss her around as her older sister. *Nothing* works. And since the entire damn town's on her side I can't get anywhere. Whoever said small towns were interested in newcomers was smoking crack. These people won't give an inch."

"They won't talk to you? What about your side of the story?"

Grier snorted. "The entire town communicates with me as little as possible. Everyone except for my lawyer cuts me a wide swath."

"The cold shoulder treatment in hopes you'll pack up and go home."

"If they only knew how little I had to go home to," Grier murmured, before adding, "Besides you, of course. And we can't forget my mother and those biannual occasions she chooses to take an interest in her only child."

Sloan couldn't stop the memory of the car ride home from intruding on their conversation. She thought back to the self-pity she'd indulged in an hour before. She might be entitled to a private moment here or there, but her night was nothing compared to what her friend was dealing with.

"So what do you say? Will you come up here and help me? You could call it research and use it to put together an article or two."

The offer was more tempting than Sloan cared to admit, and Grier had a point. Although she was fortunate with steady work, the life of a freelancer meant she was always looking to line up more. A trip to Alaska could be some good fodder for a few articles. She'd just talked to a travel editor a few weeks ago who was looking for some fun pieces with a unique twist.

Alaska.

Miles and miles away from *here*.

"I'm in."

"What?"

Now that the words were out, Sloan couldn't shake a sudden sense of optimism. She was filled with the certainty that this was not only a good choice, it was the *right* one. And it was a chance to do something out of the ordinary. And unexpected.

And it was something *she* wanted to do.

"I'll book my flight in the morning."

"You really mean it?"

Sloan couldn't stop the small laugh from escaping. "Don't sound so surprised."

"I guess I never thought—" Grier broke off and Sloan heard it. That slight hitch of indrawn breath that said her dearest friend was holding back tears.

It confirmed she was making the *exact* right choice.

"This is going to be so much fun. We'll put on our very best New York charm and work it. The people of Indigo aren't going to know what hit them."

As she hung up the phone a few minutes later, Sloan couldn't stop the flutter of hope that filled her stomach.

Maybe a trip to the middle of nowhere was just what the doctor ordered.

"Are you about done putting that woman through her paces?" Sophie Montgomery demanded of her grandson. She'd been following his work with rapt fascination, and the latest situation—what to do about the estate of one Jonas Winston—was going to get a hell of a lot uglier before it got better.

"Grandma, you know I can't discuss someone's private business with you," Walker Montgomery said on a sigh. "It's called lawyer-client privilege."

"As the mayor of Indigo, I have a right to know what's going on with my townsfolk. Especially when those townsfolk have taken such a personal interest in the situation."

Walker held back a disrespectful snort, but wouldn't back down on his point. "Your townsfolk take a personal interest in *everything*. And frankly, you only have a right to know about the things your constituents choose to tell you. Seeing as how neither Kate nor Grier have shared anything with you, I'd say that's a pretty sizable clue you don't have a right to know and are just being nosy."

Sophie did snort at that. "I'm not nosy."

Walker leveled her with a direct stare. The dark chocolate brown eyes that stared back at him were so similar to his own he could have been looking in a mirror. "Yes, you are. Just like every other person in this damn town."

"Fine. I'm quite sure I can find out whatever I need to know from someone else."

Walker wasn't so sure about that. Grier Thompson was a tough one. The petite frame and large doe eyes hid a spirit far heartier than her half sister, who'd spent her entire life calling Alaska home. Although he'd admittedly judged Grier as a bit soft, his first impression had rapidly changed over the past month.

The little New Yorker had a spine of steel and she wasn't budging on what she rightfully believed was hers. Certainly not in the wake of the news that she had a sister up here in Alaska, nor the fact that she had to find a way to divide the inheritance from her father with the woman.

Anxious to change the subject, Walker zeroed in on the one topic sure to drag his grandmother away from the relentless gossip she delighted in. Even if he was throwing himself on a sacrificial altar to bring it up. "Why don't you worry about that ridiculous competition you've got going on?"

"It's hardly ridiculous. It's the reason your parents met."

Walker raised his eyes to the ceiling of his grandmother's office. "So you remind me every year."

"And you could meet someone and be equally as happy if you'd open your eyes and look around. Women from all over the Lower Forty-eight have heard about my *ridiculous* competition. This is the third year in a row we've got over thirty entrants."

"Whatever will the Indigo Blue do? Do they have enough rooms?"

"You know very well that hotel was built to accommodate our tourist trade."

Walker couldn't resist one more poke to really get her going. "We have one of those?"

"Oooh. You're a cheeky pain in my ass."

"Yeah, well, it's a rare gift."

"It's genetic," Sophie added matter-of-factly. "You're just like your grandfather."

If she only knew. The man he'd been named for had been a no-nonsense sort of guy who believed as definitively in the law as his grandson did. What his grandson didn't have, however, was an avowed belief in the need to love, honor and cherish one woman for the rest of his days. He could thank his father for that one.

The fact his grandmother couldn't understand why he was happy with his life just the way it was fell squarely into the category of *her* problem, not his. Until early December rolled around each year, and her little competition became *his* problem.

The chatter around town was relentless, coalescing to a fever pitch every time he got within earshot of another person. His grandmother's cronies were the worst, but a new generation had gotten in the game in the last few years as they, too, were anxious to see their daughters paired up.

"That Walker Montgomery, a bachelor to the core."

"Sophie's grandson is harder to pin down than an avalanche on Denali."

"Maybe Walker's just trying to come out of the closet."

Walker Montgomery could not give a shit how anyone else—gay or straight—lived their life. So why the hell wasn't he given the same courtesy?

On a sigh, he pushed off of the large credenza in his grandmother's office, reached for the wool jacket he'd thrown on one of her visitor's chairs and stalked across the room to press a kiss to her cheek. "I'll see you later."

"Are you going to the town hall meeting this evening?"

He nodded as he pushed his arms through the sleeves. "I'll be there."

"I'll see you later, then." His grandmother patted his cheek and pulled his lapels closer. "I love you, Walker Montgomery. Every stubborn inch of you."

He leaned in. "I guess that makes us a matched pair, because I love your stubborn soul to distraction."

She giggled as she bestowed one last kiss to his cheek. "Go on. Get out of here."

It was surprisingly easy to book a trip to the middle of nowhere, Sloan thought with no small measure of amusement as she stepped up into the cold vestibule between train cars.

Grier had peppered her with a nonstop barrage of information and instructions for the past two days as she'd booked her flight and made her travel arrangements. Apparently, a train from Anchorage to Indigo was the recommended mode of travel by the local tourist board.

Sloan couldn't say she was all that upset to miss out on flying in a puddle jumper–sized plane to the town her best friend was presently calling home, but she was admittedly tickled at the idea of a local tourist board.

She knew from her editorial work that Alaska had a booming tourism industry, but a tourist board for a small outpost virtually in the middle of nowhere? It was serious overkill.

The train let out a loud, piercing whistle as they pulled away from the station, and Sloan huddled down in her coat. It was surprisingly cozy in the train car, but she couldn't quite shake the chill that had permeated her after a few moments on the station platform.

She shot a quick text to Grier, letting her know she was on the train and headed her way, then pulled out a book to sink into for the ride. She'd barely gotten through a page when her gaze caught a reflection out the window.

Endless plains of white, snow-covered ground, framed by impossibly tall mountain peaks, were set off by the dusky haze of sunset. Grier had given her a heads-up on the weird daylight she'd find at this time of year—a sort of perpetual twilight that hung around for about five to six hours in the middle of the day before darkness descended for another eighteen.

Her eyes roamed over the landscape again and a small thrill shot through her as she noticed a herd of moose in the distance, their large antlers a distinct identifying marker, as if their long, knobby legs and oversized bodies weren't a dead giveaway. And behind them, growing closer with each passing mile, was the mountain referred to as Denali by the locals.

A small curl of anticipation unfurled low in her belly as Sloan stared at the mountain that dominated the entire landscape. It hadn't escaped her notice they shared a name, and she'd come to think of it as *her* mountain as she'd read up on Alaska over the past few days.

Mount McKinley.

Of course, her mother was anxious for her to get rid of the name and Alaska natives preferred the mountain's given name—Denali—to the politically charged Mount McKinley, so maybe it was apropos she felt this odd kinship.

Or maybe it was just a funny coincidence, she berated herself for her fanciful notions.

A sharp spike of nerves ran the length of her spine as Sloan burrowed down in her oversized sweater—one of five she'd purchased specifically for this trip. The land and the enormous mountain behind it were impossibly beautiful.

And impossibly hard.

How does anyone live here?

She knew that's what people thought about living in a city like Manhattan, but easy transportation, food on every corner and ready access to any type of entertainment imaginable didn't seem nearly as challenging as miles and miles of barren land.

Pulling her gaze from the impressive sight, she turned back to her book. A sense of anticipation filled her in a sudden, steady throb she couldn't ignore and the words lay unread on the page.

Purpose.

It was something that had been missing from her life lately.

This trip had it in spades.

She'd help Grier. She'd pitch a few stories. She'd relax and get out of New York for a few weeks.

The twilight sky spread out on the horizon before her as Sloan turned back to her book.

It was perfect.

Chapter Two

Sloan knew she'd be forever grateful for the random gift of fate that had somehow threaded its way through the decision makers on the residential selection committee at Vassar. Whatever random accident—or star alignment—had been responsible, her college housing department had done her the biggest favor of her life when they placed Grier Thompson as her roommate.

The two of them had already spent two minutes squealing and embracing on the train station platform—the month they'd been apart had felt more like a year.

Sloan gave those slim shoulders—covered with enough layers to make her look like she belonged on the Giants' offensive line—one last squeeze. "Okay. I love you, but I need to go inside. It's freezing!"

"We need to get you a better coat. I told you to pack warm."

"I brought my wool coat."

"You're going to need more than that."

Sloan linked arms with the sister of her heart and hot-footed them to the station's waiting area. "I can already see that."

They moved into the lobby as Sloan awaited the arrival of the heavier bags she'd checked before boarding the train. After a quick look around, she had to admit some surprise at her surroundings.

The station depot was a large, log cabin–like structure, with exposed wood-rail walls and a tall fireplace on the far side of the room. Beautifully woven rugs in varied colors covered the floors, and the waiting room furniture had been designed to keep with the log cabin theme. The seats were oversized and looked—was it really possible?—plush.

"This is quite a place."

"Wait till you see the rest of the town. This isn't even the half of it."

Grier nodded at the waving hand of a man bundled up like he was heading out for a week in the woods and started in his direction. Sloan followed, but not before her eye caught on a large, vinyl sign tied down on the wall above the baggage claim area.

INDIGO WELCOMES ALL OUR FUN-LOVING BACHELOR-ETTES. WE'RE HAPPY TO HAVE YOU.

"Grier." Sloan leaned over and whispered as she pulled a ten out of her wallet. The two suitcases and large overnight bag seemed like an unfair extravagance now that she realized someone had to haul all of it in this weather.

"What?"

"What's this sign about bachelorettes? Am I doomed to be reminded of my single status everywhere I go?"

"It's not for you, silly." Grier dragged the overnight bag onto her shoulder as she reached for the extended handle of one of Sloan's suitcases. "It's for the big competition next week."

"What competition?" Sloan reached for the bag on Grier's arm. "Here. You don't have to drag that around."

"Apparently it's this huge thing where women from all over come and compete for bachelors."

"Oh my God, my mother's influence extends all the way up here."

Grier had set off ahead of her, dragging one of the large suitcases and talking over her shoulder. With no choice but to follow, Sloan dragged her second, equally large suitcase, her carry-on bag from the plane and her overnight bag, which was now strapped to the handles of her suitcase.

"Thankfully it's not your mother's influence, but it is about mothers. From what I can gather, there's a group of close-knit town grandmothers who cooked this up a long time ago and it's stuck."

"You're serious about this? It's a real competition?"

"Serious as a heart attack. They've got something like thirty women signed up for it."

"Wow." What did that say about being single? Were women really so desperate to find love they'd travel to the middle of the wilderness for men? Amend that, Sloan thought as they moved through the open door toward the snow-covered parking lot. The *frozen* wilderness.

And then a quick image of Trent and his groping hands flashed in her mind's eye and Sloan had to grudgingly admit the idea had merit.

Although, as she followed Grier out toward a waiting truck, painted with the logo from the Indigo Blue Inn and Suites, Sloan had to acknowledge that some of the hopeful spirit that had gripped her on the train had fled on lead feet.

Like some huge conspiracy designed to keep the ever-present fact she was single in the forefront of her mind, it looked like Indigo would offer no escape.

It took all of a five-minute ride in the battered truck to get to the Indigo Blue. Sloan shook her head as another preconceived notion was shot to dust as they pulled up in front. The hotel's method of transportation might look as if it belonged in a junkyard, but the hotel was like something out of a movie. The large, lodgelike structure rose several stories into the night sky and was about as wide as a New York City block.

"They use this place as a community space, in addition to as a hotel." Grier added color commentary as they collected Sloan's things.

"There's no town hall?" Sloan had pictured the dedicated denizens of Indigo meeting regularly to discuss everything from spring plantings to waste removal.

"There's one of those, too, but this seems to be a major entertainment destination in town."

Sloan followed Grier into the lobby, stamping her feet on the large mats set up just inside the front hall to capture the elements. "It's beautiful." With a quick glance down at the leather of her boots, she offered a moment of silence at the realization she'd be tossing them before she headed back to New York. And damn it, they were cute boots, too.

At Grier's poke in the arm, Sloan looked away from

the ruined leather of her boots and straight toward the large glass sculptures that covered one wall of the over-sized, rustic hotel lobby.

"Oh my God," Sloan breathed reverently. "Is that Chihuly glass?"

"Yes," Grier confirmed. "Wait till you get a load of this place."

Drawn to the sculptures like a compass to true north, Sloan left her bags and walked toward the glass. Large swooping swirls in bright, vibrant hues of reds and greens, oranges and yellows, blues and purples met her gaze.

Sloan turned to find Grier and another woman right behind her. "Were these commissioned?"

"Sort of." The woman's bright eyes, along with a broad smile, held a distinct note of pride. "They're a gift from my son." With another welcoming smile, the woman stuck out her hand. "I'm Susan Forsyth. I own the hotel."

Sloan offered her hand and a quick introduction in return before turning her attention back to the glass sculptures. "That's a pretty incredible gift."

"He's a pretty incredible young man." With that, Susan gave a warm wave to suggest they come along and headed toward a sullen-looking girl at the counter.

Grier rolled her eyes in the direction of the check-in desk as they followed behind Susan. With a small whisper—*sotto voce*—Grier intoned, "She's been pretty nice to me so far, but she's totally been giving us the evil eye since we walked over toward the glass."

Shifting so she could look at the piece from another

angle, Sloan darted her gaze toward Susan's retreating back, giving the woman a few extra steps to get her out of earshot. "The girl at the counter?"

"Yep."

"What could she possibly be upset about? It's not like we can steal it or anything."

"I'd say it's the fact that *I'm* here, which seems to be a total burr in everyone's ass, but she's been friendly. I don't know. Maybe it's the annual competition."

"Why would she be upset about the competition?" Sloan focused her attention on the earthy-yet-pretty athletic blonde at the counter, then turned her full attention back to Grier. "You'd think they would want to stay as far away from the competition as possible."

"Look at it from her position. I mean, if I were them, I wouldn't be too jazzed to have women from all over coming in here to steal the guys from me."

"True."

Grier's expression turned thoughtful. "Even if they haven't rolled out the welcome mat, I can see how this chafes. It's like they're not good enough so the men have to look outside town. Heck, outside the entire state."

Sloan rolled that one around in her mind, considering it as a story angle. "It *is* sort of insulting."

Grier gave her a speculative look. "I know that tone, Sloan McKinley."

With a big hug, Sloan side-armed her dearest friend and pulled her close. "Yep. You've just given me a brand-new story angle. Let's make friends with her. I want to hear about this event from her point of view. There's an editor who's looking for a story and I think I just found it."

Grier tossed a wry glance back toward the front desk. "I'm not sure that's going to be an easy task." As they stood there, watching the exchange between Susan and the young woman, Grier added, "She doesn't look all that interested in making friends."

"Well, then, let's put on our New York City charm and fix that." Sloan tugged on Grier's arm. "Come on."

Susan gestured to the front desk as they got nearer. "Sloan. Grier. I'd like to introduce you to Avery Marks."

"Welcome to the Indigo Blue." Frost edged Avery's words in the same snotty tone perfected by Saturday-night restaurant hostesses the world over.

"Thank you, Avery." Sloan made a great show of looking around. "It's a beautiful hotel."

"Susan has worked very hard to make it so. And we're all pretty fond of its rustic charm." Her enthusiasm ran around the same level as junior high school kids' for gym.

Sloan kept her smile friendly but didn't try to hide her interest as she sized Avery up. Something else was going on here, and it went way beyond a bit of annoyance at Indigo's annual tourism infusion.

Sloan also didn't think it was bitterness over money, because Avery didn't even blink as she swiped Sloan's platinum American Express for the room.

So what did have the resentment blooming all over Avery's face?

"Thanks for everything, Susan," Grier added. "Sloan and I will just get settled in and freshened up before the town hall."

Susan shot a pointed look at Avery that wasn't quite

annoyance, yet held a distinct note of dissatisfaction. "It's our pleasure, dear. I'm actually going to head over to the town hall myself. My mother-in-law asked if I'd help her get ready."

As soon as Susan was out of earshot, Sloan went in for the kill. For reasons she couldn't quite explain, even to herself, she felt a kinship with the sullen woman. Sort of like the odd kinship she felt for Denali.

Both were unforgiving.

And, oddly enough, Sloan found she liked it.

Leaning over the desk, she shot Avery a friendly, sisterly smile. A smile that promised bonding over ice-cream sundaes. A smile that said, we're all in this together. A smile that said I'm hell-bent on making you a friend, whether you want one or not.

"Give it to me straight, Avery. You've given us the evil eye since we walked into this place. So who lit the fuse on your tampon and what's it going to take to prove neither of us is the enemy?"

"You sure you want me to open another bottle?" Avery asked, her brown eyes narrowed in question. "The town hall starts in fifteen minutes."

"Definitely." Sloan and Grier's voices rang out in unison.

"I work in magazine publishing," Sloan added. "I *know* how to hold my liquor. Besides, what we don't finish now we can pick up when we get back."

Avery shrugged, then got up and crossed to the lobby bar, a big laugh racking her shoulders. "I still can't believe you said that."

Grier raised her half-full glass and added a merry chortle to Avery's. "Me, too. Seriously, Sloan. That's a real classy way to get to know someone."

Sloan felt a small blush creep up her neck. "Well, I wanted to make an impression."

Avery uncorked a new bottle of cabernet and walked back toward them, fresh glasses in hand. "You managed that."

"You just looked all stuffy. And I figured I'd either insult you or make you laugh. I'm glad it's the latter. And, for what it's worth, I meant what I said. Neither of us is the enemy."

"I'm glad, too." Avery smiled as she poured, sincerity riding high in the depths of her eyes. "And I can tell."

As Avery finished the pours, Grier started peppering her with questions. "Tell us about this competition. I've been seeing signs for the past month, but since I'm persona non grata around here, there haven't been a lot of people to ask."

Avery winced at that. "Kate's been making it pretty hard for you."

Grier downed the last of her existing glass and reached for the new one. "You could say that again. That woman is a wicked iceberg with sharp edges."

"I'd like to tell you she'll come around, but . . ." The word hung there between the three of them as Avery reached for her own glass. "Kate Winston came into this world a prickly bitch and not much changes her direction when she's decided she doesn't like someone. Seeing as how you're directly in line to take something she wants, that makes you public enemy number one."

"Fabulous. Just freaking fabulous. I can't go home and I'm not welcome here."

Sloan patted Grier's arm, surprised her friend had even hinted at the incident that had her fleeing New York and heading for the Alaska wilds.

Not sure if it was the liquor causing her friend's tongue to loosen or a month of loneliness and rejection, Sloan decided a change in topic might keep Grier from saying anything else she might regret later. "So this bachelorette thing. What's it about?"

"It's all cooked up by the town grandmothers."

"Is this one of the women Susan just mentioned helping out at the town hall?"

"Yep." Avery nodded. "Exactly. Julia Forsyth, who is Susan's mother-in-law. Then there's Mary O'Shaughnessy and Sophie Montgomery. Three more determined women you will never meet."

Any number of images filled her mind's eye, but Sloan just couldn't understand why a bunch of old women would be interested in such a thing. "What could these women possibly care about a bachelorette competition? It sounds like something cooked up by a beer distributor for Friday-night wet T-shirt contests."

"They care because they have three grandsons." Avery leaned forward and reached for her wineglass, a dark mask descending across her gaze. "Three very *eligible* grandsons."

"This is all an exercise to get their grandsons married?" Grier's eye widened. "This big thing they keep talking about that's so great for tourism is all about getting these guys married off?"

"Pretty much," Avery agreed. "And from what I've heard, all three ladies are spitting mad it hasn't paid dividends yet."

"Does it bother you?" Sloan swirled the rich red wine around in her glass and watched as the long legs coating the bowl reflected the light from the lobby's oversized fireplace.

Avery's eyes narrowed. "Does what bother me?"

"This whole thing. That women come from around the country to snatch up eligible bachelors from *your* town."

Avery's eyebrows told Sloan all she needed to know, even before her pointed words. "Is this the magazine writer talking? Or my newfound friend?"

Sloan leaned forward and laid a hand on Avery's forearm. "I'm a friend first. And the whole 'come up here to find a bachelor thing' sort of has me a bit freaked out, even as I'm intrigued. So yeah, this conversation is off the record. And when I do want something on the record, I'll make sure to tell you."

Avery breathed a soft sigh as her shoulders relaxed. "All right. To tell you the truth, it doesn't bother us nearly as much as we'd like people to think. The local girls, we all subscribe to the code and act like it's a serious affront so everyone goes out of their way to treat us well. But truly—we women of Indigo—we're a hearty bunch. Most of us aren't afraid to go after the men we want."

"Most?" Grier added.

Avery's smile was tinged with sadness. "Most."

Grier just nodded. "Believe me. Sometimes you're better off not chasing. Or forgiving, come to think of it. I've come to the educated conclusion it lets a man get off way too easily."

"No doubt." Sloan waved her glass at her best friend. If Grier was going to spill the deets on that one, it wasn't her place to stop her.

At Avery's questioning glance, Sloan added, with a nod in Grier's direction, "I believe she means 'get off' in the literal sense."

"Aha." Their new friend nodded sagely over her wine and Sloan knew there had been some chasing in Avery Marks's past. What she also knew was that now wasn't the time to go poking at wounds that clearly hadn't healed.

Sloan glanced toward the lobby door. "So I guess we should probably bundle up for the walk to the town hall."

"You really want to go?"

She'd known Grier far too long not to notice the reluctant tone in her voice. "Let me guess. Your newly discovered half sister will be there."

"Yeah." Grier stared miserably down into her wine.

"Well, then I definitely want to go."

"Are you sure? We can sit here and drink more wine and gossip."

"Oh no. I'm going." Sloan stood, pleased to see her boast had been correct. Three glasses of wine and she could still stand tall on her stilettos.

"You sure about this?" Avery asked, standing up to

collect their spoils. "I can store all this until you get back, or we can just stay right here and enjoy our cozy little wine klatch."

"Nope." Sloan grabbed Grier's discarded coat from a nearby couch arm and shoved it at her. "Come on, Grier. Let's go light Kate's fuse."

Chapter Three

Walker adjusted the microphone and watched as the Montgomery Meeting and Recreation Center filled up with the citizens of Indigo, Alaska, population seven hundred and twelve.

No matter how old he got or how many years he lived here, there was something odd about seeing your name associated with large gathering places. And while it might have been in tribute to his grandfather, he was the one who carried the name now.

"Is everything ready, dear?" His grandmother stepped near the podium. She'd just finished up a conversation with the two women he considered her partners in crime—Julia Forsyth and Mary O'Shaughnessy—and a broad smile creased her face into warm, welcoming lines.

"Yep. Just as you like it, Mayor Montgomery. Your adoring fans await."

His grandmother swatted him on the arm. "You try saying that without the cheek next time."

Walker leaned over and flipped the switch to ON, unable to hold back the smile. He did love to tease his grandmother. Partly because she was so easy to trip up and partly because she enjoyed it so much. "You're on."

As the reading of the last meeting's minutes washed

over him—a recap of the town budget, whether to do an expansion of the high school's locker room at the hockey rink and how to deal with an errant moose who had been making a nuisance of himself in the wee hours of the morning at Patty's General Store—Walker found his usual seat at the back of the room.

He had a quick handshake with Mary's grandson, Mick O'Shaughnessy, and then dropped onto the cold, unforgiving metal of a shiny folding chair. Before he could answer his friend's whispered "Yo," Walker's gaze caught on about a mile of blond hair a few rows in front of them.

Long, artful waves tripped down her back, and even without a view of her face, Walker knew he'd never seen the woman before.

His grandmother's voice filled the meeting hall as she moved from a reading of the minutes into new business, but Walker heard none of it. All he saw was the long luscious fall of hair as he waited for the woman to turn her head.

Who was she?

From the corner of his eye his gaze snagged on Mick's fists, where they were balled on his knees. "You okay, buddy?"

"Hmmm?" His old friend was looking in the same direction Walker had been.

Was Mick as enamored with the blonde as he was?

And how in the hell had he managed to channel his high school self and get angry at that fact?

"You okay?"

"Yeah." Mick nodded his head ever so slightly at the women.

"So why do you look like you're ready to do battle with Patty's moose?" At his friend's wry stare, Walker added, "And who's the woman who's got you all torqued up?"

"I don't know who the blonde is, but the little ball of fire next to her is Grier. Jonas Winston's daughter."

Walker heard the barely suppressed note of longing in his friend's voice and felt his stomach muscles unclench. "I know who Grier is. I've been representing her."

Mick rubbed a hand over the three days' growth of beard on his face, then turned to face him. "Right. Right."

"They seem awfully tight."

Mick's gaze returned to the women. "The blonde just arrived today. It was all anybody over at the landing strip could talk about. They were rather offended seeing as how she took the train up from Anchorage."

Ah, yet again, the small-town grapevine was in full swing. How could he have thought it would be anything but ripe with information?

"Maggie needs to get that stick out of her ass and spend a bit more time focused on air traffic control and a little less time on gossip. The train ride up is beautiful and a hell of a lot easier on the stomach for a newbie."

Mick held up his hands, but a small smile played at the corner of his lips. "I've had far too many pukers to argue with that."

"So do you know who she is?"

"Grier's friend from New York. That's about all I know. Since the entire town's taken Kate's side, no one's bothered to talk to Grier. Therefore, no one's got the gossip on exactly who the friend is or why she's here."

"Maggie must be dying to know the details."

Mick nodded, the smile moving into a full-on grin. "Pretty much. I'm hard-pressed to complain since it's taken her attention firmly off the grandmothers' competition."

As if on cue, Sophie's comments to the assembly shifted into a series of instructions for the coming days.

Walker let out a light groan. "Every time I think they're going to give this damn game up, they ratchet up the stakes. Do you know my grandmother actually tried pitching this to the morning shows?"

"Tried?"

"Editorial killed it at the last minute."

"You know why?"

Walker thought about the discreet phone calls he made to a few old friends from college. "Let's just say I still know a few people and know how to pull a few strings."

"Fuck me," Mick whispered. "That fancy Ivy League education of yours is clearly good for something."

Walker settled back in his chair, his gaze unwillingly drawn again to Grier's friend. "Damn straight. I may choose to live in the wilderness, but I've made sure my contacts extend far beyond here."

"I really don't know what's gotten into you." Grier's heavy whisper floated over Sloan as she resettled herself on a hard metal folding chair. She'd already introduced herself to five older couples and three teenage boys dressed in full hockey gear who'd seemed impressed with the attention.

"You text me four days ago with a desperate SOS message to come help you. That's what I'm doing. Helping you."

"You call this help?" Grier managed to maintain a whisper, but her darting eyes had the slightly glazed look of a pixie on a wine bender.

Good.

It was about damn time Grier had someone to share the burden with.

"Seriously, Sloan. Attending the town meeting of an entire city full of people who'd like nothing more than to see the back of me as I walk out of here? Oh yeah. This is a great idea."

"You're showing your interest in the community and its well-being and you're meeting some people in the process. How could that be a bad thing? Besides, it's all Kate's fault you're in this mess."

"Actually"—Grier waved her hand—"it's technically my absentee father's fault."

"True. But putting that aside, everyone seems quite lovely. Chooch and Hooch are absolutely darling, and I love the fact they're celebrating their fiftieth anniversary. Could you imagine?"

Grier nodded, a small smile breaking through the mask of anxiety that tightened her bow-shaped mouth. "It is pretty amazing."

"Besides." Sloan took a surreptitious glance around

the rapidly settling room. "We need to make the town realize that *you're* the sister they need to side with. I think this is a damn good place to start."

The more Sloan thought about it, the more she had warmed up to the idea. Grier wasn't the problem. Her rotten sister was. Speaking of which . . .

Where was this sainted martyr who the whole town had sided with?

Reaching back to fiddle with her coat, discreetly rearranging it on her chair, Sloan allowed her gaze to roam the room with a bit more focus. She started with the back, having already realized the majority of the chairs in front of her were taken by the town's old-timers.

Although she saw several younger townsfolk, no one face stood out as a likely sibling. There wasn't one single woman who resembled Grier. And now that she was taking a closer look, Sloan realized no one was even looking their direction. Surely, if Kate were here, she'd be staring daggers at Grier by now.

Sloan continued her quick perusal, knowing she was close to blowing her cover. There was only so long a person could reasonably take to hang their coat behind them, even if you did fiddle with your purse straps around the thick material. She was about to turn back toward the front when her gaze hit a freaking brick wall of masculinity.

The two men sat side by side, their shoulders so broad they'd pushed their chairs apart to accommodate their size. Her gaze roamed over the first, a long, rangy sort with a few days' worth of scruff.

Hot. Definitely.

Her type? Not so much.

Even if he had been her type, Sloan acknowledged a moment later, it wouldn't have mattered once her eyes met those of the large man sitting next to him.

A heavy navy blue sweater framed his broad shoulders and zipped up into a collar that set off his thick throat and hard-planed jaw. A firm nose filled his face— just the wrong side of too large—but oddly, it kept his face from veering into pretty-boy territory.

Oh no, this one screamed one hundred percent male, and there was nothing pretty about him.

There was something magnetic.

Compelling.

Sexual.

But *pretty*? Not a chance.

Sloan swallowed around the lump in her throat and determined to turn herself back around. She'd nearly dragged her gaze away when those molten chocolate eyes of his darkened in interest, his eyebrows winging up.

She felt the answering tug at the corner of her lips, had nearly offered up a large smile when Grier tugged so hard on her arm Sloan was practically thrown sideways.

"What is it?"

Grier's hand tightened on hers, her wide-eyed gaze focused firmly on the doorway. A small, petite brunette a few inches taller than Grier walked in the door.

Even if she hadn't known her best friend for over fifteen years, Sloan would have had no problem pegging the woman who stood in the doorway as her sister. They even walked the same way—head held high as they took a quick look at their surroundings.

They were *perky*, even though Grier hated the word with a passion.

The entire room erupted in a chorus of whispered murmurs. Grier's arch nemesis—and little sister—had just arrived for the town hall.

For all his grandmother's talk about his "advanced age of thirty-six," Walker Royce Montgomery had never actually witnessed a catfight. Based on the tension that had suddenly gripped the room, he suspected the possibility had just gone up considerably that he'd see one before the evening was out.

"I'll lay you odds this isn't going to go very well," Mick intoned in Walker's ear as Sophie's voice continued to drone on from the podium at the front of the room.

"You know I don't take sucker bets."

Walker watched as Kate Winston navigated the room, cherry-picking a seat two rows in front of where her sister sat. The resemblance between the two women was uncanny and, although he was as interested in the drama unfolding as the rest of the room, he couldn't quite tear his gaze away from Grier's friend.

The long blond hair had made him instantly think of a fun-loving beach girl. But it was the hard set of her jaw as Kate took a seat two rows in front of Grier that suggested something else.

A warrior.

An avenging goddess.

Shit, when had he gotten so fucking fanciful? He gave himself a mental slap. She was ready to defend her friend, pure and simple.

His grandmother's voice rose in pitch as she realized her audience's attention was waning. "We'll begin welcoming all the new bachelorettes next Thursday evening."

"Sophie, one of them's already arrived," Chooch McGilvray interrupted from the front. "Hooch and I just met Sloan over there."

Sloan.

Walker rolled it around in his mind, marrying her name to the image of the avenging goddess, and found he liked it.

A lot.

What his grandmother lacked in subtlety, she made up for in good manners and a smooth ability to set anyone at ease. With a broad smile, she gestured their new arrival forward. "Sloan, then. Please come on up here."

A light pink blush crept up Sloan's face, but she stood and moved through the room toward the podium. Walker only felt a brief moment of guilt while watching the sexy glide of her hips as she walked toward the podium in jeans that molded to her firm ass.

"What's your grandmother up to?" Mick's voice nudged him out of his daze.

Walker reluctantly dragged his eyes away from the luscious view and turned toward his friend. "I suspect she's about to make the entire town feel bad about itself."

"What?"

Walker nodded toward the podium. "Just watch."

"Welcome to Indigo, dear. Please tell the folks a bit about yourself."

The flush crept higher, turning Sloan's cheeks a warm pink that only made her glow under the bright lights that spotlighted the front of the room where the town council sat in a row behind the podium. "Hello, everyone. My name is Sloan McKinley."

"And what brings such a lovely young woman like yourself to Indigo?"

"I'm here visiting my best friend, ma'am."

Ma'am.

Walker knew his grandmother's old-fashioned notions about respect and courtesy just shot to attention at that one.

"You mean you're not here to compete in next week's games?"

"Oh no, ma'am. I'm here to visit Grier."

Walker groaned inwardly as *the look* descended over his grandmother's face. He'd spent his entire adult life in receipt of it, that look that said Sophie Montgomery knew far better and was about to poke her nose in exactly where it did *not* belong. "Perhaps Mary, Julia and I can change your mind."

At that suggestion, a loud chorus of wolf whistles went up from the various bachelors scattered throughout the room.

His tolerance for his grandmother's antics evaporated at the obvious interest in Sloan displayed by the bachelors of Indigo. His gaze shifted to her and the small, confused smile riding her features didn't quite say uncomfortable, but it didn't exactly broadcast pleasure at the sudden show of testosterone-laden appreciation.

Nothing could have prepared Walker, though, for what came next.

Sloan McKinley smoothed her hands over her sweater, planted a large smile on her face and turned sweetly toward his grandmother. "I'm not easily convinced, but you're welcome to try."

His grandmother let out a great whoop of laughter and pointed toward the audience. "It looks like you're going to give the bachelors of our fair town a run for their money, whether you compete or not."

"Thank you for the warm welcome, Mayor Montgomery. To show my appreciation, I'd love to get to know everyone. I'm staying over at the Indigo Blue with Grier and we'd love it if you all came on over and joined us in the lobby for a few drinks."

Another loud round of whistles went up and Walker could only imagine the line that was going to form around Sloan McKinley.

With a sideways glance at Mick, he folded his arms across his chest. "Looks like we're headed over to the Indigo Blue for a drink."

Mick's eyes never left the back of Grier's head. "Bring it on, buddy."

Sloan wasn't sure what had possessed her to invite the entire population of Indigo, Alaska, to join her for a drink, but she never regretted acting on impulse and wasn't going to start now.

She'd already been introduced to about twenty more

people as she'd made her way back across the room from the podium to gather her coat. Sophie had clearly seen drinks as a fitting end to the meeting and had struck her gavel before Sloan had even left the stage.

"What are you thinking?" Grier whispered as she kept a smile firmly planted on her face.

"It just came out. Let's call it good instincts."

"But the entire town, Sloan?"

"You wanted to meet people. This is a good way to tell them your side of the story. Besides, people get a hell of a lot nicer once they've had a few drinks in them."

Sloan didn't miss Grier's frown as she bent down to retrieve her purse from underneath her seat. She also didn't miss the conversation that drifted in their direction from several rows away.

"Like buying us off's going to help."

"Her friend sure seems to think so."

The first voice piped up again. "She's awfully persistent. You'd think she'd realize by now we don't want her here. The poor little orphan who thinks she's entitled to something that's not hers. Her father clearly could not have cared less about her. First anyone heard of her was the reading of the will."

Sloan's back stiffened as the words floated toward her. Although the speakers weren't quiet, the women weren't broadcasting their conversation either and Sloan suspected they were unaware their comments had been overheard.

But she *had* heard. And if Grier's frozen position as she leaned down for her purse was any indication, she'd heard, too.

Sloan couldn't stop the wave of nausea that filled her as she immediately found herself back in her parents' kitchen on Thanksgiving.

Those low tones, dripping with false sympathy, smacked far too closely of Betsy and Mary Jo. The dulcet cadence of their words suggested the object of their comments should be scraped off the bottom of a shoe. A warm flush crept across her face and, unlike the slight embarrassment on the stage of the town hall, this had a distinctly different feeling.

Like she was ready to do battle.

Kate Winston came up behind the two women, rapidly shrugging into her padded winter coat. Her voice was stern, but her eyes were focused on Grier. "Come on, Trina, Sherry. Let's get out of here."

Unwilling to leave the subject alone, Sloan turned toward the trio of women. The panic that had immobilized her in her parents' kitchen, making her unable to defend herself to her mother's friends, fled as her concern for Grier took over. "You sure? It sounds like you've all got something to say. There's no time like the present."

Grier stood up, purse in hand, and reached for Sloan's arm. Ignoring the tight grip that suggested she shut the hell up, Sloan kept her gaze level with Kate as she tried to avert her eyes.

"She's not welcome here," one of the women added.

Before Sloan could answer, Kate grabbed the red-head's arm in a gesture surprisingly similar to Grier's. "We're leaving, Trina."

"But you were just—"

"Leaving. Come on. Now."

The pack of women who'd surrounded Kate Winston when she'd sat down followed her out of the room. None but the redhead, Trina, spared them a backward glance.

Was this really what Grier was dealing with up here? "What the fuck is wrong with them?"

Grier dashed at the corners of her eyes. "I don't know and I really don't want to talk about it."

"But, Grier. This is ridiculous. You didn't write your father's will. Hell, you didn't even know the man existed."

"She did."

Sloan caught the misery in Grier's tone. "She did what?"

"She did know my father. Because he was *her* father. Each and every day of her damn life."

"But—" Before she could finish the thought, the large man with the three-day scruff of beard walked up to them. Sloan didn't miss the concern he focused on Grier as his gaze searched her face.

"Everything okay?"

The stiffening of Grier's spine was the only indication she was rattled, but her tone was calm and cool as she turned toward the man. "Everything's fine."

"You sure?"

"Positive."

With that, Grier slammed her purse over her arm and marched determinedly toward the door.

The gesture was so out of character for her friend that Sloan didn't know what to do except follow Grier's retreating form. She tossed a small, apologetic glance toward the guy as she wended her way out of their row of chairs.

As she turned to offer him one last contrite smile, his friend walked up behind him.

The breath caught in her throat as her gaze once again locked with his. Heat suffused her, even as the harsh winds of early December wrapped around her body from the open door.

With one last glance, Sloan turned her attention to Grier. And wished like hell the big guy with the shoulders would choose to spend his evening in the lobby of the Indigo Blue.

Chapter Four

*F*irmly pushing aside the unpleasant moments churned up by Kate's bitchy friends, Sloan went into full-on hostess mode the moment she and Grier returned to the Indigo Blue. She'd play the room, introducing herself to everyone and flashing them her biggest, warmest smile. The one that said Sloan McKinley was both full of girlish charm as well as a damn good time.

Ha.

Fuck Trevor Stuart Kincaid the Fourth and the rest of the Scarsdale assholes who thought she was over the hill *and* a blight on their little high society.

"Do you really think this will work?"

Sloan stood at the bar next to Grier, surveying the townspeople as they filled up the lobby of the Indigo Blue. "Of course it will."

"But you invited the entire town back to the bar to drink for free on your tab."

"Only the ones who were at the town hall."

"Yeah, but I'm sure they called their friends who weren't there to come on down."

Sloan shrugged, unwilling to be deterred. She had a freaking trust fund, for God's sake. It was about damn time she put some of it to good use. "We're mixing with the locals."

"It is sort of like Kate's friend said. You're bribing them."

"Grier! I am not."

"You are, too. And it's not very ..." Grier's voice dropped off as the two large men from the town hall came through the lobby doors.

"Friends of yours?" Sloan couldn't keep the interest out of her voice. She was still surprised Grier had been so cold and unfriendly to them, but she couldn't hide the burst of pleasure that the two men had come to the hotel anyway.

"Not exactly."

"Who are they?"

"Two of the three town grandsons."

Sloan ran through Avery's comments from earlier over wine. "*They're* the grandsons?"

"In the flesh." Avery came up to them from the other side of the bar.

"And the competition's for them?" Grier asked, her gaze never leaving the men.

"Well, let's make no mistake about it," Avery added drily. "The competition's for their grandmothers, who have visions of great-grandbabies. But yes, they're the reason why it's held each year."

"What do the bachelorettes compete for?" Sloan wondered aloud as she tried to be discreet in her observations.

"The competition's actually in two parts. The day is a test of skill for the women. You shoot fake skeet birds, carry pails of water down Main Street. There's even a mini-Iditarod. It's presumably to see if you could survive in Alaska."

"You shoot a lot of birds, Avery?" Sloan couldn't resist teasing.

"Don't you know it. Anyway, then in the evening, things switch to the guys. There's a bachelor auction and dance for the women to bid on the men."

"What do you do with them?" Grier's eyes widened and Sloan couldn't help but giggle.

"It's not a bordello, Grier."

Avery laughed at that one. "No, far from it; although, what happens at the auction stays at the auction, if you know what I mean. But no, the proceeds go toward a town fund for needed items. They've given scholarships out of it, helped out a family who had a fire. Lots of different things. It's for the good of the community."

"That's rather nice," Sloan added, impressed the grandmothers had found a way to make their little hobby useful.

Before she could ask any more questions, Sophie Montgomery approached and asked for a moment of Grier's time. As Sloan watched her friend move to the end of the bar with the mayor, a shot of pride filled her that her plan was working out so well.

Pleased Grier's community inroads were moving along, she turned her attention back toward the two men. With a glance toward Avery, she said, "The grandmothers can't get those two married off?"

Avery leaned over the bar and refilled Sloan's wineglass. "I think it's a matter of neither of them wanting to, despite their grandmothers' best efforts."

"Who's the third one?"

"He doesn't live here anymore."

The tightening of Avery's voice put Sloan on high alert and she deftly ignored the two men who seemed to have taken over the hotel lobby with their very presence. "Where does he live?"

"Your neck of the woods, actually. His name's Roman Forsyth."

Sloan had followed the New York Metros a few years back when she wrote a series on rink bunnies and she still remembered the names of most of the team members. "You mean Roman Forsyth is the third grandson?"

"Yep."

"The NHL MVP two years ago?"

"That would be the one," Avery whispered as she suddenly took an intense interest in polishing a spot on the bar where she'd spilled a few drops of wine.

Sloan wanted to question her further, but saw the bleak, ice-cold heartbreak in the young woman's gaze. "Roman?"

Avery gave a quick nod before heading back toward the opposite end of the bar. Sloan didn't need any more information—the reaction, coupled with the odd remark earlier—told her all she needed to know.

Avery Marks was nursing one hell of a broken heart.

Walker nodded around his longneck, feigning interest in whatever it was his law partner, Jessica McFarland, was saying.

"It's getting uglier by the day, Walker. Isn't there something we can do? Kate's been here a lot longer. She's entitled to stay in her father's home."

"She's got a home and she can stay there until we get this figured out. Until then, the house is under an injunction and neither of them can live there." He turned his gaze on Jess. "You damn well know that, so why the argument?"

"It hardly seems fair."

"We're not tasked to judge what's fair; we're tasked to do our jobs."

"But she just came waltzing up there and thinks she has a right to Jonas's things."

"*She* is Jonas's daughter, Grier." The small burn of annoyance that had dogged him since the start of the case—that Jonas had ignored said daughter for her entire life—shifted into a simmering fire. "And, Jess. If you can't separate your personal feelings from this one, maybe you need to extricate yourself from it."

She held up a hand, her cocktail sloshing dangerously close to the rim of her glass. "You think I can't handle it?"

"I think you need to stop thinking like Kate Winston's friend."

"Easy for you to say."

"It wasn't a suggestion, Counselor." Frustrated that someone he respected as much Jess couldn't separate the small-town life from her job dogged him as he headed for the bar, intent on getting a refill for his beer.

When he had Avery's attention, he pointed to his beer. "I'll have another longneck and snag me one for Mick while you're at it."

He allowed himself to casually look around the large lobby, now packed to the brim with Indigo's finest. Before he could stop himself, his eyes alighted on the woman at the center of this evening's little tête-à-tête.

"You sure can't seem to stop looking at her, Walker Montgomery." Avery's whisper floated over his left shoulder. He turned, careful to keep his manner casual, even as he questioned how she had noticed.

"I'm just taking in the view. And there's a lot to take in this evening, seeing as how we've suddenly got a few party girls in our midst."

"I'd hardly call them party girls. Grier Thompson's been given the bum's rush by this town and her friend just wants to help her break the ice." Avery shot a dark glance across the room at a gaggle of women wrapped in a circle around Kate.

"Kate'll thaw out."

"She's not acting like she'll thaw out." Avery reached under the bar and pulled out a bottle of wine, pouring herself a glass. "In fact, she's getting colder and meaner by the day."

"She's still here drinking the free liquor."

Avery nodded toward a short line of glasses at the bar—two to be exact—holding credit cards wrapped in receipts. "Oh no. She's got her own tab going. Made sure several people saw her do it, too."

Walker shook his head at the small-town politics. Truth be told, they weren't all that different from large-town politics, but it was a lot easier to show your hand up here.

Kate and her friends sashayed to the bar and ordered another round.

Or to show off your hand, Walker thought as the women made another production of ordering on *their* tab. Loudly.

He moved away from the bar, his interest in getting caught up in conversation about the same as getting cornered by a grizzly on his way home. Instead, he moved determinedly in the direction of Grier Thompson and her friend.

Sloan.

Why couldn't he stop thinking about her? It was a name to be whispered in the wash of moonlight coming into his bedroom as his mouth did dark things to her body. A name that matched a woman who fired his interest and drew his attention like a magnet.

Setting a determined path, Walker made his way across the room.

"You're really writing an article?"

Sloan had decided to take the bull by the horns and had inserted herself into Grier's conversation with the mayor. It hadn't taken her long to weave in a small mention of her profession and after that, she could have scripted the discussion, it moved so smoothly to her benefit. "Well, I still have to pitch it, but I think this is exactly what the editor is looking for." Sloan watched the rapturous expression spread across Sophie Montgomery's face and mentally tallied a point in the outsiders' column. It might not be as hard to charm the town of Indigo as Grier had feared.

"What do you mean 'pitch it,' dear?"

"I'm a freelance journalist, Mrs. Montgomery. Although all writers have to pitch their stories, my process is a bit more complex."

"I'm sure it will sell, dear." Sophie patted her arm. "People are awfully interested in what happens up here. I was this close"—the woman squeezed two fingers together, leaving minimal space between them— "to getting one of the morning programs to cover our competition. There's interest. Mark my words."

Sloan certainly hoped so. With an ear to the conversations around her, she allowed the article to take shape in her mind. The people she'd met, even after only three hours, had defied her expectations and she was already excited to do the piece. "That's what I'm planning on, Mrs. Montgomery."

Although the idea for the drink invitation had been pure impulse, Sloan had quickly realized the benefits of the plan.

And it wasn't a bribe, damn it.

Not in the least.

Clearly, she needed to get on the good side of the town if she had any intention of writing a story about them. And it was the perfect excuse to introduce both herself and Grier to everyone, helping to drum up some sympathy on the part of her friend.

While she admired the town's insistence in taking care of one of their own, Grier was one of theirs, too. Jonas Winston had seen to that when he decided to live here. Too bad if Kate had gotten here first. She might have home-court advantage, but Grier was entitled to a shot at the game.

Pasting on a broad smile, Sloan turned her attention to the two women who had moved up next to Sophie to join in the conversation.

The first woman extended a withered hand. Despite her age, the handshake was firm. Solid. And a clear indication that the women who chose to live in Alaska had a hearty bent to them. "I'm Mary O'Shaughnessy. It's lovely to meet you."

"You as well."

Sloan was then introduced to the third member of their triumvirate, Julia Forsyth. "I met your daughter-in-law earlier when I checked in. I understand your grandson's a hockey player."

"Yes, that's my Roman."

"I did an article on the team a few years back. He was having quite the season." Sloan elected not to mention that Roman Forsyth was one of the hockey world's hottest commodities that season, sought after by women from New York to Los Angeles.

"That *was* you." Julia's eyes lit up. "I thought I recognized your name. And thank you for bringing to light the disgusting habits of those rink bunnies. Goodness, you'd think young women would know how to be more subtle than all that."

Sloan nearly choked on her mouthful of wine. Did the woman honestly think the rink bunnies were the only ones to blame? While she'd never had a problem acknowledging the healthy appetites of red-blooded American males, what was with these women? Were they truly so besotted with the image of great-grandbabies that they couldn't honestly assess the somewhat improper behavior of the men they loved so well?

"So the three of you are behind the annual competition?"

Three nodding heads and broad smiles greeted her inquiry.

"When did it start?"

"Oh goodness, we married our sons off with a version of the competition, going on almost forty years ago. But the current competition is about fifteen years old."

Sloan's eyebrows rose at that one. "Wow. That's some longevity."

"Well, it's grown over time," Julia added. "When our kids were young we just sort of added on to an existing town dance we hold every winter. But when our grandsons proved to be so reluctant to settle down, we decided it needed resurrecting."

"Our grandsons are particularly stubborn," Sophie added with a wry glance across the room.

Sloan followed the woman's gaze, not surprised when she locked eyes once again with the large guy from the town-hall meeting. With a slight nod of her head, Sloan added, "I take it that's your grandson."

"My bull-headed grandson, Walker."

"Walker." As his name left her lips, recognition hit. "Grier's lawyer?"

"Yes, dear."

Like a deflating balloon, Sloan couldn't stop the rush of disappointment as it burst the tentative interest she'd had in the man. As far as she was concerned, Grier's lawyer was a good portion of the reason her friend was in this mess. The man had advised Jonas Winston for years and he couldn't be bothered to encourage the man to reach out to his daughter?

What the hell kind of legal advice was that?

"Oh."

If she heard the distinct chill that had frosted Sloan's words, Sophie paid no attention as she waved her grandson over. With a wry grin, he accepted his grandmother's invitation, crossing the room in confident strides.

Sloan submitted to yet another round of introductions, but instead of the anticipation that had flowed through her earlier like warm honey at the prospect of meeting this man, all she could manage was the dull facade she'd honed for over a decade and a half in polite society.

It also didn't escape her notice that the grandmothers had found excuses to slip away before the introductions were complete.

"Grier didn't mention a friend was joining her. How are you finding Indigo?"

Sloan couldn't pinpoint why she was so disappointed; all she knew was that she couldn't quite keep the righteous anger from seeping out. "Maybe if you spent more time with your client you'd have known I was coming up here."

His eyes clouded in confusion. "I do spend time with my client. She simply hasn't mentioned your visit."

"Are you representing her sister, too?"

"Not that it's any of your business, but no, I don't. It would be a considerable conflict."

"So why have you allowed the entire town to side with the sister?"

Walker tried to reconcile the virago in front of him with the sloe-eyed beauty from the town-hall meeting and found himself coming up short. "Is there a problem?"

"I think you've been shortchanging Grier."

"I'm sure you and Grier share a lot. And if that's how she feels, then you should suggest to her she take it up with me."

"*I'm* taking it up with you."

"It's really none of your business."

A small line furrowed her brow and Walker saw a mixture of sympathy and anger in the blue depths of Sloan's eyes. "She needs someone to stick up for her."

"I think she does just fine by herself. And I'm following the letter of the law in the execution of her father's will. I'm sorry if you feel that's somehow shortchanging her."

"And this"—Sloan spread an expansive hand out to the room at large—"these people don't seem all that happy to have her here."

Walker turned to the spot in the room he'd noticed Grier had drifted to earlier. Truth be told, the woman had drifted among different groups of people all evening. "She seems to be doing just fine, mama bear. Your little experiment here is working wonders."

"Experiment?"

"Sure. Butter up the locals. Flash a bit of cash and a few smiles. Great tactic, I'll give you that. Most folks around here don't get treated to whatever they want at the Indigo

Blue. Although—" He broke off, nodding in the direction of the bar. "You'd better keep an eye on Hooch. He's been drinking their single-malt Scotch like it's water."

Walker couldn't suppress the smile at her wide eyes and dropped mouth when she zeroed in on Hooch and his wife, Chooch, laughing merrily at the bar. "What?"

"They don't call him Hooch for nothing, after all."

He was impressed when she didn't move to give an early end to the old couple's evening, instead turning her attention back to him. "I'm not flashing cash, as you so rudely put it. And even if I were, it doesn't change the fact these people hadn't given her the time of day until someone poured a bit of liquor in them."

"So you're going to play the avenging angel and make it all better?"

"No."

"Then what are you doing here?"

"I'm lending some support."

"Let me give you a hint, Princess." He leaned forward, not quite sure why he had gotten engaged in this idiotic battle of wills in the first place. "Your friend's a lot tougher than you give her credit for. Why don't you just try being her friend?"

Sloan knew she should be feeling profound joy that her idea had taken off, but all she felt was a sensation of dark melancholy working its way through her. Her little ploy had worked. They'd been in the hotel for only an hour and already Grier was the center of attention, the townspeople anxious to meet her, introducing themselves in groups as they sought to get acquainted.

She should feel joyous and happy for her friend and all she felt was the one-two punch of bitchy and manipulative.

And where in the *hell* had that come from?

Grier was an awesome person and these people had judged her without benefit of a fair trial or even a friendly conversation. All she'd done was facilitate a few meet-and-greets, letting everyone get a chance to hear Grier's side of the story.

A father she'd never met. A sudden inheritance that necessitated a trip as geographically far away as she could get from home and still stay in the United States. And a new family member who'd decided she was no more interesting—or welcome—than a pile of moose droppings.

So why were Walker's comments so upsetting?

Why don't you just try being her friend?

Damn it, that *was* what she was doing. Grier deserved better treatment than she'd been receiving from the townspeople of Indigo.

And if the sense of anger and annoyance she felt for her best friend matched the disappointment Sloan felt at being an outcast in her own hometown . . .

Well.

She just wasn't going to go there.

And as for the disillusionment she felt in finding out the hot man with the broad shoulders and warm brown eyes was Grier's useless, good-for-nothing lawyer, well, she just wasn't going there, either.

On a whispered *shit*, she discreetly dragged her coat out of a pile in the far corner of the lobby and headed for a side exit of the hotel. A few minutes of fresh air would clear her head and kick whatever glum ache had settled itself in her heart to the curb.

A few minutes to gather herself.

A few minutes before she had to get back to being the gracious hostess with the burning platinum card.

"That really is quite the party you've got going on in there. Although, you'll be pleased to note Hooch and Chooch just bundled themselves up for the walk home."

Sloan shrieked as she whirled around to see Walker's large silhouette framed in the doorway. Before she could reply around the pounding in her throat, he moved forward, the door closing gently behind him. "You're going to freeze yourself. Here. Put this on." He held out a large man's coat to her as he shrugged into his own.

"I have a coat," she informed him primly.

"And you need another one. Put it on."

She took the offered garment, already understanding his point as the frigid night air seeped through the wool of her dress coat. "Thanks."

"You need some new things. That coat won't do up here and those boots"—he gave the stiletto heels a nasty glare that let her know *exactly* what he thought of them— "really won't do."

"Thanks, Mr. Gunn. So glad to have the fashion lesson. Now I know exactly what does *not* work." The confused look in his eye both reassured and brought a small smile to her face. "Not a *Project Runway* fan?"

"Um, no."

"You're more the man-cave dwelling, let-me-watch-my-football type instead of the Heidi-and-Tim type?"

"You could say that." A small smiled hovered over his lips as he fastened the last button on his coat. "Maybe we could try this again?"

"Try what again?"

Walker extended his hand. "Walker Montgomery." When she just stood there staring at him, he reached for her arm, dragging her hand toward his. "And you are?"

Sloan tightened her grip. "Sloan McKinley."

If she hadn't been standing, frozen to the very depths of her impractically clad toes, Sloan wouldn't have believed it. But as Walker's hand enveloped hers for the faux introduction, a shot of electricity tripped along each and every nerve ending she possessed.

As waves of warmth flooded her wrist and traveled up her arm, settling somewhere in the center of her chest, she tugged lightly and tried to pull back her hand. Despite her best intentions to stay immune to his charm, the warmth continued to fill her, spreading out like ripples on a pond from her very core.

Oh man, was this guy lethal.

When he wouldn't release her hand, she opted for bored disdain. "You make it a habit to follow women out into the cold, stealing men's jackets for them?"

"Only when it's women from the Lower Forty-eight, who don't seem to know how to dress for the temperature."

"Sounds like you get a lot of them up here, from what I've heard. That big competition next weekend is all anyone can talk about."

Walker moved forward and Sloan had to tilt her neck to look up at him. She wasn't a small woman—and the heels on her boots only added to her height—so the sensation was as unfamiliar as it was welcome. Up close, he was even bigger than he looked. "Tell me about it."

There was something so manly—so physical—about him, Sloan was torn between taking a few steps back or tackling him to the ground and having her way with him.

Where had that thought come from?

As unexpected as the idea of tackling him was the bubble of laughter that threatened at the dismal note in his voice.

"You're not all that crazy about the event?"

"Would you be?"

Sloan tapped a thoughtful finger against her lips. Although the gesture had been innocent, she didn't miss the way Walker's eyes grew even blacker in the reflection of the light, his gaze following her fingertip with rapt attention. "So the men don't like it and the local women don't like it. Seems like that would make for more trouble than it's worth."

"That's not exactly how my grandmother sees it. And several of the men actually look forward to it."

"You're just not one of them."

"No."

"And the other grandsons?"

"Mick and Roman?" Walker let out a harsh bark of laughter. "They'd prefer a trip to the dentist, too."

"Oh, come on, it doesn't sound that bad. It is for charity." Sloan had paid attention to Sophie's little PR piece during the town hall, where the woman attempted to explain her grand vision of what the competition was *really* all about.

Charity.

Yeah, right.

Sloan tried to focus on the conversation at hand, though Walker's strong physical presence was doing a number on her. A town full of marriage-obsessed matrons, desperate to marry off three men who had no interest and willing to go to great lengths to achieve it.

"So my grandmother hasn't tempted you to compete in the event yet."

Horrified at the thought, Sloan firmly pulled her hand back, suddenly remembering it was clasped tightly in Walker's very warm palm. "No."

"She's awfully persuasive. Besides, how are you going to write about it if you don't compete in it?"

"I'll be interviewing the competitors for the piece."

Walker shrugged, but she saw the light of battle in his eyes. "Seems like a cop-out to me."

"I hardly think so."

"Oh really. You come up here and claim the entire town's out to get your friend. Then you decide to make a few bucks at our expense writing about us. Maybe you need to put a little skin in the game."

Chapter Five

"Skin in the game?"

Walker watched the red already in her cheeks from the biting night air turn a deeper shade. It wasn't until Sloan echoed his comments that he realized what his words might have implied. A distinct warmth settled in his core and his body tightened uncomfortably at the image of her exposed skin that lit up his mind's eye. "Some commitment from you. Especially if you want to write a well-rounded article and all."

"I don't need to be *in* the competition to do that. I'm going to interview town residents, the competitors, as well as the bachelors. It will be a very well-rounded piece."

"Sitting on the sidelines?"

"It's a reporter's job to watch and listen."

Walker shrugged, enjoying the conversation—and baiting her—far more than he'd expected to. "I just think you could write a stronger piece if you put yourself in the game. If it's too much for you, that's another story."

The hands she'd been rubbing together to keep warm slammed on her hips as her eyebrows rose. "Reverse psychology, Counselor?"

Damn it, but this was fun. It didn't hurt that the light

in her blue eyes offered an enticing challenge. "I'm simply making an observation."

"Sure you are."

"Come on. You heard the lineup of events during the town hall. It's all done in a spirit of fun. None of the games are hard, per se. And the best part is that all the money raised goes into a town fund to help the community."

"From what I've also heard, you've never been a huge champion of the contest. Right this moment, you sound like the tourism board."

"What my grandmother and her friends have cooked up is sort of amazing." As the words left his mouth, he had to admit they weren't lip service. His grandmother *had* created something pretty amazing.

Why hadn't he ever noticed it before?

And why did it take someone—even a someone as enticing as Sloan—to make him realize it?

"For the record, the bachelors don't actually compete. They're just the recipients of the attention."

"But there is an auction, right? Do you participate in that? On a stage, in front of everyone."

He ignored the neatly tossed jab. Clearly, Avery must have already been sharing stories. "I leave that to the younger guys."

Sloan snorted, the uninhibited gesture pushing an extra puff of breath into the air. "Yeah, right."

"Just because I choose to humor my grandmother doesn't mean I have to actually be in the contest."

"Play the tough guy all you want, Counselor. I don't think you're quite as immune to all this as you say."

"Oh, really?" Walker stepped closer, seized by the urge to reach out and touch her. He moved before he could question the impulse. "And what gave you that impression?"

"I think you like being an object of such intense attention. All those women fawning over you. You and your buddies, the eligible bachelor brigade, on display."

Walker took the last few steps to close the gap between them. Despite the heavy layers of clothes—and the oversized coat she'd wrapped herself in—he could still smell her captivating scent. The rose notes that must be her shampoo filled his senses. "Why don't you compete and find out?"

"You may not like what I write about you."

"That's a risk I'm prepared to take."

"I refuse to be influenced by my subjects."

Walker leaned down to press his lips against her ear as he settled his hands on her waist. "I can't promise I won't try to influence you."

Her voice fell from her lips in a hushed whisper. "I wouldn't be a very good reporter if I allowed myself to lose my objectivity."

Sloan's head fell back slightly, allowing him better access to her neck, and Walker reached up to lay his hands on either side of her throat. He shifted so his mouth hovered over hers, anticipation humming through his body with eager pulses that matched the beat of his heart. "You can remain as impartial during the competition as you'd like, Ms. McKinley. Just so long as you don't remain impartial to this."

With a tenderness that belied the crazy, raging need

that gripped him, he pressed his mouth to hers and plundered.

Sloan had never felt blindsided by a kiss before. Excited, yes, even thrilled.

But gobsmacked?

Absolutely not.

The reaction of shock, adrenaline and pure, unadulterated feminine pleasure rocketed through her system as the firm press of his lips quickly gave way to the heated assault of his tongue.

The cold that had seeped into her bones from the moment she'd fled outside was rapidly replaced with a liquid heat that spread through her like a wild blaze and she knew—with absolute certainty—how the denizens of Alaska stayed warm.

As his mouth played over hers, she dimly registered the fact that her hands were hanging by her sides, so she lifted them to settle at his waist. His hips were solid, thick with muscle as her fingertips sought purchase under the fabric of his coat.

Glorious need filled her. It beat within her and matched the want she felt emanating from the solid planes of his body. Although some dim recess of her brain warned her this likely wasn't the brightest idea she'd had in a long time, she couldn't quite muster up the will to push him away. In fact . . .

Sloan's grip tightened on his waist, pulling him closer as she tilted her head to allow him greater access to her mouth. He explored her with his tongue, their mingled breaths and sighs warming up the frigid night air.

A loud burst of laughter broke the sensual haze and Sloan pulled her head away as reality interrupted their stolen moment.

"Um. Yeah. Okay."

Damn it, was she so desperate that a few good kisses could scramble her brain?

As her gaze returned to his lips, seductive in the light of the parking lot, Sloan couldn't miss the satisfied smile that spread across his face. His dark eyes promised it wouldn't be the last moment—stolen or otherwise—they'd share.

"Think about it, Sloan."

Oh, she'd think about it, all right.

"I mean it. Think about the competition."

"Of course." Of course he meant the competition. "I'll definitely give it some thought."

"Come on. I'll walk you back inside."

Sloan glanced down and realized she was wearing someone's coat. And from the increasingly loud sounds coming from the direction of the parking lot, the towns-folk had clearly had enough of her hospitality.

"Walker! Washa ya doin' over there?" a man she'd only heard called Bear hollered from across the parking lot.

Okay, Sloan amended her first notion. Avery likely shut down the bar, hence the departing guests.

"I'm just seeing Ms. Sloan back inside, Bear."

"Youz sure thaz all?" As several people near Bear let out a loud burst of laughter, Sloan realized these last few moments with Walker likely weren't nearly as private as she'd thought.

Walker's hand settled low on her back, the insistent pressure her cue to walk toward the side door she'd escaped out of only minutes before. "I was just giving Ms. Sloan a tour of our evening sky. Alaska's too pretty not to share it with the tourists."

"Thaz for sure." Bear nodded good-naturedly.

"You be careful getting home. All of you," Walker hollered from behind her as he pushed her through the door.

Suddenly nervous, Sloan wasn't sure how to handle the attack of nerves that began dive-bombing her stomach. "No one misses much up here, I guess."

"I think it has less to do with up here and more to do with the fact that Indigo is a small town."

Sloan thought of her own relatively small town and the individuals who fought for dominance there. "Too true. There are no secrets in small towns."

Dark eyes narrowing, Walker's voice was a husky mix of desire and—annoyance? "Are you interested in keeping this a secret, Sloan?"

"It was just a kiss." Was it? Even as the casual response left her mouth, she was regretting the words.

"Of course. Here you are. And there's Skate Mac-Intyre." Walker pointed in the direction of a big guy looking determinedly through the now dwindling pile of coats in the corner of the lobby. "He probably wants his coat back."

Did no one in this town have a real name?

Before she could ask or say anything else, Walker had moved away to help his grandmother with her coat.

Shrugging quickly out of the oversized wool, she offered a small smile to the man standing there with an expectant smile. "Skate?" At his nod, she continued. "Sorry about that. I ran outside for something and realized I should probably layer. I just grabbed the nearest one I could find."

"No problem, ma'am." Skate nodded his head, a dark red flush creeping up his neck even as he smiled broadly. "You warmed it up for me."

She glanced down at the coat in her hands, thrusting it at him as if it had suddenly turned into a snake. "Oh. Sorry."

His large bear-sized hand closed over the collar of the coat, his fingers just brushing hers. "I'm not."

"I hope you enjoyed this evening."

Before he could say anything, she excused herself and crossed the room toward where Grier stood at the bar with Avery.

"Someone's quickly making an impression." Avery smiled as she handed a bill across the bar.

"What?" Sloan clamped down on the impulse to screech when she saw the total on the bill.

"The town's bachelors certainly seem taken with you. Skate's notoriously shy, but there he was, talking you up." As if reading her mind, Avery added, "And while the Indigo Blue appreciates your patronage, I figured you'd like me to call it quits after the bill hit a grand. Otherwise a few more might have gotten up the courage this evening."

"The bill's for almost fifteen hundred."

Avery smiled broadly. "I said I *figured* you'd like me to quit after a grand. Then I called last call and everyone got busy. I did throw in a few freebies, I'll have you know. Susan won't mind a few free bottles of wine in exchange for a bar tab like this one. Oh, and gratuity's included."

"How thoughtful," Sloan said drily as she reached for the pen Avery had laid beside the bill. On a small mumble, she added, "Besides, I only had his coat."

"What'd you have of Walker Montgomery's?" Grier added in a slightly tipsy voice.

"G!" Sloan whirled on her friend, midsignature on the bill.

"It's a fair question." Avery made a good show of collecting glasses off the bar, but Sloan didn't miss the broad smile that lit up her face.

"More than fair." Grier waved a hand as she reached for a bottle of water. "I saw your face when you walked back in that door over there. Fess up. The man charmed your panties off, didn't he?"

"Grier!"

Avery held up a hand and Grier smacked it with the age-old high-five motion. "Told you."

"Do not tell me you two were betting on this."

" 'Course not," Avery added. "I don't take bets I'm sure to lose and that absolutely would be one. But I can tell you that man is fuckalicious and he's got his eye on you."

"What have the two of you been up to in here?" Sloan wanted to be angry, but she couldn't seem to conjure the proper emotion as she took in the matched looks of merriment on both women's faces.

It was funny, she mused, how easy it was to laugh with both of them. "And tell me how I can possibly go from having you stare daggers through me mere hours ago to telling you deep, dark secrets?"

Avery shrugged. "I'm irresistible."

Sloan laughed and took a seat. Before she could say anything, Grier interrupted around another swig of water. "Seriously, though, Avery. I feel like I've known you forever. It's nice."

"It is," Avery agreed. "Speaking of nice—I want details."

Avery's dark gaze caught the overhead lights of the bar, reminding Sloan they were still sitting in a recently full room. With a quick glance around—and to ensure they had privacy—she leaned forward. "He kissed me. Well, after he challenged me. Then he kissed me."

"Whoa, whoa." Grier waved a hand, her water bottle now empty. "I think this calls for more wine. I finished my water like a good girl and this is too juicy for another bottle of H-two-O."

"My thoughts exactly."

Avery was already reaching under the bar for a bottle when the label caught Sloan's attention. "You've got Mouton-Rothschild?"

"Holy shit!" Grier leaned forward. "I've never had that before."

"Me either," Sloan admitted, even as she watched Avery expertly uncork the bottle.

"Then you're in for a treat." Avery's smile broadened as she poured small amounts into two glasses, offering them forward to Grier and Sloan for a taste.

Sloan swirled her wine, the ritual of tasting a pleasant diversion from the grilling on her kiss with Walker she knew was still to come. As the first drop hit her tongue, she closed her eyes at the sheer magnificence of the wine. "It's gorgeous."

"Every single time." Avery leaned forward and poured a full glass for each of them, raising her own glass in their direction. "To a good story and one I hope is rather juicy."

On a soft clink, Sloan touched the rim of her glass to theirs, then took another sip, releasing a small sigh as she set her glass back on the counter. "Truly amazing."

"That it is." Avery swirled her glass, holding it up to the light.

As she took another delicate sip, Sloan's thoughts tripped over everything that had happened since her arrival. "Avery. Wait a minute. This stuff is like liquid gold. And that's Chihuly glass in the lobby. What's going on around here?"

Avery took a sip of her own wine, but Sloan saw a slight wariness that tightened the corners of her new friend's mouth. "So we have some nice things. We may be a bit out of the way, but we're not complete hicks."

"I wasn't suggesting you were. But this is extreme. Come on. This is a thousand-dollar bottle of wine. Most people don't have this lying around, and if they do, they sure as hell don't just open it up over a chat. What gives?"

"What gives is that this is all"—Avery waved a hand to gesture to the room at large—"how Susan's son assuages his guilt. Expensive gifts that arrive with an alarming degree of regularity."

Sloan's heart turned over as she heard the note of

unbearable sadness that tinged Avery's words. "Roman?"

"Yes."

"And yet you stay here? Near it all?"

"I do."

"But he broke your heart?" Sloan phrased it as a question, but even as the words left her lips she knew it was more of a statement.

"That he did. But, despite that small fact, I can't leave."

"Sure you can," Grier urged. "You don't have to stay here."

Avery's eyes were bright as she stopped staring at the wine in her glass for a few seconds to look up. "Actually, I can't leave. Maybe someday, but not today. So in the meantime, I'm going to enjoy my Rothschild and my view of the Chihuly glass and my new friends—especially my friend who has a kissing story she's putting off telling."

Sloan knew a closed subject when she heard one and Grier did as well. So they both lifted their glasses toward Avery and smiled.

"So are you going to keep us in suspense, especially seeing as how I bribed you with this amazing stash?" Avery stared over the rim of her wineglass, whatever sadness that had lingered firmly extinguished in the light of a good gossip session.

"You can't possibly want to know the details."

"Oh, yes we do."

On a long-suffering sigh, Sloan leaned in to tell her story. "It was probably the most amazing kiss I've ever had."

"Hot?" Grier probed.

"Sexy?" Avery added.

"Passionate? Oh, and masterful?"

"Masterful?" Sloan couldn't help but giggle at Grier's adjective. "What have you been reading lately?"

"You probably don't want to know. So let's just say I've been in the middle of Alaska for the last month, freezing my ass off during the long winter nights. What do you think I'm reading?"

Sloan waved a hand. "Say no more."

"And I say 'masterful' is the right word since you walked in here with a dazed expression on your face and a light blush that can be put there only by someone as supremely masterful as Walker Montgomery."

"Actually, I think you had it right before. What was the word? Fuckalicious?" Sloan asked.

Avery lifted her glass and Grier quickly followed. "Sometimes it's the only word that fits." Avery shrugged.

It was Grier, though, who added the toast. "Amen to that."

For about the nine millionth time since her freshman year of high school, Jessica McFarland wondered why she hung around with Trina Detweiler.

"Buying off the town. As if." Trina led their merry little parade down Main Street, with her faithful cohort, Sherry, close on her heels. Kate hung back slightly. Even if there wasn't a physical distance between them, it was clear Kate was a million miles away.

"I don't feel bought off," Jess said reflectively as she brought up the rear. "I just feel buzzed." She watched as various townsfolk walked down the streets. Avery had kept a close eye on the ones she knew had to drive and cut them off early or enforced designated driver rules. For those who lived within walking distance, the taps had flowed freely.

"Is that Mr. Rivington peeing against the side of the gas station?" Sherry pointed.

"That should be illegal, pulling that shriveled old thing out in public." Trina—ever the soul of logic and kindness—quickly chimed in.

"He's old, Trina. He obviously just has to go." Jessica wasn't sure why she was defending the guy, especially seeing as how he was technically committing a crime, but something about Trina's attitude just set her teeth on edge.

"It's gross."

Unable to let it lie, Jessica pushed back. "Oh, and you vomiting in Mrs. Riley's rosebushes this past summer after Louise Kent's bachelorette party was the height of class."

"I'm not dignifying that with an answer," Trina *tsk*ed over her shoulder. "However, I do think we need to have a discussion about your loyalty, Jess. Why'd you drink *her* drinks?"

"It was me and the rest of the town, in case you missed it. And it was free booze, Trina." Although she didn't want to come off as cheap—and she knew she made a solid living compared to much of the rest of the town—it was damn nice to be treated for the evening. "And besides, if you had that big a problem with the whole thing, why'd you even go? Just so you could rub in the fact you bought your own?"

"It was a strategic choice. Hello, as a lawyer I'd have thought you knew the difference." Trina let out another huff before whirling around and coming to a dead stop in the middle of the street. "Whose side are you on, anyway?"

"It's not about sides, Trina."

"Actually, it is. Here Kate is in her time of need and all you can do is side with her sister. It's hardly fair and it *is* taking sides."

"I'm legally representing her against the estate of their father. I have to act appropriately."

"But you don't have to drink with them."

Jessica sighed, not sure how she'd become the villain in this little set piece. "Look. I'm just doing my job."

Before Trina could repeat her perspective, Kate stepped up between the two of them. "Trina. Leave it the hell alone."

Trina took a few stomping steps backward before glaring at the two of them. "Fat lot of thanks from you. What's gotten into you tonight, Kate?"

"Nothing." Kate sighed and Jessica thought she caught a glimpse of tears filling the corners of her eyes. "Nothing's gotten into me. I'm just tired and so over this subject. I'll talk to you tomorrow."

"Whatever. Come on, Sherry. Maguire's is still open. Let's head over there. If you two change your minds and decide to find your senses of humor, come join us."

Jessica watched the two women stomp off through the snow under the light of the streetlamps that ran down Main Street and wondered when their lives had reverted to the seventh grade. "What's her problem?"

"I can't say that I care."

"She's not being fair."

"None of it's fair." Kate kicked at a slick of ice on the sidewalk. "Most of all, it's not fair my father thought ignoring the fact he had another child was the right thing to do. And now he's dumped me with her."

"Kate. He didn't dump you with anything. He—" Jessica broke off, but both of them knew her next word would have been "died."

"Actually, he did dump me with her. And based on tonight, it looks like she brought in reinforcements."

"Grier's not bad, Kate. Actually, she's kind of nice. You might be surprised if you gave her a chance."

"Jessica." Kate shook her head, and this time Jess didn't miss the sheen of tears—or the few that fell from the woman's eyes. "I'm not going to like her and nothing you can say will change that. I can appreciate her life is as unpleasant as mine right now, but I've spent twenty-six years without a sister and I'm not starting now. And for the record, even if I did accept that I have a sister, I sure as hell don't want her in my town."

"Then why don't you resolve all this and she'll leave? I can't believe she wants to stay here any more than you want her here."

"Because she doesn't deserve anything from a father who didn't even know her. He was *my* father. And if I give in, it's like I'm saying she does."

Jessica had seen tough cases, but there was something wrong with Kate's insistence that her sister deserved no part of their father's estate. "That's not for you to say."

"If not me, then who?"

Kate moved on ahead and Jess realized she really didn't want to follow her. Although she'd known Kate Winston since they'd both been small, their four-year age difference had ensured they really hadn't gotten to know each other until they were both older. Add in the current situation and all Jess could stomach was a small moment of sympathy, mixed with a huge wash of annoyance as she watched the younger woman walk away.

"Fuck."

A discreet cough from several feet behind her had Jess whirling around. Her heartbeat sped up immediately, but she honestly couldn't blame it on being startled. "Oh. Jack. Hi."

Jack Rafferty, widower and "the-man-who-would-never-love-again," as Jess had dubbed him, was illuminated by the light of the streetlamp, a small smile ghosting his lips. "That's not a very ladylike word."

A weak laugh escaped her. "It's not a very ladylike situation."

"No, it's not."

Jessica's eyes roved over his face. His head was covered with a knit cap and the layers of fabric insulating him from the cold gave him the same padded look as everyone else in town, but she still felt her pulse throb. "I suppose you saw the drama back at the hotel, only reinforcing the reason for my unladylike remark."

"Me and half the town. Most people haven't been crazy about Kate's attitude in all this, but they've gone along out of loyalty. After tonight . . . well, I'd say Grier made an impression. A good one, too."

"Getting to know her tonight makes it that much harder for them to ignore her."

"They already know they shouldn't ignore one of their own. Tonight added that sweet touch of guilt that will ensure they don't any longer."

Jessica stared down at her boots, then caught herself and brought her gaze back up. Damn it, why did he always make her tongue-tied? "I hope so. Grier deserves better."

"I doubt if Kate agrees with you." Jack glanced in the direction in which the woman had taken off. "And I don't know if anyone's going to be able to change her mind."

"Grief makes people do funny things, I guess." As soon as the words were out of her mouth, Jessica wanted to bite her tongue off. Jack Rafferty knew *exactly* what grief did to people. "Well, I'd better get home. Good night, Jack."

He didn't say anything else, just nodded at her, his big gray eyes clouded in mystery as he stared at her.

As Jess walked away, she wondered if Jack was watching her. Despite the curiosity, she resisted the urge to turn around, afraid he'd already moved on.

Chapter Six

"That's not warm enough, Sloan. If you're not padded like the Michelin Man, you're not going to be warm enough." Avery flung a coat at her from an overstuffed rack that looked like it belonged in Mrs. Claus's closet.

"I'm going to look ginormous." Sloan held up the thickly padded coat that resembled a down comforter and sighed. "At least it's black."

"Oh, give in, Sloan," Grier shouted from a nearby rack of ski sweaters. "It's cold and everyone looks the exact same. It beats having your extremities turn black and fall off due to frostbite."

Sloan shivered at the unpleasant image, even as she knew Grier had a point. "Fine, fine, fine." She dragged her arms through the sleeves as the shop's proprietor, Sandy Dunbar, walked over.

"Can I help you gals with anything?"

"Hey, Sandy." Avery's voice held the comfort of a lifetime of knowing each other as she greeted the shop owner. "We're just outfitting Sloan properly for her stay here in Indigo."

Sandy picked up a colorful scarf off a nearby accessories table, the gleam of a sale in her eyes. "I saw that wool coat you were wearing last night, dear. It's just not warm enough for Alaska."

"I've quickly come to the same conclusion." Sloan offered up a rueful smile as her eyes alighted on Grier across the room.

With an inspiration born of years of shopping, Sloan made her move. "Oh, Grier. Bring that sweater over here. I love how it complements your eyes."

Sloan saw Avery's eyebrows shoot up where she stood behind Sandy, but she caught on quickly. "Yeah, Grier. Grab the lavender one, too."

The previous evening had gone a long way toward helping Grier make some allies in town, but there was nothing like full-on support of a business—and a little gossip with the owner—to cement the relationship. With Avery as their sponsor and Sloan and Grier's credit cards picking up the rear, they were sure to win a loyal ally over to their side.

"It's a beautiful shade." Grier held up the sweater as she walked toward them.

"I knit it myself," Sandy added in a proud voice.

Avery's smile widened like the Cheshire cat and Sloan knew—with such certainty that she would bet every last penny in her bank account—their hometown girl had known that little tidbit, too.

"It's gorgeous, Sandy." Although Sloan felt a small shot of remorse at her battle tactics, it was fleeting. The sweater *was* gorgeous and the expert knit meant Grier would have the piece for a long time to come. "And, Grier, you need both of those."

Grier's eyes widened before one dropped into a wink. "I need a scarf to match."

"Oh, well, then come on over here, dear." Sandy waved her over. "I have the perfect shade to match your eyes."

Sloan stared at the breakfast menu at the Indigo Café and ordered the short stack and bacon along with her black coffee. She'd never have considered the carb-laden meal at home, instead opting for her usual egg-white omelet, but for some reason, the fresh, cold morning air made her feel like pancakes.

Although she was initially surprised Sandy's shop opened so early, Avery had explained that they tried to take advantage of the daylight and most of the stores got going early and then shut by midafternoon.

Whatever the reason, Sloan took in the crowded café as she looked up from her menu. She could eat her breakfast satisfied she'd made another inroad on Operation Grier this morning.

And now it was time for a little reconnaissance as she ate her pancakes.

Some mixing with the locals would let her know how successful she'd been the previous evening. Especially since the object of their previous hostility had gone back to their hotel to nurse her hangover.

With a smile for her departing waitress and her first sip of coffee, Sloan took in her surroundings. The café was clearly the place to be at eight on a weekday morning. The tables were packed and there was the loud hum of happy, optimistic conversation.

As an idea formed, Sloan scratched down the words "town life," "slice of life," "day in the life" in her ever-present notebook. No reason she couldn't jot down a few notes on her freelance piece. She could see it now. She'd open the piece talking about the daily life in Indigo and then segue into the craziness that became the town during the competition.

At least she assumed it would be crazy.

The enthusiasm for the event would *have* to leave a mark. It was up to her to capture it, before and after, pre and post.

Warming up to her subject, she realized the idea really did have legs. What if there was even a wedding or two out of the whole thing? She could come back in the spring and do a follow-up piece.

"Ms. Sloan? Do you mind if I sit down?"

Sloan was pulled from her musings by the sweet voice and even sweeter smile of the man who'd hollered in her and Walker's direction the evening before. "Of course. Please sit down."

The large man sat, his hand extended across the table. "I'm Bear."

"I'm Sloan."

Another broad smile cracked his face. "I know."

The idea that this stranger did know who she was gave her pause before she brushed it off. She might enjoy anonymity in a city of eight million, but there was just no such thing as anonymity in Indigo, Alaska, population seven hundred and twelve.

As she pushed aside her city-girl distrust, another thought took its place.

"So, Bear." Sloan leaned forward with the air of a co-conspirator. "I realize we just met, but I need to ask you a question."

"What's that?"

"Does everyone in this town have a nickname?"

"What do you mean?"

Sloan almost laughed at the confusion stamped across his face, but decided to chalk it up to research and kept up the questions. "Well, everyone I've met seems to go under a name I find very hard to believe is written on their birth certificate. You. Skate. Chooch and Hooch. What's up with it?"

A few women sitting in the booth behind them had overheard because they turned and chimed in. Sloan recognized them from the hotel lobby but couldn't conjure names out of the soup of introductions she'd had the evening before. "It just sort of happens," the smaller brunette said.

"To everyone?"

"Well, the men mostly," her friend added. "But several of the women do, too. Like Chooch."

"Where did she get that nickname?" Sloan probed, anxious to know how the sweet woman she'd met could possibly have a name like that.

"She doesn't say. I think it's private."

Sloan nearly choked on her coffee at that news. Private?

Although she knew names were personal—hers had always been a source of conversation as it wasn't the most typical name—but for no one to know where a fellow townswoman had gotten her name? "But why would it be private?"

"Likely on account of the pillow talk," Bear added, his face a blazing shade of red as he reached quickly for his coffee cup.

"Excuse me?" Sloan had the sudden feeling she'd fallen into some parallel universe. What kind of pillow talk could possibly result in a name like Chooch?

"You know, pillow talk. Don't tell me a big-city girl like you has never heard of it."

A long, slow roll of desire filled her as Walker Montgomery's deep, husky voice registered somewhere around her stomach. "I think I've heard of it."

"Then you know how it works." Walker dropped into the booth next to her and Sloan quickly made way for him as his thigh touched hers. "Private moments. Private conversations."

"If it's so private, how does Bear here know how Chooch got her name?"

A slight frown marked Bear's forehead—Sloan wasn't sure if it was the conversation or Walker's arrival that had put it there—but his affable smile didn't take long to return. "Hooch brags about it pretty often."

"Ah." Sloan nodded, the image of the couple she'd met engaging in sex rapidly forcing a subject change.

The waitress arrived with her breakfast and Bear glanced at the meal being set down, then back up to Walker before his gaze settled on Sloan. "Well, I'll let you get to your breakfast."

"You're welcome to join me if you'd like."

Bear eyed Walker, looked as if he were about to say something, but then thought better of it. "Thank you, but

I've eaten. I just wanted to come over and introduce my-self properly."

"It was lovely to meet you, Bear." Sloan held out her hand to shake his, fascinated when her hand disappeared in his palm.

"You, too." Bear got to his feet. "Walker."

"Bear." Walker's voice was smooth, but the note of implacable steel was evident underneath.

Sloan watched the interesting byplay between the two men and knew there was some sort of unspoken pissing match going on. Although she was tempted to say something, a small voice reminded her she wasn't back home any longer.

This was a different sort of place and she was fast coming to realize she wasn't entirely sure of the rules.

As Walker ordered his breakfast and Bear headed toward his companions to retrieve his coat, her thoughts drifted to an image of Trent, with his smooth words, practiced smile and two-hundred-dollar haircut.

The epitome of the suave, wealthy American male. If she hadn't known him well—or his reputation—she'd likely have thought him charming. The man who had a ready quip and quick comeback for any situation.

Her gaze caught on Bear's large, burly frame as he exited the diner and then on to Walker's linebacker-sized shoulders as he stood to slip out of his coat, and she realized these men had a different sort of charm.

Rugged.

Weathered.

Real.

Walker took Bear's spot and reached for a glass canister of sugar. "So you're curious about nicknames?"

She watched, fascinated, as he dumped the equivalent of four spoonfuls into his coffee.

The waitress returned with Walker's stack of pancakes and a side of bacon, dropping off both along with a wink for Sloan.

With a mental head shake and the acknowledgment that nothing seemed to escape anyone's notice, Sloan refocused on Walker. "Lots of people seem to have them."

"I guess. You just get used to them. I remember lots of guys from college who had them, too. It's not exclusive to Indigo."

The syrup bottle came next as Walker covered his pancakes in about twice the amount of sugar he had just shoveled into his coffee.

"No, but you have to admit it's a bit unique."

When he only shrugged, she added, "Where'd you go to school?" Sloan reached for the syrup, indulging the sudden urge to add pure sugar to the light layer of butter that had melted into the stack.

"Dartmouth for undergrad. NYU for law school."

"Really?" She cut a small bite of pancake and almost groaned in ecstasy as the first fluffy taste of carbohydrates hit her tongue.

Walker kept his gaze level on hers as he reached for his coffee and took a large sip. "Just because I live here doesn't mean I never wanted a chance to see something else."

"That's fine. I was only wondering. I'd have likely said the same thing if you were from California."

"Not likely."

Her eyes widened as his words registered. "I'm sorry?"

"You came here with a set of preconceived notions. Admit it."

"I did not."

Even as she defended her comments, Sloan could admit he had a point. While she wasn't one of those people who believed anyone outside Manhattan couldn't possibly be interesting, she also didn't expect to come to Alaska to drink Rothschild, look at a Chihuly and flirt with a Dartmouth grad.

Which didn't make her a snob, damn it.

"Sure you did. It's okay. We get it all the time."

"If you'd pull that prickly stick out of your ass, you'd see that I was simply making conversation."

Coughing around a bite of bacon, Walker let out a belated chuckle. "Prickly stick?"

"Sure. You've got a few preconceived notions yourself. About my expectations and the fact I'm a city girl and all."

Walker leaned forward, his broad shoulders taking up her entire field of vision, just as they had the evening before. Fascinated, she couldn't help the quick peek she gave them—measuring their width with her eyes—before turning her gaze back to him.

He was so large. So imposing. So undeniably male. Talk about a strong sexual presence. She tried to refocus her scattered thoughts.

"Are you going to make me change my preconceived notions, Blondie?"

"You don't think I can?"

"Are you signing up for the competition?"

Dropping back against the padded vinyl of the seat, Sloan let out a small groan at how neatly he had boxed her in. "Are you back to that? Why do you care so much?"

"I think it'll be good research."

"Or a raging humiliation." Where the hell did *that* come from? Sloan wanted to slink down lower in the booth as he keyed in on her slip.

"What are you scared of?"

"I'm not scared. Not exactly."

"It sounds like it."

"If there's any fear, it's fear of humiliation."

He kept his gaze on his plate, forking up his last bite of pancake, but Sloan didn't miss the speculation in his tone. "It's all done in fun."

"Fun for who? Because it doesn't sound like a whole lot of fun to drag heavy pails of water down Main Street."

"We don't make you go very far."

"We?"

"I meant the collective we," Walker said, pointing his fork outward. "As in the town."

"Well, then. From the collective *we*, I hear, there's a dinner dance and bachelor auction after all this not-so-horribly-difficult set of tasks. Are you participating?"

"I'll be there to support my grandmother, but I don't go on the auction block."

"Oh no?"

"No."

Sloan didn't miss the hard edge to his words. "So who does participate?"

Walker's gaze followed the same path as his fork, skipping around the room. "The guys. Bear. Skate. Tommy Sanger. Chuck Bartlett. Pretty much that entire row of booths back there."

The urge to turn around was strong, but Sloan kept her attention on Walker. "Not afraid of a little competition, are you?"

"I don't go on the block. It's a matter of principle."

"A lawyer with principles?"

"Damn good ones, too," he growled into the top of his coffee cup.

"Are you embarrassed, Counselor?"

"It's undignified."

Her mouth fell open at his pronouncement. "This from a man who thinks it's all right to compete in bachelorette events up and down Main Street."

"It's not the same. It's not your grandmother watching the proceedings like a hawk."

With an unladylike snort, she reached for her coffee cup. "I'd pit my mother against your grandmother any day."

Sloan didn't even realize the import of her words until Walker's dark chocolate gaze turned assessing. "Would you, now?"

"Oh, yes. Don't you know, dahling"—Sloan dropped her voice to a mock whisper—"it's simply scandalous that Winifred McKinley's daughter is still single. An absolute horror."

"And what would Winifred McKinley think about her

daughter competing in something as crass as a bachelorette competition?"

Sloan forked up another bite of pancakes. She'd already sinned for the day—might as well enjoy every last, delicious bite. "She'd be mortified."

"Isn't that reason enough?"

The dare hung between them, like a live wire sparking in a puddle.

Sloan had never used her mother's behavior as a catalyst for her own, but in that moment, the thought of doing something so outside the bounds of propriety suddenly seemed like a very good idea.

Inspired, actually.

Sort of like the pancakes, only better.

More delicious.

More sinful.

As her gaze roamed over Walker Montgomery, she realized something else. While there were implications to her behavior in front of Scarsdale's elite, no one here knew her.

Or cared about her background. Or, frankly, cared about her future. They just seemed pleased she was here now.

Oddly enough, she suddenly realized, that made all the difference.

"Tell you what, Counselor. If you're in, I'm in."

Aside from the fact that Mick would brand him a traitor to the cause *and* that his grandmother would think she'd finally won in their annual battle of wills, Walker considered the challenge.

Maybe it was the sleepless night, courtesy of Blondie here.

Or maybe it was finding Bear sitting opposite her with damn cupids floating in his fucking eyes that set him off.

Either way, something deep down inside him—something *primal*—had him unwilling to leave her exposed to the rest of the men in this town, all of whom were eyeing her like a brand-new Zamboni for the town rink.

A bright, shiny Zamboni with a heartbreaking smile, warm blue eyes and truly superior breasts.

And that, my friends, was the sign of a man completely losing it.

That he'd dare compare the woman to a *Zamboni* was bad enough. That she'd torqued him up so much he was willing to concede to his grandmother . . .

Well, fuck.

"I'm in."

Those blue eyes widened at his words. "That's it? You're in?"

"It's relatively simple. In or out."

"For someone who's pushed back on this annual tradition for so long, you're awfully quick to concede."

"Maybe I've just never seen such healthy competition before." Or a reason to jump in with both feet.

One perfect eyebrow rose above that cool blue gaze. "You already said the women don't compete with the men. They compete with one another."

"Yes." Walker leaned back in his chair, unable to keep the satisfied smile from his face. "You're all competing for me."

Although he'd always had a fairly healthy ego, even he wasn't smug enough to think that wasn't going to get a rise out of her. Which is why her burst of laughter— loud and husky and so damned sexy that his body went on red alert—shocked him.

"Well, there's one stereotype I got right."

"What's that?"

"The 'I'm man enough to live in the wilderness and nothing can touch me' stereotype. Rugged, wild and God's gift to women, despite long stretches without bathing or general grooming."

"Hey. I showered this morning. And so did the guys back there." Walker shot a look toward the back of the restaurant, satisfied to see that everyone looked reasonably clean. "Well. Most of them, anyway."

"Yep. Ego and long stretches of loneliness are a dangerous combination."

"I'm not lonely." And he wasn't. He could find female companionship when he wanted it. He lived life on his terms. He was happy.

And damn it, he wasn't lonely.

The laughter had stopped, leaving in its wake a broad smile that lit up her face. "Then you make up for it with ego."

Walker couldn't resist smiling back. "You have that right."

Their waitress arrived, putting down the check. He reached for it automatically, causing another raise of those sleek eyebrows.

"I'm here for research. I can get it."

"You were here to eat. With me. So I've got it."

"Walker." She extended a hand. "I don't want to make a stupid deal out of this, but I *am* working."

He already had the cash out of his pocket and the bill back to their waitress before Sloan could protest any further. "So come on then and work. I'll give you the downtown tour. I need to walk off these pancakes."

Without waiting for her to agree or disagree, he stood and shrugged into his coat, then held hers out to her. "I see you remedied your coat situation."

"Just this morning. Sandy was more than happy to oblige."

"I've no doubt of that. Did she rake you over the coals?"

"It's a price I paid willingly."

He leaned down and whispered in her ear, "Sucker!"

Even as the word lingered between them, Walker knew the moniker was far more applicable to him.

Sloan ignored him and pulled her hair from where it was stuck in her collar, the long fall of blond drawing his attention like a compass to true north. Mouth dry, he struggled for some response that wouldn't give away how thoroughly she affected him.

And as they stepped out onto Main Street a few minutes later, he was still trying to come up with something.

Chapter Seven

"Tour" wasn't really the right word, Sloan thought reflectively a half hour later as they passed a monument that stood at the far end of town. A love letter would have been a better description of her walk through the town of Indigo with Walker Montgomery.

He'd guided her from one end of Main Street to the other pointing out landmarks, from where the town's most ardent moose liked to come cozy up while looking for love, to the place he, Mick and Roman got drunk (and sick) for the first time.

It was interesting, she mused, as they neared the far end of town, how much pride she could hear in his voice when he spoke of these things.

He loved living here. Really, truly loved it.

"What's the monument for?"

She expected him to say it was a war memorial and yet again, had to change her expectations at the answer.

"Love."

"Really?"

"The grandmothers commissioned it."

"An entire monument?" Sloan had to tilt her head back to see the top of it. Who did that?

"Julia's husband died when she was only thirty-six."

Pulling her gaze away from the top, she turned toward him. "Losing a spouse at any age would be hard, but to lose someone that young—it must have had a huge impact on her."

Walker nodded and an unexpected softness tinged the hard edges of his jaw as his mouth curved into a slight smile. "It had a huge impact on all three of them."

Sloan moved forward to look at the monument, glancing over her shoulder as her boots crunched on the snow. "Is that where the competition came from?"

"In part. They wanted a celebration to kick off the unveiling of the monument. And at that celebration, my mother and father hooked up after the dinner and dance that was tied to the festivities."

"So you've got quite a legacy to live up to."

"At times."

As she walked around the base of the monument, she couldn't stop the warmth that filled her as she observed the smooth lines and curves of the granite. Again, another assumption blown to bits. She'd seen the monument from a distance and immediately thought it was a war memorial.

And instead it was the antithesis.

The monument suggested a man and a woman wrapped around each other, even though it was more an abstract sense of movement than two clearly defined bodies. Long, curving lines matched with hard-edged corners. A sensual feast chiseled out of one of the most unyielding substances on earth.

As she simply stood and soaked in the sensuality the piece evoked, she wondered if she was as unyielding as the granite that arched before her. How could she have—even for one moment—thought it was a war memorial?

It was yet another testament to assumptive thought and a stubborn close-mindedness that seemed to have gripped her since stepping off the train the evening before.

"Do you like it?" Walker's breath puffed out in front of him, the husky timbre of his voice magnified by the biting cold.

"It's beautiful. And unexpected. Pretty much like everything else in this town."

"You haven't been here that long."

"And hardly anything is what I thought it would be."

"What were you expecting?" Sloan turned his words over in her mind, unable to decipher a lick of snark in them. He must have sensed the question in her gaze because he added, "And there's no prickly stick in my ass prompting the question."

No, there wasn't.

"I've spent my life in an environment that's all about expectations. And I guess I never realized how many of them I had myself. It's sort of an irritating discovery, truth be told."

"Irritating?"

"Deeply." She sighed and kneeled down as her gaze landed on the edge of a carving etched in the marble base of the monument. With her gloved hand, she brushed away the snow caked there to reveal words.

The rush of emotion caught her—blindsided her, actually—square in the throat. On a whispered breath, she read the engraving. "'For those we aren't allowed to keep.'"

Silence descended between them and in the still quiet, Sloan heard the distant honk of a car horn, the light punctuation of shouted conversations farther down Main Street.

"You should probably stand up. Your jeans aren't made for kneeling in the snow." As Walker extended his hand to her, helping her rise, Sloan couldn't quite keep the unexpected sentimental tears from spilling over.

With a peculiar clarity, she couldn't help but compare these tears to the ones she'd shed only a few nights prior, after her encounter with Trent. Where that had left her empty and sad, this left a different sort of mark.

Something quieter. Deeper. And oddly, more hopeful.

True love *did* exist.

It lived and breathed, floating on the air and dancing a merry tune between those lucky enough to find it.

"Thank you for bringing me here."

Walker removed one of his gloves and ran a finger from her chin to her jaw, then over her cheek to catch a tear on the tip. Her stomach tightened at the tender ministration, the barely-there touch registering with the force of a hurricane.

A lock of dark hair blew against his forehead in the light breeze that swirled around them as he reached toward her other cheek. With the same tenderness, he brushed away another tear as she fought the urge to lean in to him. Caught in the moment, need rose up to replace the nerves in her belly with a growing, greedy desire for more of his touch.

She wanted to take, but something held her back. Nerves? Fear?

With one last glance toward the monument, she stepped back, turning herself in the direction of downtown.

"We should get back."

He gave a short nod and a simple, husky, "Yes."

But as she walked next to him down the frozen sidewalks of Main Street, Sloan felt the heat of desire that burned the air hot between them.

The words blurring before his eyes had Walker reaching for the pair of wire frames that lay next to his coffee mug. With the reluctant grace of someone who knew he was losing the battle, he shoved the glasses onto his nose and stared down at the brief that awaited his attention.

"You wearing those to poker night, Mr. Professor?"

Walker glanced up to see Mick O'Shaughnessy standing in his doorway, a leather jacket slung over one shoulder and a steaming mug in the other hand. "Who the hell let you in?"

"The ever-delightful Myrtle."

Far too many manners had been drilled into him— and the door stood way too open—for Walker to laugh at Mick's description. However, Walker suspected the word "delightful" had never made it into the same sentence as the name Myrtle Driver in all the woman's sixty-plus years.

"She got you coffee, too?" Walker gave a dry stare at his own now cold mug, acknowledging the fact that in the decade he'd employed Myrtle, the woman had never so much as brought him a glass of tap water.

"What can I say?" A broad, cocky grin spread across Mick's face. "It's damn good coffee, too."

"Nothing. You can say nothing." Walker crossed the room to the small sink in the corner of his office, dumping the cold coffee and then pouring a fresh cup from the perpetually full pot he kept on the small counter next to the sink.

After dumping in a liberal amount of sugar, he grabbed the seat next to Mick, stretched out his legs and balanced the mug on his knee. "What's up?"

"I finished up my runs early today. Thought I'd see if you wanted to grab a beer."

"I could be persuaded." Walker thought about the work he'd drowned himself in since his morning walk with Sloan and nodded. The legal brief on his desk was his last chore of the day and it would keep. "In fact, it's inspired. You, however, may not want to go with me once you find out I'm a traitor to the cause."

Mick took a sip of his coffee, his gaze speculative over the rim. "Because you're entering the auction?"

"Fuck." Walker scrubbed a hand over his jaw, the day's stubble making a satisfying scratch. "There really are no secrets in this town. How'd you find out?"

"The note I got in study hall pretty much tipped me off."

"Smart-ass."

"It's all anyone out at the airstrip could talk about."

"You're kidding."

"Hell no. I barely had the damn plane on the ground before Maggie was chattering in my headset. She claims she heard it from Renee who heard it herself at the diner this morning."

Of course. Even he wasn't dumb enough to think he and Sloan had any privacy during breakfast. "At least she let you land."

"True," Mick added drily. "She's actually quite smart and pragmatic under that mile-long streak of gossip she's always spouting. She's already working on me. And then she got Darlene in on it; she harangued me some more while signing off on my paperwork."

"Work? There couldn't have been much of that going on today."

"Other than my paperwork, I don't think she did a lick of it. Instead, she spent the day making a list of the women who are landing in a few days' time so she can pass out a checklist. Apparently she's created some bachelorette scoring system and everything."

"Does TSA know she's copying their names for a distribution list?"

Mick raised an eyebrow. "What do you think?"

"Shit." Walker did another scrub with his fingers, this time over his suddenly aching temples. "What the hell have our grandmothers wrought?"

"The apocalypse."

"You competing?"

"I think I'm rearranging my sock drawer that day," Mick drawled.

"Now that Sloan's in, Grier may not be far behind."

Mick shrugged as he lifted his coffee cup to his lips for

another sip, but Walker didn't miss the stiffening shoulders or the slightly too-casual tone. "Doesn't mean I should give my grandmother the satisfaction of actually entering the auction."

"Suit yourself."

Mick stood and grabbed his jacket. "Come on. Let's go."

A quick knock on the doorframe stopped them. "Walker. I need two minutes."

With a glance at Jessica, he nodded. "Sure. What's up?"

"More affidavits from the men on Jonas's crew. All of them claim he talked about a daughter." Walker took the papers from her, eyeing Mick before scanning the information quickly.

"I'll give you two some privacy. Walker, come meet me at the Indigo Blue when you're done."

Walker didn't miss the smirk on his friend's face but refused the bait.

If Mick wanted to spend the evening in the company of some New York bachelorettes—which he had no doubt the man did—who was he to argue? With an eye to the affidavits, he glanced up at Jessica. "They don't say which."

"No, but based on the timing it had to be Grier. Kate wasn't even born yet." Jessica waited a moment before adding, "So what do you hope to do with this?"

"It's further evidence he cared for her. Further evidence Kate can't stand in the way of Grier's half of the inheritance. And further evidence they have to split the house."

"I'm sure Kate's lawyer will see it differently. Especially since she practically moved in there during Jonas's convalescence." Jessica's defense of her childhood friend hadn't completely vanished, but it had far less fire than the evening before.

Walker ran a hand through his hair, grabbing at the strands with clenched fingers. "Let him. It's all gotten too carried away, anyway. Kate shouldn't be contesting the will, but because she is, it's screwing both out of them out of grieving and putting this behind them."

"They're both shell-shocked, Walker. It makes it difficult to think straight."

"That's why we're here, Jess. To do the thinking and keep it straight."

"Of course."

Walker eyed his partner, the dark circles under her eyes catching his attention. "You doing okay?"

"Of course."

"You sure?"

"It's just . . ." She broke off as a frown marred the smooth lines of her face.

"It's just what?"

"I don't know. Petty, and at the same time, understandable. And it's not my job to judge petty, I know."

"But it's hard to watch a friend suffer."

"It's hard to watch anyone suffer."

The misery stamped on her face tipped him off, but it was her words that finally had him cluing in to the fact there was something else going on. "Why does my Spidey-sense tell me we're not talking about Grier and Kate anymore?"

"I don't know what you're talking about."

"Sure you do. And that faraway look in your eyes tells me you're thinking about one person."

"Damn it, Walker. I'm entitled to my own thoughts."

"Didn't say you weren't."

"So what the hell do you want?"

"I want to know why you don't just bite the fucking bullet and ask Jack Rafferty over to your home for dinner. If something consenting happens afterward, even better."

The dark circles only highlighted the light sheen that filled her eyes. "He's not interested."

"I think he might surprise you."

Jess looked him straight in the eye, whatever momentary grief she'd felt sparking over to anger. "I don't believe in surprises."

Walker's mind filled with an image of Sloan McKinley wrapped in his arms the night before outside the Indigo Blue. The heat of her mouth and the immediate, desperate longing that had filled him without warning slammed into him again at the force of the memory.

"Well, that's the funny thing. Just when you're convinced they don't exist any longer, one comes right on up and bites you in the ass."

"You're really going to do it?" Grier's smile was infectious as she poured the first glass of wine. "I can't believe it."

"Believe it." Sloan reached for her wine, holding it until Grier had finished pouring for all of them.

"It's all anyone's been able to talk about today," Avery

added as she picked up her own glass. "You are a hot commodity here in Indigo, Sloan McKinley. The whole town's talking about you."

"Which is a refreshing change from them talking about *me*." Grier held up her glass to toast. "To the town's new point of interest."

Sloan reveled in the merry clinking and thought about the call she'd had a few hours before with the travel editor. She'd bought the piece, just as Sloan had expected. What she hadn't expected was that the woman would fall so in love with the pitch—"Getaways with Girlfriends"—that they'd spend nearly an hour on the phone.

Before the call was over, she'd committed to an ongoing series, to be done over six months' time with unexpected travel destinations for single women.

"So what's the really big news?" Avery gestured with a pretzel she'd lifted from a small bowl on the cocktail table between them.

"How'd you guess?"

"You practically danced into the lobby. I just don't think the prospect of dragging pails of water down Main Street can put that sort of swing in your step."

Unable to keep the grin from her face, Sloan let it all out in a giddy rush. "I just sold a series of articles."

Grier's mouth dropped before she settled her glass on the table and leaped out of her chair. "Sloan! Oh wow! Wow, wow, wow!" Sloan felt herself being pulled forward and just barely got her wine out of the way before Grier upended it on both of them.

Avery took the glass with one, smooth, practiced

move as Sloan moved into Grier's arms for a hug. "Thanks."

"I am so proud of you." Grier gave her one final hug before dropping back into her own seat. "Come on. We want deets."

Sloan ran through the conversation again, still in shock the idea had been so well received.

"Where else are you going to go?"

"We talked about that, too. We actually agreed that one of the columns should be on New York—more of an insider's guide. And she's also going to let me use the trip Grier and I took to Bora-Bora last year as one of the stories. But I've got to think of the other three."

"Australia," Grier supplied. "Or New Zealand?"

"France?" Avery added.

"Oooh. No. Spain. All women need to go to Spain and find a Spanish lover for the weekend. Armand. Yes," Grier snapped her fingers. "That's it. Armand."

Sloan laughed. "I've been to Spain and didn't meet anyone named Armand. In fact, I didn't meet anyone at all."

A light touch covered her forearm as Grier reached for her. "You were still in your awkward stage. Besides. Sixteen-year-olds don't need to be hunting up Latin lovers while touring Europe."

"Awkward stage?" Avery's eyes were wide with curiosity. "No way."

"Oh God, yes. I was the ultimate ugly duckling. From head to toe." Sloan was surprised by how easy the words came. How far away it all seemed, even though it always felt like yesterday when she was at home.

"I know that look."

"What look?"

Grier sighed. "The one that says you're thinking very deep thoughts."

"Then I must have worn it all day. I can't stop thinking about how different I feel up here."

"Different how?" Avery reached for another pretzel.

"I can't quite explain it." How did she put into words what she was only slowly figuring out herself? "But I feel more grounded here. More, I don't know, *real*, somehow."

As the words came out, Sloan realized they weren't quite right. "No. No, I'm not explaining it the way I mean it. It's less about being real or fake, and more about looking at things a little differently."

"Such as?" Grier munched on a pretzel.

"It's like all these ideas I've held in my head forever—even the things I didn't know I was holding on to—are changing. My expectations are blown but that's a good thing."

"Unsettling, too," Avery added as she reached for more wine.

"It's like I said to Walker this morning: I've been walking around with this set of expectations I didn't even know I had and it's humbling to—"

She broke off at the twin looks of wonderment that stared back at her.

"What?"

"As you were saying. To *Walker*?"

Grier's emphasis on his name jarred Sloan back to

reality. "Yeah. He was kind enough to give me a tour of town this morning."

"My lawyer hit on you and it took you a half hour to tell me? When did this happen?"

"This morning."

"Sloan! Scratch that." Grier waved a hand. "It took you all damn day."

"I was busy, Grier."

"You should never be too busy to spill details about a man."

"I'll remember that from the *Best Friend Handbook* and file it away for next time."

"There's going to be a next time?" Avery's provocative tone dragged them both from their faux argument.

"I meant it figuratively."

"Well, I mean it literally."

"No." Even as the words were out of her mouth, Sloan realized they weren't entirely true. "Yes. I guess. He's taking part in the bachelor auction."

It was Avery's turn to look stunned. "You promised blow jobs, didn't you?"

"I did not!" Even as she pretended indignation, Sloan couldn't stop the warmth that flooded her belly. The man did . . . *something* to her. Something she hadn't felt in an incredibly long time.

If ever.

And the prospect of getting very intimate with him had crossed her mind more than once in the last twenty-four hours.

"Walker Montgomery has been a stubborn holdout,

along with his partners in crime. Well, partner. Singular. The other one hides out for as much of the year as he can get away with, and he sure as hell doesn't come to town during bachelorette season."

"He mentioned he doesn't participate in the auction."

"Nope. He, Mick and Roman humored them the first few years, but have stubbornly refused to take part in quite a long time. Their own little rebellion."

"If the grandmothers' whole purpose is getting them married, doesn't that sort of defeat the point if they don't show up?"

Avery turned toward Grier. "It's a valid question, and they do technically show up, but they refuse to participate. At this point the whole thing's sort of taken on a life of its own. And neither side is willing to concede. Until now, it seems."

Grier nodded sagely. "I knew he liked her."

"He does not." Even as she said the words, Sloan knew he didn't *not* like her. The kiss they'd shared the evening before hadn't held the mark of disinterest. Nor did his dismissal of Bear that morning in the diner.

"I wouldn't be so sure. Especially since he practically sucked your brains right out of your head last night."

"Avery!" Sloan turned on her new friend, only to see the woman's eyes twinkling with merriment.

Unaffected by the death glare Sloan was trying her hardest to deliver, the twinkle spread across her entire face. "I even saved the security tape."

"I want to see it." Grier was already up and out of her chair, striding for the front desk, her gaze focused over her shoulder. "All the gory det—"

Grier's comment—and forward movement—was stopped by the solid wall of Mick O'Shaughnessy's chest.

"Well, would you look at that?" Avery whispered the words in a hushed breath as she leaned toward Sloan. "Is it just me or is the lobby suddenly on fire?"

Sloan watched with interest as Mick's large, rangy frame collided with her friend's tiny, petite one. The bush pilot—she'd found out his occupation the evening before—wore a day's growth of beard along with a tattered leather jacket, faded jeans and work boots. His long-fingered hands rested on Grier's shoulders a few extra moments as he held her away from his body, concern etched across his features.

The air practically crackled between them as Mick dropped his hands and shuffled from foot to foot while Grier pushed her hair behind her ears in an endearingly nervous gesture Sloan had seen more than once over the years.

"On fire and I think the roof just collapsed," Sloan collaborated, curious to see how Grier played it. She knew what hell Grier had lived with for the last three months and also knew the damage it had done on an emotional level. Mick O'Shaughnessy was definitely not Grier Thompson's type.

And as she watched her friend take a few nervous steps backward, Sloan realized he might be exactly what she needed.

Avery stood with a light sigh. "Much as I hate to interrupt, I need to get on bar duty. Make sure you save some of the juicy stuff for me."

Before Sloan could ask her what she was after, she

walked straight up to the two of them. "O'Shaughnessy. A beer?" When he nodded, she added, "Take my seat. It looks like we're about to get a repeat crowd."

Grier shot Avery a look that indicated dire retribution, but Avery ignored her, moving behind the bar with practiced ease and a keen eye as she welcomed a few people who sat along the length of the bar.

As Sloan watched her, she couldn't stop the thought that Roman Forsyth must really be an inconsiderate asshole to have let this one get away.

Chapter Eight

The cold December air swirled around Walker as he headed toward the Indigo Blue. Although it wasn't even six, the sky had long since darkened and now a blanket of stars twinkled overhead.

He said hello to fellow townsfolk, even stopped for a quick catch-up with Rose and Mark Paxton, who wanted to see if he'd be willing do their wills now that they were expecting their first child.

As he walked away from them, he couldn't keep the same unease from washing over him again. Damn it, why was he so turned around? It was just a kiss last night and a walk down Main Street this morning. Nothing more, nothing less.

A few shared moments that didn't add up to anything significant. All that consenting stuff he'd just lectured Jess on.

So why could he still picture her shining eyes? That liquid blue, covered with tears as she stared up at the love monument that seemed to define the town.

Fuck.

The lights of the Indigo Blue washed over him as he walked up to the hotel. The lobby glowed with an indefinable cheer, Christmas decorations adding bright splashes of color where Susan and Avery had put up a tree and several wreaths.

And then the wash of color faded away so that all he saw was *her*.

Sloan.

A bright smile lit up her face, her head tilted back in laughter. His stomach tightened painfully when he realized she was laughing with Mick, but he quickly tamped it down when he saw Mick's gaze shift. Darken. And stay firmly and fully on Grier.

The same thought that had struck him earlier—that his friend had the hots for Grier Thompson—went from a vague thought to a dead-on conclusion as he watched the way Mick looked at her. Devoured her, really.

Oh yeah, he had it bad.

Stepping through the door, he caught Avery's eye from across the room and she held up a beer she'd just opened for another patron in a very clear signal to ask if he'd like the same. His affirmative nod ensured she handed him a cold one as he approached the bar.

"Looks like you guys need to brace for another crowd tonight."

"And there's one person we can place our thanks to for that." Avery nodded in the direction of Sloan and Grier. "Bachelorette week's starting earlier than usual."

Walker eyed her speculatively, but he couldn't detect any notes of sarcasm. "You're not wearing your usual annoyance on that subject."

On a light shrug, Avery drank a sip from a bottled water she kept under the bar. "I like Grier and Sloan."

"That's a change of pace. I thought I distinctly remembered you telling me the annual influx of visitors were pond-scum-sucking interlopers."

"These ones aren't interlopers. They're friends."

Not entirely sure why he felt honor bound to let her know, he nevertheless found himself adding, "Speaking of friends, Roman's coming in next weekend."

"Oh?"

"It's his one long weekend off this season and he decided to make the most of it."

"How nice for him."

"Susan hasn't mentioned it to you?"

"No, she hasn't." A few hand waves from the opposite end of the bar caught her attention and she excused herself.

And with that confirmation, he was glad he said something. Roman was one of his best friends, but he'd always thought the man had acted like a perfect asshole when it came to Avery. And, in true matchmaking form, Roman's mother couldn't see it and opted to blindside Avery each and every time Roman decided to drop in to town.

So yeah.

He was glad he said something.

Good deed done for the day, he walked over to grab the empty seat next to Sloan. "I can only assume he's told you so many tall tales by now you're ready for some real stories."

"Ah." Mick sat back and cracked his knuckles. "Are you about to regale us with some deeply fascinating legal stories, Abe Lincoln?"

"Let me guess. You've heard about the bear at the

base of Denali who decided to use part of his plane as a scratching post. And then you probably heard the one about the salmon he caught too large to fit in the back of his plane. And I bet he's also told you the one about the moose who decided to head butt one of his propellers on the runway last spring."

Mick reached for his beer, taking a long drag before adding, "All true stories."

"So there was this case I was trying down in Anchorage," Walker started.

"Here he goes." Mick groaned.

Sloan's laughter interrupted them both. "So how long have you two been doing this routine?"

"Off and on since puberty."

"Routine's the same; the script has changed a bit," Mick added.

"It figures."

Walker's gaze jumped from Sloan to Grier and back to Sloan again. "How long have you two known each other?"

"Since the first day of college."

"We were roommates," Grier added.

"That's amazing. Most people hate their first college roommate."

"Not us," Grier said firmly. "We were a match from the start."

Even their physical appearances made them a pair, their differences lending an odd sort of symmetry. Grier, petite, with dark chestnut hair and smoky gray eyes. Sloan an all-American blonde with piercing blue.

As if uncomfortable with the scrutiny, Sloan's gaze

turned speculative as she deftly changed the subject. "So, Walker of the legal tales. Have you ever gone head-to-head with a moose?"

"It's an ugly story."

"That only makes it all the more important you tell it."

Walker tossed her a speculative look of his own. "You can't be interested in something that happened when I was a young buck, convinced of my invincibility."

"You'd be surprised." Sloan leaned forward slightly, her eyebrow going up in a seductive challenge.

Before he could answer, a loud throng of voices assaulted him, breaking him out of the moment.

Slamming him out of it, actually, with the force of an oncoming freight train.

Mick groaned under his breath, the sound not carrying farther than the four of them as the men's grandmothers walked toward them.

"Good evening, everyone." Walker didn't miss that his grandmother spoke first.

"Grandmother." Walker nodded as he stood to kiss her cheek and take her hand to lead her to his seat.

Grier and Sloan started to stand to give their seats before Mick leaped up, landed a quick kiss on Mary's cheek, then muttered something about "grabbing more chairs."

The small conversation circle quickly expanded to include the three women and Walker couldn't help but think of his earlier description to Avery.

Interlopers.

He'd always felt an edge of annoyance at his grandmother's matchmaking efforts, but for all his complaints, he'd never felt intruded upon.

Until now.

Sloan saw the change in Walker immediately. Although she'd enjoyed teasing him about his grandmother's interfering ways, she hadn't really sensed he minded all that much. But the dark look that rode his face went way beyond a slight irritation.

If she wasn't mistaken, he was mad.

The only question in her mind was whether he was mad over the arrival of the grandmothers, or if it was something else.

She'd seen his face when he'd strode into the lobby of the Indigo Blue a short time ago. There was a hardness in the set of his shoulders that spoke of frustration. And then those few moments at the bar with Avery, when her carefree expression turned decidedly troubled. She hadn't missed the dark look that crossed Walker's face once Avery turned away to help some patrons at the end of the bar.

It had captured her interest, even though it really wasn't any of her business to wonder about him.

So why was she still thinking about it?

Silence descended among the group. Grier shot her a look that Sloan immediately interpreted to mean *What the hell do we do now?*

Before she could think of anything, Grier took over, her smile bright with excitement. "I think you'll be excited by Sloan's news."

Sophie turned toward her, just as Walker returned with drinks for the three women. "What news, dear?"

"I'm writing an article about the town. The event that's coming up. It was just accepted today by a travel editor."

"On our town?" Mary interjected, her gaze pulled from its laser focus on her grandson and Grier. "In a magazine?"

Sloan brought them all up to speed, pleased when their excitement and enthusiasm seemed to lift the collective focus off of matchmaking and firmly on what it all meant for Indigo.

"You'll be nice to us, won't you, dear? With what you write." Julia's smile was soft, but Sloan didn't miss her firm resolve.

"Yes, Mrs. Forsyth. I'm writing a piece that will encourage visitors, not keep them away."

The answer seemed to satisfy as the woman sat back and took a sip of her drink. Sloan watched her as the discussion swirled around them, remembering her conversation with Walker that morning. Julia Forsyth was the first widow.

At thirty-six.

Sloan just couldn't imagine it. She was only three years away from that age and the couple part of her life hadn't even started.

And she still felt like she had so much time.

Didn't everyone feel that way?

She watched Julia a few more moments. There was a way about her. Not sad, really, but *quiet*. Like she was marking time instead of living it.

Sloan was pulled out of her reverie by the arrival of Susan, who planted herself on the arm of her mother-in-law's chair, leaned down and gave her a quick kiss on the cheek. "I can see the troublemakers have arrived."

Julia glanced up at her daughter-in-law and the quiet shifted, brightened. "I thought it was your night off?"

"Nope. I couldn't leave Avery by herself with the up-tick in business." Susan's gaze flicked briefly toward Avery before turning back to Julia. "Besides, Roman's in next weekend and I want to take a bit of time to visit with him."

Sloan shot Grier a look at that and suddenly the exchange at the bar made a bit more sense. Although they didn't know Avery well, Sloan had to believe the woman would have mentioned if the one who got away was coming back for a visit.

Which made her think that Walker was the one who had imparted the information.

The hard set of his shoulders confirmed it.

The conversation spun out, changing topics as Grier kept things moving, peppering the grandmothers with questions about the competition itself.

"Mick and Walker and a few others are helping set the course tomorrow," Mary interjected. "You two should come watch."

"Won't that give me an unfair advantage?" Sloan couldn't resist teasing. "I mean, if I know the course, won't it be easier to carry my pail of water?"

"Pails. Plural," Walker corrected her with a dry tone.

Sloan shook her head, once again boggled she'd agreed to this. She was a professional, for heaven's sake.

And she knew damn well there would be a ton of pictures taken for the event.

Pictures that would, no doubt, end up showcased on some Web site somewhere.

Good Lord, what had she gotten herself into?

And then she caught sight of Julia's face again.

With a disturbing flash of insight, the answer to why she was competing was crystal clear.

Mark time or get in the game?

Jessica stared at the phone, studying it with deep concentration. They'd upgraded to office phones a few years ago at Walker's insistence and it had taken Myrtle six months to even learn how to use the damn thing.

Now you'd have thought it had been her idea, since the woman knew how to use each and every feature. Voice mail. Conference calls. Even the horrific paging system, which she used with frightening regularity.

A particularly pointless exercise, since their offices were basically three large rooms.

It really was a beauty of a phone, though. Six lines, with buttons for each one. And then a whole panel of buttons to do everything from transfer calls to launch a guided missile.

And she was stalling.

With a deep breath, she lifted and dialed, the number flying from her fingertips with the taunting clarity of memory.

"Hello."

"Jack?"

"Yep."

"It's Jessica. McFarland."

A light laugh rumbled through the line. "I know who you are."

"Oh. Well. That's good."

Silence hummed for a moment and every thought she'd ever had about him—every moment of need and longing and desire—seemed to stick in her chest as she waited to see if he'd say anything.

"Where are you? I don't recognize the number."

"I'm calling from the office."

"It's awfully late." It wouldn't have been if she hadn't sat there for almost two hours trying to get up her nerve.

"Yeah, well, we've been working on a few things. I'm trying to get ahead before the holidays and all."

"Sure. Busy season is coming. Sounds like for both of us."

"You and Mick have a lot of trips coming in?"

"We do. Lots of corporate stuff again this year, which is good. We've missed that the last few years."

"I'll bet."

Small talk.

That's all this was and they both damn well knew it. Seeing as how they'd covered jobs, all they needed to do was to discuss the weather next.

"Storm's scheduled for early next week. I hope that doesn't put a dent in things, making it hard for folks to arrive."

And there it was, the proverbial conversation time waster.

On a rush, she decided to get it over with, possible

humiliation preferable to a discussion on rising storm fronts and weather systems.

"So, Jack. I was wondering. If you're not too busy. I'd like to have you over for dinner." And then for some other things. *Consenting* things, as Walker had dubbed it. And oh, I don't know, for the rest of my life sounds pretty fabulous, too.

"Thanks, Jess. Thanks. But. Well."

She heard the fumbling, the flat tones of his voice, and knew what was coming.

Knew there would be no dinner.

"Look, if you can't, I understand."

"You do, don't you?"

"Sure I do."

"It's not a good time right now."

"Got it. No problem. Look. Know that the invitation's always open. That's what friends do, you know."

"Yeah. I know."

"Well, it sounds like you've got a busy week and I've got about another hour of it here before I close up for the night. I'll catch you around town."

"You, too."

She would not cry.

She would *not*.

To her great relief, she didn't. But as she replaced the expensive phone in its high-tech cradle, Jessica fought the urge to throw it across the room.

The hotel was in full swing for the second night in a row, the lobby almost bursting with the denizens of Indigo. Sloan again found herself mingling, saying hello to some familiar faces from the evening before and meeting those who hadn't made it or whom she simply hadn't met yet.

All the conversations were filled with warmth.

And welcome.

And a whole lot of speculation.

The triple crown of that very friendly nosiness small towns were known for.

Why was it that since she hadn't grown up with these people their interest felt almost charming somehow? If she'd been at home, she knew it would have made her feel oppressed and rather annoyed.

A quick glance at Walker—and the hard lines that still marked his face—suggested he fell very squarely in the oppressed and annoyed camp this evening.

And it had all started when his grandmother came in.

With a gentle tap on her elbow, Sloan turned to see a very refined man with jet-black hair streaked liberally with silver and dark skin the color of a perpetual tan. "I wanted to introduce myself. I'm Ken Cloud."

Sloan put together various stories she'd heard over the past two evenings. "Dr. Cloud?"

"Yes."

"It's lovely to meet you."

"You, as well."

"How are you getting on? With the inquisition, I mean?" A smile played the corners of his lips as he eyed the seats Mary, Julia and Sophie still occupied, holding court with the town.

"I'm doing all right. Still puzzled by all the fuss, but no

complaints. Everyone has been so warm and welcoming."

"The grandmothers. They like you. And your friend Grier."

"They seem to like everyone."

"Don't let those sweet faces fool you." Ken's gaze roamed over the group of women, his eyes stopping on Julia. "Underneath there's pure steel. Pure, *stubborn* steel."

"You sound like you speak from experience."

On a nod and a last look, he added, "Perhaps."

"Dr. Cloud, I hope I don't seem rude, but maybe you'd answer a few questions for me."

He shifted his focus and Sloan felt the power of his direct gaze. Quiet and solemn, his dark eyes bespoke a knowledge and awareness and, if she wasn't mistaken, a secret or two. This was clearly a man who kept his own counsel and liked it that way.

"If you don't mind."

"No, not at all."

"Well, it seems like there's all this stuff going on underneath the surface. And I can't figure out if the contest brings it out or if it's there all the time and the contest simply heightens everyone's longing."

"Everyone yearns, Sloan."

"Do you think so?"

Again, those mysterious eyes stared back. "Don't you?"

"Yearn? For what?" The idea itself was silly. Yearning suggested unfulfilled desires and an unhappy life.

She was happy. And, well, she would admit to having a few unfulfilled desires—regular sex for starters.

But *yearning*?

"For whatever we most want in the world."

She turned over his words. "Is that what you think the contest is about?"

"On some level. The women who come yearn to find love; the men who enter the auction are looking for the same. The grandmothers yearn for great-grandchildren." With a small smile, he added, "The town yearns to send them all home again. Again, everyone wants something."

"But if that's true, then what happens when someone gets what they most want?"

He shrugged. "They want something else."

"Are we really as bad as all that?"

"I've spent my life studying people; it's the mark of the physician. I see them at their very best and, often, at their very worst. Trust me, my dear. Everyone's searching for something."

Mischief sparked somewhere inside of her as she allowed his words to sink in. Maybe she was looking for something. Something she hadn't found yet in the insular world she'd built back home. The narrow world she'd been raised in.

But she was here now and all the rules had changed. That glorious sense of freedom she'd felt earlier came back in a sudden rush.

She could be anyone here. Could do anything. Or she could just be herself.

The best version of herself.

With a nod in the direction of the women, Sloan reached for his arm. "Let's go have a chat with the grandmothers. I'd like to get a sense of what's going to happen over the coming days. Brace myself for all that yearning."

Chapter Nine

*A*very slammed the glasses into the dishwasher, barely taking care not to break anything. It would feel good to break something.

Good to finally let it out.

In a week, he'd be here.

Roman.

The raging asshole who'd broken her heart and who continued to do so with an alarming degree of regularity.

Every present that arrived at the hotel was like a slap in the face. Even on the few occasions she'd managed to date—had managed to enjoy the company of another man—his name had inexorably come up.

Roman Forsyth. Hockey god and local legend.

All it took was for her to mention she worked at the Indigo Blue and the questions fired in.

Yes, isn't his record amazing?

Of course he's destined for the hall of fame.

No, I don't think New York's going to trade him this year.

Damn it, even a few orgasms at the hands of another man couldn't purge him from her mind.

Or her soul.

And didn't that just suck.

*   *   *

Sloan wandered down the hall, the dull light from underneath the kitchen door catching her attention. The lobby was finally quieting down and she needed a few minutes to herself.

Her conversation with Dr. Cloud had been interesting, but it was the chatter afterward—once they sat down with the grandmothers—that truly grabbed her attention.

The entire town might be lovesick at the moment, but Sloan would bet her fifty-dollar entry fee a hundred times over that Dr. Cloud's interest in Julia went way beyond the temporary.

It was sweet. And just a little more of the unexpected.

A loud clatter had her moving into high gear, pushing through the swinging door into the kitchen. And straight into the middle of a full-on cry fest.

"Avery!" Sloan rushed over, grabbing Avery's hand before she stepped into a pool of shattered glass. "Stop. Just stop a minute."

Gently pulling her backward, then around the glass, Sloan led her to a small alcove and a kitchen table. "Here. Sit down. I'll take care of it. Just tell me where the broom and dustpan are."

"Pa-pa-pantry cl-closet." Sloan didn't miss the heavy hiccup that ended the mumbled words, indicating she hadn't come in on the beginning of this.

"You want to tell me what's wrong?"

"Like you can't figure it out."

Sloan shot her another glance as she turned back from the pantry door, broom and pan in hand. "Why don't you tell me instead of me making an assumption? Which I'm finding I do rather often—and I don't like it."

"Not all assumptions are bad. Especially when you're right."

"Or self-righteous, which is the usual angle. So tell me what's going on."

"Roman's coming back. Next week. Oh fuck." Another round of tears bubbled up. "He's coming *here*. And I have to paint on a smile and act like I don't have a care in the world."

The urge to move closer and offer comfort filled her, but Sloan stayed focused on her task. Unfortunately, this was one road that Avery walked alone, no matter how much Sloan wanted to fix the situation for her. "So it bothers you that he's coming back?"

"No." A loud sniff. "Yes." Another loud sniff. "Hell, yes. It bothers me a lot. And it bothers me how everyone feels they have to tiptoe around me all the time about it. He's been gone for thirteen fucking years. I've had time to get used to the idea."

Sloan kept sweeping, chasing the shards of glass that were scattered far and wide on the floor. "If you've gotten used to the idea, why are you still here?"

"What's that supposed to mean?"

At the indignation, Sloan smiled to herself. Good. This was good. "Well, I just mean that you could go somewhere else. Do something else instead of sit in his backyard. I assume he stays here when he's in town to visit Susan?"

"Yes."

"So why do you stay?"

"Because I have nowhere else to go."

Sloan bent down with the dustpan to sweep up the

small pile. "Surely that can't be true. There's a big world out there. Heck, there's a big state out there. Anchorage has to have something. Juneau, maybe, too? If, you know, you didn't want to leave Alaska."

"I mean I can't leave. Or couldn't leave up until about a year ago."

With a heavy sound, Sloan slammed the dustpan against the lip of the wastebasket. "Why?"

"My mother."

And now they were getting somewhere.

After a quick wash of her hands, Sloan left the broom propped against the counter and took a seat opposite Avery at the table. "Why don't you tell me about it?"

"What? My clichéd life? How my mother's alcoholism fucked up her life and mine. How she's been in need of almost constant care for the last decade. How relieved I was when she finally died last spring. What the hell does that make me, Sloan? Bitter? Ungrateful? Or worst of all, a horrible child who couldn't honor my parent."

"If you stayed, it seems like you honored her plenty."

"Yeah, well, that's for me to figure out. But it's why I stayed. And it's why I'm now stuck here."

"Stuck is a choice, Avery."

At the well of tears that filled her friend's eyes, Sloan patted her hand again. "It's taken me thirty-three years to recognize that, but I finally do. Stuck is a choice."

"That belongs on a T-shirt."

"We could make millions."

"Don't forget mugs and notebooks, too." Avery hesitated a moment. "Is everyone still out there?"

Sloan thought about the dying crowd she'd passed on her way to the kitchen. "There are still quite a few there, but not nearly as many as last night. Susan's got the bar. They'll keep."

The two of them sat there quietly for a few minutes as Avery pulled herself together.

"What did it feel like?"

"What?" Avery dragged her gaze back from where it had hung on a light over the industrial-sized sink. "What did what feel like?"

"Being in love like that."

Avery's face changed in that moment. Softened. "It was wonderful."

Sloan waited a beat, allowed Avery a moment to savor the memory. "Is that all?"

A shout of laughter rang out as Avery's dreamy gaze focused, then sharpened. "Yeah, be-atch. That's all."

"Thanks for clearing that up." Sloan patted her hand, then stood and crossed to the door. Pushing slightly on the swinging door, she turned her head. "I still hear party noises. I'd take another few minutes if I were you."

"I think I'll do that."

Sloan was nearly through the door before she turned around again.

"Avery?"

"Yeah?"

"There's more wonderful out there, you know."

Walker was a grown man and it chaffed to admit it, but he longed. For the feel of a woman. The taste of her. The promise of her.

And it doubly chaffed to admit that it was Sloan McKinley who'd gotten under his skin.

The one thing he owned—controlled—was his personal choices. He'd never regretted coming home to Indigo after college and law school. He had enjoyed the life he'd built here.

But damn it, he was entitled to build the life he wanted.

And it didn't include being tied down to anyone.

So how the hell did perfection manage to walk into his town on a pair of sexy legs and highly impractical designer heels?

This couldn't go anywhere.

And more than that, attempting anything would surely result in ties he not only didn't want, but didn't need.

Grier Thompson wasn't going anywhere. Even if she shook the snow off her boots as soon as she could escape Indigo, there was a connection to the town now.

She was bound to Indigo through her father.

And because of it, he couldn't think about simply doing a bit of screwing around in Sloan's hotel room.

He wasn't callous and he wasn't cruel. He entered into things with women who knew the score, knew what he was looking for and were seeking the same. A mutual good time and no strings.

And fuck it all, Sloan McKinley had strings written all over her.

Commitment strings.

Good girl strings.

Best friend strings.

And about a million others he couldn't—and shouldn't—ignore.

What was he thinking coming here, anyway? He'd been roped into acting as bellhop for Susan when a few guests arrived early. The women—a pair of friends from Chicago—had eyed him like he was a box of Godiva.

He pulled the crumpled note out of his pocket—one of the women had included it along with her tip when he'd dropped her off at her room. He'd tried giving both back, to no avail. She'd taken the money, but wouldn't take the folded paper.

Nor the hint, apparently, as she managed to run her fingers over his ass as she closed the door behind him.

Crumpling the paper, he saw a trash can in an open conference room doorway as he walked the first-floor hallway back to the lobby.

He needed to leave.

Sloan had disappeared a while ago and it wasn't his business to know where or why. Or to care about, either. So he would leave.

"Walker." Her voice floated out to him on a breathless whisper.

And there she was, walking through the swinging doors to the kitchen not ten feet away from him.

"What are you doing here?"

"I could say the same for you."

She hesitated for the briefest of moments. "I was just helping Avery with something."

"Me too. Susan asked me to help a few people up with their bags."

"Full service."

"It would have been fuller, had the guest gotten her way."

Sloan's eyes widened on that bit of news. "Oh."

"Yeah. Oh."

Before he could stop himself—before he could argue his way through all the pros and cons—he had her by the shoulders, pulling her against his body. His hands reached for her hair, fisting all those long blond strands as he walked backward toward the conference room he'd just passed.

"Walker—" Her whisper of his name ended on a moan as his mouth crushed hers, devouring her with a mix of tongue, teeth and lips.

She responded with reckless need, her mouth firm on his as she took, as he took, as they pushed each other on.

He had the presence of mind to slam the door as they tangled their way through the entrance, then continued moving them across the room. His spine hit the padded back of a conference table chair and Walker blindly reached for it, unwilling to break contact with her. With his free hand, he swirled the chair into position, then sat down in it, pulling her toward him by her hips.

Like a sexy fantasy come true, Sloan straddled him, her ass in perfect position for him to get a grip on it as he pulled her against him. With his mouth, he continued the assault, dragging a series of moans from her throat that grew in intensity.

Desperate for the feel of her skin, he skimmed his fingers along the waistband of her slacks. The light cashmere sweater she wore was soft as he lifted it, but nowhere near as soft as the skin he revealed underneath.

He let his fingers roam over her lithe body—the slender hips, the slight curve of her belly, the indentation of her belly button. Over and over, he stroked as his mouth moved on hers.

He felt her hands moving over his shoulders in eager caresses that slowly drove him mad. From his neck, over his collarbone, to grip at his shoulders. The fervor in her fingertips was like a sexy brand and he enjoyed the restless motions of her hips as they both fell deeper into the kiss.

Deeper into each other.

Sloan didn't know how it had happened. One minute she was thinking concerned thoughts for Avery and the next she was straddling Walker Montgomery in the middle of a conference room.

Oh God, she was straddling Walker Montgomery in the middle of a conference room.

Thankfully he'd had the foresight to close the door, because she knew she had none. All she could manage to conjure up besides mind-numbing need was the abstract thought that this was a great idea in theory but probably not a great idea in practice.

And then his devious hands were dipping down under the waistband of her slacks and *in practice* suddenly seemed like a marvelous idea.

Inspired.

Phenomenal.

Sparks of desire shot through her body as his fingers unbuttoned the waistband of her pants, then dipped lower to brush over her pubic bone as he undid the zipper. She shifted to allow him better access, but those clever hands kept on moving, up under her sweater, his thumbs pressing the underside of each breast as his palms gripped her rib cage.

All the while, his mouth stayed wild on hers.

She was the one to break the contact of their mouths first, her head falling back as his fingers played over her nipples. The aching tips grew hard under his ministrations as he encouraged sensation after sensation deep inside of her. Liquid heat traveled down her spine in sensual waves, coalescing in her belly in raw, aching need.

Unable to contain her light moans, she took her pleasure, grinding more forcefully against the hard length of his erection where she was seated against him. A low growl rumbled in Walker's throat and she was glad when he got her intent, his hands shifting from her sensitized breasts to the aching needs of her core.

She emitted his name on a sigh as his fingers dipped below the thin elastic of her panties and nearly groaned with satisfaction as he ran them along the folds of her body in one long, satisfying stroke. As his finger dipped inside of her, beckoning with deft movements, Sloan felt the world simply melt around her.

With a maddening exactitude that screamed lawyer—and a delightful devotion to his task—he didn't let her rest as he dragged wave after wave of pleasure from her. One finger became two as he plied her body with unerring precision, long, swift strokes dragging her up, up, up and then holding her there, prolonging the moment until she wanted to scream from the exquisite need.

On a ragged whisper, she heard his voice as if from a long way away. "Sloan. Look at me."

She opened eyes she hadn't even realized she'd closed, staring into the dark orbs of his. Pleasure and satisfaction mixed as he kept his gaze focused on hers. "Come for me."

"Walker." She breathed his name, reaching for what he offered, desperate to take it. And then there was no more waiting—nothing more to do but simply shatter.

Walker held her as her body convulsed with pleasure, his strong hands an anchor as she left her body for a few brief, glorious seconds. Falling forward, she buried her face in his neck as her orgasm receded, the lingering shocks of pleasure still trembling through her.

She felt him move his hand, shifted to allow him to withdraw and reached for the hem of his shirt, intent on drawing it up. Great, giddy waves of happiness suffused her as she smiled down at him. "Is that what they call full service?"

His answering, sexy smile was the epitome of male satisfaction. "You could say that."

"Well, then. Baby, you haven't seen anything yet." Her fingers fumbled with dragging his shirt up, her movements clumsy as her body still shivered with the aftershocks of pleasure. He leaned forward to help her when the distinct sound of the door clicking open stilled them both.

"Who's in here?"

"Avery," Sloan whispered against Walker's chest.

A muttered "shit" was all she got in return.

"I'll give you thirty seconds to get out of there."

"Avery. It's me."

"Sloan? Oh. Good. I figured somebody'd snuck in here to get it on." The door inched open as Avery reached in and flipped the switch. The bright overhead lights marred the ambience of muted light coming from the parking lot through the slats of the window blinds.

"Actually . . ." Sloan peeked over Walker's shoulder, their bodies firmly shielded by the oversized conference room chair as Avery walked through the door.

"Oh God! I'm so sorry." Avery spun on her heel, slamming the door in her wake.

"Well, that wasn't awkward," Sloan muttered against the side of his head.

"Not much."

He gently maneuvered her off his lap, struggling to stand around the painful erection that would likely haunt him for the rest of the night.

"You okay?" She glanced up from zipping up her slacks.

"Fine. Good."

"Good." She reached up to smooth her hair. When she missed a large piece that flew out sideways, he lifted his hand to assist her.

He straightened his own clothes, smoothing the material over his waist.

"You sure you're okay?"

"I'm fine, Sloan. We should get going."

She shrugged and left the room in front of him. As he watched the light swish of her hips, he couldn't stop the clench of his hands as his mind went straight back to the feel of her hips in his palms.

What the *hell* was he thinking?

The fucking conference room?

With his grandmother down the hall?

Part of the joy of being footloose and fancy free was that he kept that area of his life separate.

In a life that didn't have much privacy, this was one area he owned. And he'd be damned if he was going to give it up.

Sex in public in front of the entire town was hardly the way to keep that part of his life private.

He followed Sloan down the hall, not surprised when she stopped at the bank of elevators instead of returning to the lobby. "I think I'll turn in for the night."

"Probably a good idea."

When her gaze ran the length of him, his traitorous body—already walking the tightrope of barely banked desire—nearly ignored any and all sense of caution in favor of dragging her back against him.

"Would you like to come up?"

"I should probably leave you here."

"Sure. Right. Nothing like an interruption to spoil the mood."

"It's probably for the best."

"Excuse me?" Her voice came out on a strangled moan, and if he hadn't already known the words were the wrong ones, her reaction ensured it.

"You know. Things happen for a reason. There's a lot going on here. You're visiting. You deserve better."

"I know I do."

"Well, then. Good."

The elevator pinged open, saving both of them from any further awkwardness.

She stepped through the doors, her spine stiff. With anger, no doubt, and a good dose of pride to back it up. "Good night, Walker."

"Good night, Sloan."

As the doors swished closed, he told himself it was for the best once again. There was no way he was turning his life upside down for a woman.

But as he walked back toward the lobby, he couldn't stop the image of her in his arms from assaulting him.

How right she felt.

And how very wrong it felt to leave her to go to bed alone.

Chapter Ten

The knock came sooner than she thought it would, but she was deeply grateful to find Grier and Avery at her door. And they came carrying cookies. Still-warm chocolate chip cookies with little flecks of toffee in them.

"You don't fight fair," Sloan muttered as she reached for one.

"This isn't about fair. It's about details." Grier ran across the room and hopped onto the bed. "Spill."

"I think I'll just sit here and savor my cookie for a minute." Sloan took a bite as she walked to the bed, the warm chocolate on her tongue providing a temporary balm to make-out-session interruptus.

Unfortunately, a whole tray of cookies wouldn't make up for the brush-off at the elevator Walker had delivered after.

Grier's gray eyes darkened like storm clouds. "What happened, Sloan? You're totally missing the smug happiness people who just had sex have. And actually, what the hell are you doing texting us to come up and talk? Avery told me in the elevator you were, um, conferencing."

"The conference ended."

Grier's eyes widened. "Was he bad? Because he

doesn't look like he'd be bad. Oh wow. That's so disappointing."

"Grier." Sloan finally had a chance to get a word in. "He wasn't bad. He wasn't anything. We didn't have sex."

"Before you tell us"—Avery held up a hand as she moved to sit on the edge of the bed, laying the platter of cookies in the middle between them—"I owe you an apology. I've had to knock off things in that conference room more than once and I figured it was someone else. Had I known it was you I would never have interrupted."

"Don't worry about it. It was probably for the best."

"Sloan. Why?"

"Because he gave me the brush-off right after delivering the best fucking orgasm of my life."

Grier and Avery leaned forward as a pair, eyes wide. Grier was the first to speak. "Okay. Sorry, but you need to back up. What happened?"

"I'm not sure, to be very honest. One minute I'm heading into the hallway after talking to Avery in the kitchen and the next he's got me moving backward down the hall and into the conference room, kissing me senseless. And then . . ."

Sloan broke off when the memories threatened to overwhelm her. No matter how comforting it was to share, some of the specifics had to remain private.

Especially with the mortifying way it all ended.

"And then we screwed around a bit in the conference room." Sloan reached for another cookie. "And that's basically it, culminating in an ending that means Princess Dry Spell isn't quite dry-spell free."

"I'm sorry you're still sitting in the castle. But you did

get an orgasm out of it. A good one if the color on your cheeks is any indication," Grier pointed out helpfully, laying a hand over the top of hers.

"That I did." Her body was still overly sensitized from his touch, the energy that followed a really good orgasm still firing through her nerve endings.

"This is my fault, Sloan. I'm really sorry."

"Don't be, Avery. If this is the way the man reacts to a willing woman, I probably got off lucky."

"Well, you got off," Grier added with the dry wit that usually managed to cheer her up.

"Again, your statement of the obvious is oddly comforting while annoyingly accurate." Sloan tamped down on the tears that threatened at the base of her throat.

Avery must have sensed the threat of tears because she passed the plate of cookies again. "I know we're all brand-new friends, but I'm forbidding any tears. Because if you start, I'll start, and I refuse to shed one more tear over Roman Forsyth."

"Did something happen?" Sloan was grateful for the change in topic and the chance to focus on someone else's problems instead of her own.

"Nothing since I last updated you."

Avery quickly got Grier up to speed, fleshing out the same details she'd shared with Sloan earlier, but with a succinct and emotionless monologue. "Of all weekends. With the competition we've got a full house, so there's no way Susan will let me off."

"Surely she understands," Sloan argued. "I mean, what does she do for help when you're not around? Can't she ask them?"

"They're already here filling in to help with the over-flow. And no, she doesn't understand. She sees me as the one who got away."

"Oh, Avery. That's awful." Grier shifted positions, laying a comforting hand over Avery's. "Can you try and talk to her about it?"

"Nothing works. She claims she knows best when it comes to her son."

"Which obviously she doesn't." Why was it, Sloan mused, most people—even well-meaning people—just didn't know how to mind their own business?

"Do you guys have any sort of reunion sex when he comes back?" Grier reached for another cookie.

The misery stamped across Avery's face gave all the answer she or Sloan needed. "No. Never."

"That's too bad," Grier mentioned as she took a small nibble. "That means the last time you two had sex together was when?"

"My nineteenth birthday."

"Ooooh." Grier winced. "And you've had several birthdays since then."

"Thank you, Grier. That would be correct. Thirteen more of them, to be exact."

"Then I say it's definitely time for some grown-up reunion sex."

Sloan had no idea where Grier was going with all this and was about to interrupt when Avery's phone went off. Glancing down at the text, Avery jumped up. "Shit, shit, shit. Drama. I'll be right back."

"Saved by the bell," Grier hollered after her as she ran out the hotel room door.

"Grier. What the hell was that about? We're supposed to be giving her a listening ear."

"I was helping. I'm way better at sex now than I was at nineteen."

"And your point is?"

"She needs to stop thinking of the two of them when they were kids. They're grown-ups, with very grown up parts they both now know how to use."

"I swear, you need your head examined."

"Probably." Grier nodded with a smile. "But I bet I gave her some food for thought."

"Closer together, Walker. They're running an obstacle course on ice. We don't want them falling."

"Yes, Grandmother." Walker repositioned the bright orange cones he'd already moved three times as his grandmother marched around the obstacle course they'd set up at the far end of town.

"It doesn't look like last year."

Tamping down on the urge to yell, Walker gritted his teeth and smiled. "You didn't want it like last year because that girl from Arizona fell during the third turn."

"Oh, that's right dear." Sophie patted his arm before turning at the sound of her name. "Well, I know you'll do what's best. I need to go."

Walker watched her walk away before glancing down at the paper map he'd been given earlier that morning.

"She making you nuts?"

"It's an annual tradition." Walker glanced up to see Jack Rafferty, an armful of tools in his hands. "What did she rope you into?"

"I'm hammering bleachers for the next hour. Or until I freeze my ass off, which, based on the temperature this morning, will likely happen in the next ten minutes." Jack glanced in the direction of Sophie's retreating form. "How the hell is that woman so hale and hearty?"

"She made a deal with the devil." At Jack's bark of laughter, Walker added, "It's the only reasonable explanation."

"I hope you know I mean no disrespect to your family if I agree with you."

"None taken." Walker refolded the paper and shoved it in his pocket. "Here. Let me help you with that. Hammering something may put some feeling back into my limbs."

"You're on."

The two of them walked to the far side of the course, where a series of poles and metal forms had already been laid out. "You've done this before?"

"This isn't the first year your grandmother roped me into this."

"I guess not."

Jack pointed to a few poles that were separated from the rest. "We start with those."

They worked in companionable silence for a few minutes as Walker followed Jack's lead. In a relatively short time, the framework began to take shape.

"Your grandmother's a wily one. She put me to work last year on this. Thought getting me out in the community would do me good dealing with Molly's passing."

Walker cast an eye toward Jack as he tightened a bolt. "Was she right?"

"Not much helped then, but it was the first time I got out. Funny what a year does. Or doesn't," Jack added quietly.

Walker thought about his conversation the evening before with Jess. He kept his tone casual while violating his personal rule of staying out of other people's business. "You been doing much of that? Getting out?"

"Nah."

With a final twist, Walker tightened the bolt he was working on and started for another. "Any reason?"

"I get out plenty with the flying. Mick and I have so many runs we're thinking of expanding. And the rest of the time—well, there's not a whole lot to get out for."

"You sure about that, Rafferty?"

"Yeah." A loud pounding echoed as Jack hammered on a post. Walker figured the movements were deliberate and he almost let the whole thing drop. He would have except that he caught Jack's suddenly still form from the corner of his eye.

Across the square, Jess tromped out of their offices, her hands full of packages. Likely doing errands for Myrtle again, Walker figured, so the older woman wouldn't have to go out in the cold. Jack's gaze never left Jess until she turned the corner onto Indigo Avenue, out of sight.

Purposely keeping his tone light and casual, Walker reached for another bolt, not even looking at Jack as he spoke. "Seems to me you could do some getting out if you were up for it."

For a few moments, it seemed as if he'd overstepped his bounds because Jack stood there in stony silence. Just as well. It wasn't any of his damn business anyway. Besides, who the hell was he to be giving out relationship advice?

"Time's just not right, Walker."

Well, that was one bit of logic he couldn't disagree with.

"Guess so, Jack. I guess so."

As the frame of the bleachers went up between the two of them, taking shape and form with each passing minute, Walker ignored the clench in his gut that told him he'd made a mistake the night before with Sloan.

The timing was just off.

That was all.

If being snubbed via make-out-session interruptus by Walker Montgomery was the height of feminine embarrassment, breakfast at the Indigo Café was its antidote. Sloan and Grier were immediately seated at a table in the dead center of the dining room, amidst table after table of men.

All of whom were focused on the two of them.

"It's like a dream come true." Grier leaned forward over her menu, her voice barely above a whisper. "And I never thought a dream come true would feel so weird."

"You've got that right." Sloan glanced down at her menu, the pancakes again drawing her eye with all their carb-loaded sinfulness. With a firm snap, she decided a plate full of fluffy calories was just the ticket after the previous evening. Besides, now that she was competing, she needed to build up her strength.

"What are you both having? Besides a side of bachelors," the waitress added with a wink as she filled their coffee mugs.

"Pancakes, bacon and a side of hash browns," Grier answered, as if reading Sloan's mind.

"Same."

"Good choice. The men up here like a woman with a bit of padding. And you two certainly need a bit." She sauntered away, refilling coffee as she went.

"I'm not sure if that was a compliment or not." Sloan reached for her coffee.

Grier glanced up from where she was dumping a plastic creamer into hers. "Actually, I don't think it was an insult. I think it's a refreshing change."

"Refreshing?"

"Yeah. Everything in New York is about maintaining our image. It's nice to hear a different version of perfect."

Sloan glanced into the shimmering top of her cup. Grier's words had struck a chord. "Do you really think we live that way?"

"Not you and me, in how we treat each other. But yeah, I think there's something of the rat race in how we live. Especially in our jobs. Hell, would you actually go out and buy Armani if you weren't trying to impress the latest editor you're wooing?"

Sloan thought about her latest purchase, a gorgeous charcoal suit. "Maybe."

"Okay. Wrong example, queen of the closet. But think about it in a broader sense. When's the last time you went out without makeup? Or even thought about wearing ratty old jeans to pick up Sunday-night Chinese food."

"Is it wrong to get fixed up? Or to want to look nice?"

Grier waved a hand. "No, no. That's not what I meant. I mean the whole idea of doing it because it's expected of you. Like every moment needs to be scripted to perfection."

Sloan couldn't help but think of the unscripted moments she'd shared the evening before with Walker. The all-consuming heat that had built up between them. The *immediacy* of it all. He saw her and he took her.

Which made his rejection that much more upsetting.

One moment they were so wrapped up in each other there wasn't enough room between them to slip a piece of paper and the next he was checking out and sending her back to her room.

At Grier's questioning look, Sloan returned her attention to their conversation. "You sound like you've suddenly become a fan of Alaska."

Grier shrugged. "It's not so bad. And that's all because of you, by the way."

Sloan reached out and laid a hand over Grier's. "It's all because of you. And who you are. I simply provided the liquor to drop natural inhibitions for a few brief moments so everyone could get to know the real you."

"That you did." Grier squeezed back before reaching for another creamer. "And while the people part has definitely improved, I wouldn't say much else has improved. Walker called me yesterday. Kate's still not backing down on the house."

"Do you want it that badly?"

"I don't know. Honestly, there's a huge part of me that wants to just give it to her and be done."

"So why don't you?"

"It's like he wanted me to have it, you know." Grier fiddled with the empty plastic creamer. "And I don't have a problem giving it up. Hell, a month ago I didn't even know it existed. But I can't quite shake the fact that he wanted me to see what it's like up here. Try it for a while. But no matter what I think, all I look like is the greedy interloper."

"And you think you're wrong for that?"

"I don't think it makes me very sympathetic to anyone."

"Why does anyone else matter?"

Grier's gaze tripped around the room before settling back on Sloan. "He lived here. Made a life here. I'd like to think these people he called his friends thought well of me."

Before Sloan could say anything, Grier added, "After the year I've had, I can't figure out if it's the universe kicking my ass some more or if it's a second chance. But, whatever the answer, I'm just not quite ready to give it up."

"Then you shouldn't."

Two heaping plates of pancakes were laid out before them. As the warm scent of bacon wafted toward her, Sloan couldn't help but wonder how it was that she and her best friend—two New Yorkers to the core—had ended up having a cozy breakfast for two in the middle of Alaska.

The thought didn't have much time to take root as their twosome rapidly expanded.

"Mind if we pull our table up?" Sloan glanced up at

another tree-sized man with several days' worth of growth on his cheeks. His equally massive friend hung back slightly. "You two look like you could use some company."

"Be our guest." Grier waved a hand.

After quick introductions, Sloan couldn't hold back a smile. "Tom and George. Those are your real names. No nicknames we need to be aware of?"

"No, no nicknames here."

"That must make you unique in this town."

"That it does," Tom, the quieter of the two, agreed.

As their conversation spun out, Sloan had to acknowledge that not only were Tom and George enjoyable breakfast companions, but they could provide some great material for the backstory in her article. "Do you both mind if I interview you a bit?"

"Interview us? For the story you're writing?" George sat forward, an eager smile across his face. "We're in."

The conversation Sloan thought was between the four of them was quickly interrupted by a series of shouts.

"Can we get in?"

"Hey! I want to be interviewed!"

"What about us?"

Grier's attempt at a discreet giggle missed horribly as her laughter carried across the table. "There really is no such thing as privacy in this town."

"If you want privacy, don't go out," Tom pointed out reasonably.

Sloan reached for the steno pad she kept in her purse, amusement at the sage advice lightening the mantle of melancholy she hadn't even realized hung around her shoulders. "You're all sure? You really want to be interviewed?"

A chorus of yesses came back at her.

"Let me put this another way. Who here doesn't want to be interviewed?"

When no one uttered a sound or raised their hands, Sloan shrugged. "Okay. You're my witness, Grier." She rummaged in her bag for another pad of paper and a pen, shoving both across the table. "Please take notes on who's who."

Grier picked up the pen. "Got it."

Turning back toward the crowd, Sloan jumped in with the question she'd been wondering about from the start. "What's wrong with the women right here in Indigo?"

At the blank stares, she elaborated. "That you have to look outside the town for women."

When more blank stares greeted her, Sloan wondered if there was some unspoken code she'd missed. What she didn't expect was the raised hand at the back of the room. "Yes?"

A small man stood up. He wasn't unattractive, but he didn't have the rugged presence of the others. Not just in physical size, but in demeanor as well. "There aren't enough of them."

"I'm sorry?"

"The women. There aren't enough of them. The men outnumber the women almost two to one."

"Oh."

"And then, when you factor in that there are some men who all the women seem to go for, well, it's an honor that bachelorettes come up here wanting to meet us."

An unfamiliar tightness coalesced in her chest as she watched the man standing there, his words honest and not even remotely tinged with bitterness.

Instead, he stood and spoke fact.

And in that moment, Sloan had the startling realization that loneliness could touch you anywhere, whether you were in the middle of eight million people or seven hundred and twelve.

Chapter Eleven

Walker found her at the café, surrounded by men, after he and Jack got done hammering up the bleachers.

"She's quite a looker," Jack leaned toward him and murmured. "And it sure looks like the town's taken to her."

Walker figured the man was entitled to a few jabs, especially after his own prodding and poking about Jess, but damn, if the sight didn't irritate him. "She's trouble."

"More like trouble follows her, I'd guess." Jack slapped him on the back before following their waitress to a table.

Shouts and laughter rang out through the room and Sloan was clearly the ringleader among the ruckus.

Trouble was right.

"So what happens after the auction and dinner dance?"

George Tapper admonished her. "If you need to ask that, you're not a very good reporter, Ms. McKinley. Nor do you have a very good imagination."

A round of guffaws went up and Sloan's fair complexion turned a rosy shade of dark pink. Despite her obvious embarrassment, she maintained her composure. "I meant after-after. Not right after. When the women go home."

A man in the back—Boone Fellows, Walker thought— hollered back. "Some don't go home."

"Oh?" Those bright blue eyes lit up like the Fourth of July. "What do you mean?"

George nodded sagely. "Lots of the bachelorettes have stayed up here. Margaret and Tanya stayed a few years back."

"Don't forget Marcy!" one man hollered.

Maria, their waitress, added to the list as she floated around refilling coffees. "Darla and Melissa about seven or eight years ago. And remember Wade? Up and moving off to Arizona three years ago to go with that girl from Phoenix."

"That's quite a few love matches." Sloan scribbled on a notepad in her lap. "Is that what you're all hoping for?"

Walker's gut tightened at the question.

Was that what they were all hoping for?

A wife to come home to? Someone to tie themselves to for the rest of their lives?

Commitment. The promise of forever.

There wasn't any such thing. His father had proven that one, even if no one else knew it but him.

And in keeping that secret, he'd managed to carve off his own little piece of misery. Caught between his grandmother's memories of her perfect son and the cold reality of truth.

Nope. He liked his commitment-free life just fine. No commitment meant no hurt feelings when someone moved on. No long, endless years marking time with someone you didn't really care about. And most of all, it meant there wasn't any deception.

Based on the round of resounding "yesses," "sures" and "absolutelys," Walker figured he was the only man in town who felt that way.

Roman didn't count now that he didn't live there any longer. And Mick's sudden and marked interest in Grier had him wondering if his friend's bachelorhood wasn't something he'd abandon if given half the chance.

With a glance at Jack's face as he ordered his breakfast, Walker added the man to his mental tally of confirmed bachelors.

At least there were two of them who felt the same way.

"He can't keep his eyes off of you."

"Grier. You're bordering on the way Susan treats Avery with the whole she-knows-better crap. Enough with this."

"But he likes you, Sloan. I know it."

Sloan resolutely avoided glancing across the diner. The men had proven incredibly helpful, but all had reluctantly said their good-byes as they were called off to their various jobs. And now she and Grier sat alone in the dining room along with Walker and a man she hadn't met yet.

"If he liked me, Princess Dry Spell would be sitting proudly in the brand-new castle of Princess Got Me Some. Instead, I'm nursing a serious case of postorgasm embarrassment because he ran out on me."

"You don't know why he ran off. Avery said she interrupted you guys. Maybe *he* was embarrassed."

"You seriously expect me to believe a few moments of inconvenient awkwardness will keep a man from closing the deal with a willing woman?" Sloan stopped just short of dropping her head in her hands and let out a light groan instead. "A *very* willing woman."

"There has to be a reason."

"Yes, and you're looking at her."

"No way. And if you think that then your mother's bullshit has affected you far worse than I suspected."

Sloan glanced up from her coffee. "What does any of this have to do with my mother?"

"You tell me? You've been weird for the last week and I think it's tied to what happened at Thanksgiving. Actually, for what's been happening a lot longer than that."

The eagle eyes of friendship bored into her psyche as a sharp pain hit her gut. "You know the holidays aren't easy."

"A lot of people struggle at the holidays. It's a time of joy and it's disheartening when you don't feel any."

Leaning forward, Sloan lowered her voice to a whisper, unwilling to broadcast her personal embarrassment through the diner. "I'm just so sick of it. The constant focus on being single. It gets so old, this relentless focus on something I can't control. The holidays only shine a spotlight on it."

"You don't think you can control it?"

"Do you?" Sloan wouldn't have been more surprised if Grier had asked her when she was taking her next trip to the moon.

"It's not outside the realm of possibility."

"You really think you can control who you fall in love with."

"I'm talking about marriage, Sloan. If you wanted to be married, you could be."

"But I'm not in love with anyone."

Grier sat back with a satisfied smile on her face. "Then what are you so gloomy about?"

And just like that, Grier turned the entire discussion on its ear.

Sloan *did* want to find the right man to marry, not someone who fit some preconceived notion created out of her mother's relentless need to interfere.

"Oh fine, sit there all smug. Next time I get fixed up by the Winnie McKinley matchmaking service, I'm dragging you along."

"Lucky me. Your mother picks out such charming specimens."

Sloan couldn't stop the bark of laughter at that one, and quickly focused on what was left of her now cold pancakes before the entire room tuned in to their conversation.

"And now, on to phase two of my devious plan," Grier whispered under her breath before lifting her voice several notches, putting them clearly in eavesdropping range of Walker. "Fine. Then let's talk about the bachelors. Some of them were awfully cute."

Sloan wanted to sink through the floor. Absolutely, positively sink through the floor. "Look, why don't we get out of here?"

"Not yet. I want more food."

"More?"

"Yep. George and Tom raved about the omelets."

"Then have one tomorrow."

"I want one now." Grier waved their waitress over and put in her order for gruyere, mushrooms and spinach.

Sloan shook her head as she dived into about her fifth cup of freshened coffee. "I have absolutely no idea how you eat like that."

"It's a rare gift."

"It's annoying."

"Which you've told me on several occasions." Grier's wide-eyed stare held not one hint of remorse.

"You're tiny and petite. That should be good enough. But then add in the fact you can eat like a truck driver on a three-day bender and it adds insult to injury."

"And you're long, lithe and gorgeous. Ask me if I feel any sympathy."

"Looks like you two were busy making friends." Sloan glanced up to see Walker, coffee cup in hand, standing next to them. "Mind if I sit down?"

"Weren't you here with someone?"

"Jack had to get back to the airstrip and get to his runs."

"He's the one who flies with Mick, right?" Grier's tone was nonchalant, but Sloan wanted to do a fist pump in victory. If Grier wasn't interested in Mick, Sloan would eat one of the pylons being set up on Main Street.

"He's the one."

At Sloan's pointed stare, Grier offered a small shrug. "It's starting to come together. Who's who in town, I mean."

"Looks like more than that was coming together. You two had quite a crowd."

"The men were very helpful." Sloan felt the ice in her words clear down to her ramrod-straight spine. Unwilling to show him how he'd gotten to her, she pushed as much sweetness into her tone as she could. "It's great background for my article and their enthusiasm was contagious."

"Ah yes. Your article. Was that all it was?"

"I'm sorry?" She saw the speculative look in his eyes as his shoulders stiffened to match her physical indifference.

"Oh, come on. You mean to tell me you're not sizing up the bachelors in advance? The rest of the bachelorettes haven't descended yet, so you're getting a leg up."

"I was focused on my story. Nothing more. And I've seen a few people arrive in advance."

"A few. But most wait until next weekend. I have a theory on that." He leaned forward in his chair, as if waiting for them to bite on the clue. "If, you know, you want to put it in your article."

"Well, don't keep us in suspense." Grier smiled up at their waitress as she laid down the omelet.

"I think it's because no one wants to ask for that much time off work."

Sloan watched him, not sure she'd followed his logic. "You think what?"

"I think the women who come up here to compete in the grandmothers' little game are afraid to tell their bosses they're traveling to Alaska to meet a man. So they don't take the extra time off and don't come in early. Most are on puddle jumpers or the train back to Anchorage first thing Sunday morning."

"And what about the ones who came early?"

Walker shrugged and took a sip of his coffee. "They're the rarities."

"Or maybe they don't come early because it's minus fifteen degrees and they're smart enough to stay home."

"I'm just suggesting it could be a good angle for your story."

Sloan wasn't sure why his theory bothered her. After all, he'd lived through this for several decades, from the sound of it. He knew far more than she did.

Even so, it disturbed her that was what he thought. "It doesn't make any sense. Why would someone come up here if they were embarrassed about it?"

"Sloan's right," Grier chimed in. "Why bother coming all this way if you're worried about what someone thinks?"

"The entire world's scared of being single and alone. Women especially. So they come up here but don't tell anyone."

A small tic started around the edge of her eye, but Sloan held back her thoughts, instead catching Grier's gaze. The quick wink she got in return confirmed what Sloan already thought—that they'd both let him dig his own grave before throwing on several shovels full of dirt.

"And you don't spend any time thinking about being alone. No one to share your life with? Have a family with?"

"I haven't spent all that much time worrying about it."

Could this really be the same man she'd spent those long glorious minutes with last night in the conference room? And was it possible that she was angry because his callous words flew in the face of what she hoped about him?

"Start asking around. You'll see what I mean."

Sloan finished writing the words "embarrassed to take part," followed by a large question mark, then circled the entire passage.

It was something to look into; something to ask.

As she circled the phrase one more time, she glanced up at Walker. A hard edge tinged his features, his mouth a grim line as he laid his coffee cup down.

Was she reading something that wasn't there?

Or was he hiding something? A pain he held back, behind cynical words and lackluster theories.

Or maybe his comments stung because he wasn't falling neatly into some box she'd painted him into in her mind.

Either way, the eager shovels full of dirt she was anxious to throw on him suddenly felt far too heavy.

"I'll take that under consideration." Shifting gears, Sloan laid her pen down. "Speaking of Mick and Jack, I assume it's not all that hard to book a flight to Anchorage. I want to include some sights in my article."

"I think I've seen signs at the hotel," Grier said. "Avery can arrange it for you."

"Great."

Sloan shoved the notebook and pen back in her bag, the next several days shaping up in her mind. She'd planned to spend ten days here and could easily extend it if she needed to. Maybe she'd have Avery book her a trip out to Denali as well.

"I'll take you."

"What?" The coffee she had halfway to her mouth fumbled in her hand, sloshing liquid over the rim as Walker's words registered. "You'll take me where?"

"To Anchorage. Today, if you want. In fact, if you hurry, we can snag a ride with Jack."

"I'm not going to Anchorage today."

"Why not?" Grier cocked her head. "It's a great idea. Get a jump on your story. Heck, you'll probably even fly back with a few more early-arriving bachelorettes. You can get their take on the upcoming weekend and what they hope will happen."

"Thanks, Grier." Sloan shot her a look that she'd had very little use for over the years, but which Grier absolutely knew meant she'd pay later, and dearly.

"Come on. Go back and get whatever you need and I'll tell Jack to hang on a few minutes."

Sloan glanced at the seat next to her where she'd piled her things after they'd sat down. She had the heavy padded coat. Add in the heavy, fur-lined boots and the three steno pads in her large purse and she was all set. "I've got what I need."

"No packing. Really?"

"Walker, it's a day trip, right?"

"Yeah."

"Okay. Then I'm ready."

"Well, then"—his smile was lazy as he pushed back from his chair—"there's one stereotype blown."

"Are we really back to that?"

"I guess we are. I'd have never made you for a rough-and-ready kind of woman."

"I'd hardly call a puddle jumper to Anchorage and a day in the city rough and ready."

"Suit yourself."

She cursed his name as they made their way to Anchorage. Damn fucking asshole.

The plane tilted again and her stomach tilted with it, the pancakes she'd devoured an hour earlier threatening a return trip.

"Miz Sloan. Are you all right?" Jack's voice came through on the earphones she wore.

She waved a hand back at him with a small smile, afraid to actually put voice to words for fear of what else might come out of her mouth.

Oh God, no wonder people recommended the train.

They'd left seven minutes ago and she'd spent the last six and a half in the sheer misery reserved for victims of the flu or a really awful hangover.

This felt like a combination of both.

A light tap on her arm had her turning her head to see Walker with a can of soda stretched out to her. The rough, husky tones of his voice came through her earphones and damn it if she couldn't feel a slight twinge in her belly.

It was amazing there was room to feel anything else in there, but she did. Threads of longing wrapped around her limbs like warm honey. With trembling fingers, she took the can of Coke and tentatively took a sip, the fizzing liquid a balm as it made its way down her throat.

He kept his eyes on her, their deep, warm brown color full of concern. "Have a bit more."

She nodded and took one more ice-cold sip, the fizz and the sugar going a long way toward settling her roiling stomach.

With a small smile, he pointed to the window. "Now look over there."

Sloan turned toward the window and nearly dropped the can the view was so breathtaking. Sheer icy peaks rose into the bright morning light as the impossible face of Denali stared back at them. Her thoughts immediately reverted to those moments on the train a few days earlier when she'd viewed the mountain from a distance.

She had felt a kinship.

Anticipation.

Hope.

Where had that gone?

"It's beautiful, isn't it?" Again, that amazing voice poured through the headphones, affecting her system like a drug.

"Absolutely magnificent."

"Are you okay if I dip a bit? I can show you a few things before we head on down to Anchorage?" Jack's kind voice echoed through her headset and she nodded.

"Yes, please. I think I'll be okay." Sloan took another sip of the soda, pleased that her stomach seemed to be leveling out. As Jack turned the plane, she realized that really was true—her insides took only a slight dip as the plane made a wide swoop around the south face of the mountain.

Jack narrated as they went, pointing out a base camp

for climbers, a landing area for planes and a few other landmarks of interest.

"People actually climb it?" Sloan's gaze traveled over the peaks of the mountain. The impressive height, combined with the harsh weather conditions had her questioning the sanity of those who chose to pit themselves against nature in this fashion.

"Several thousand a year, actually. It's not the season for it now. It's too cold. Fall's the peak season. Mick and I ferry at least three to four groups a day up here in season and usually as many back off."

"They do a brisk tourist trade in the summer, too," Walker added. "Lots of visitors want to see her."

"I can see why. She's magnificent." And she was, Sloan thought. A majestic example of nature's beauty and a very clear reminder to humans that there was far more to the universe than anyone could ever see, touch, know or hope to conquer.

Like staring out at the ocean or up at the stars.

For in those moments, Sloan felt very small and tiny, yet powerful all at once. These monoliths of nature had been here for millions of years and would be here for millions more, yet for that moment, she was one with them.

A part of something far bigger.

A light prickling sensation ran down her spine and Sloan shifted in her seat, turning away from the window. Walker's heavy-lidded gaze bored into hers and she saw the unmistakable stamp of desire in their dark depths. A sharp spike of feminine intuition speared through her as she allowed her gaze to linger on his. To drink him in.

To revel in the moment.

And again, she had the sense she'd become a part of something far bigger than herself.

Chapter Twelve

*J*ack took the plane down smoothly, the wheels touching down with a light grace that belied the awkward start of the trip. He still felt bad about Sloan's reaction to the flight, but knew it wasn't to be helped.

He and Mick regularly dealt with the rebellious stomachs of very unhappy—and very airsick—passengers. People accustomed to flying on 747s had no idea the experience didn't necessarily translate to the small planes they used to get around up here.

But he had to hand it to her—Sloan had held it together. The one he really wondered about was Walker. He hadn't missed the care and troubled concern he'd shown for her on the flight.

Jack shot his old friend a sideways glance as Walker helped Sloan from the plane cabin to descend down the short flight of portable stairs. If he wasn't mistaken, the stubborn son of a bitch had it bad.

"I'll see you both back here at six."

Walker shot him a thumbs-up of agreement and a wave from outside the plane. Jack had picked up his logbook to record a few details when his gaze caught on the pair. Curious, he watched the two of them walk across the tarmac toward the airport.

Although Walker didn't touch her, he hovered close and Jack saw him clench his fists a few times as the urge to settle a hand at her lower back clearly overcame him.

Yep, Walker Montgomery had it real bad.

Served him right.

Jack had ferried him down here more times than he could count. And while he liked and admired his friend, he'd always thought the man lived a very empty sort of half life.

Carefree, but an empty one all the same.

And who the hell are you to talk, Rafferty?

An image of Jess filled his mind's eye, kicking him with a swift hook to the chest that would have made David Beckham proud.

That was one fucking situation that wasn't carefree. It might have started that way, but Jack knew trouble when he saw it.

And guilt.

Oh yes, did he know guilt.

And he had a big old heaping pile of it keeping him up at night. Guilt for betraying Molly not even three months after she'd passed. And another matched serving for ignoring Jess and treating her like none of it had ever happened.

But it *had* happened. For one amazing weekend a whole lot of something had happened.

His memories traveled back over that weekend. The unexpected way things had just sort of clicked. A casual, Friday-night dinner at the diner where they'd happened to run into each other. And the ensuing forty-eight hours where they hadn't been able to keep their hands off each other.

He'd felt that weekend. For the first time since Molly's diagnosis two years before, he'd felt something other than numb.

He'd *felt*.

And damn it, now that he'd let the genie out of the bottle, he couldn't seem to find the numb again.

Walker glanced over at Sloan as they moved through the airport. "Are you sure you don't need something to settle your stomach?"

"I just ate a huge breakfast. That's probably why my stomach got so upset."

"If you're sure?"

"I'm fine. Really. The Coke helped a lot." A small, rueful smile tilted her lips. "But there's clearly a reason there's no mention of the possible side effects in the pamphlets. From the wad of airsick bags I saw in the back of the seat in front of me, I take it that's a pretty regular occurrence."

"Yeah. It's a little-known trade secret."

"Tricky."

"Necessary," he added with a nod. "Would you have gone up willingly if you'd known?"

"Touché. So, Mr. Tour Guide, where are you taking me?"

"I thought we'd start with a visit to the mayor's office."

"The mayor?" He saw the quick flash of panic cross her face as she looked down at her outfit. "I'm not dressed to see the mayor of Anchorage."

"On the contrary. You look great. And he's an old friend of the family."

"Oh God. That means he knows your grandmother, and I'm dressed in jeans and a sweater."

"Like I said. Great." He laid a hand at the base of her back and pushed her in the direction of the parking lot.

Sloan was quiet as she walked next to him and it gave him a chance to study her from the corner of his eye. She really was a beautiful woman. Long, coltish legs kept an even stride with him as they moved toward the long-term parking lot.

It wasn't her beauty, though, that had managed to grab his attention. She had something—a certain something special—that he was having a hard time ignoring.

Sloan was obviously a bright, intelligent woman. And she was sexy as hell. But above all, he found her *interesting*.

She intrigued him. Like a puzzle he was trying to solve or a mystery he wanted to figure out, beating the author to the last page. He'd been captivated from the start, and now he couldn't get her off his mind.

Why was she single, for instance? Certainly a woman as smart and accomplished as Sloan would have her pick of men. The men in Manhattan couldn't be blind to what a catch she was. Hell, he'd bet any man with a pulse would be smitten after two minutes with her.

So what was it? Was she single by choice?

Walker hazarded another glance in her direction and was slammed with the same sense he'd had on the flight. And the first night over at the Indigo Blue. There was something there. Something underneath that beautiful face and body that she kept hidden from the world.

A sadness, perhaps?

No, he amended. It wasn't sadness. It was a loneliness he couldn't quite get a handle on, but it was there all the same.

Like in the way she'd stared out the window at Denali.

Most people were awed by the sight, but he'd sensed something more in her. Her entire expression had changed as her gaze drank in that mountain. Like she was *longing* for something, if he had to hazard a guess.

"The parking lot?" Her voice pulled him from his thoughts.

"What? Oh. I keep a car here."

"Really?"

He caught the speculative look, but she didn't say anything else as they moved through the parking lot toward his SUV. He flicked the remote alarm and the taillights flickered a few spots ahead. "This is us."

"How convenient."

If there was any hidden meaning in her words, Walker couldn't find it, but he was smart enough to assume there was one. The clench in his gut was very rarely wrong when it came to reading female innuendo and her "really" had hidden meaning written all over it. "I was spending so much time on renting cars it ended up being easier to keep one here."

"Do you try a lot of cases down here?"

"Quite a few."

Their drive into downtown was quick—the time of

year coupled with the fact it was late morning ensured they had an easy drive to the mayor's office.

Walker was still puzzling through all of it as he and Sloan walked down the long corridor to the inner sanctum of local government twenty minutes later. He also didn't miss the speculative gaze she shot him. "What?"

"I don't know. You. This." She waved a hand. "I'm just surprised by your concern for my work."

"You don't want access to some contacts for your article?"

"Sure. But you could have handed me a piece of paper with a name and a phone number."

"This is more personal."

"Yes. Exactly." Sloan came to a halt a few doors short of the mayor's office. "What I'm trying to figure out is why."

"You said you wanted to come here. Jack was making a run. I spend a lot of time here. It's easy enough for me to show you around."

She cocked her head and Walker didn't miss the way the long blond tail of her ponytail flicked against her shoulders. "Is it?"

What was she getting at? He'd made the offer to be nice. To give her a chance to get her article done.

To get her out of town for the day and away from the fawning attention of the rest of the men in town.

Where the fuck had that come from?

"It isn't a big deal. So come on. I'll make some introductions."

On a soft sigh, she followed him the last few feet down the hall to the mayor's office. As the receptionist behind the counter looked up at him, recognition sparked behind her eyes.

"Walker Montgomery, in the flesh. After that last poker debacle, I figured you'd be scarce around here."

Walker put on his broadest smile. "And why am I not surprised my raging defeat has made it onto your radar?"

"I miss nothing. You know that."

He leaned down and bussed Sandra's cheek. "That I do."

"So the craziness is about to descend on town. Is that why you're hiding up here?"

"No hiding. I just brought in a friend for the day. Is he in?"

They both got a broad smile and a "Go on back."

And if the eager perusal Sandra gave Sloan as they passed suggested she bought the term "friend" about as much as she bought his prowess in poker, well then, that was her mistake.

Sloan's head spun as they walked back to Walker's car. "I can't believe all there is to do up here. It's like a paradise for those who love the outdoors. And all the cultural events. It's incredible."

"Alaska's a lot more than people think it is."

She couldn't resist a small jab, but she made sure to deliver it with her broadest smile. "Not, however, in early December."

"A lot of stuff closes down during winter."

"You could have told me and saved us the trip."

"I enjoy coming down here and getting out of town for a while."

"It seems like a lot of effort."

"Have you met my family?"

She couldn't stop the giggle as she imagined his grandmother. "Sophie must be in full-on general mode by now."

"You have no idea."

The alarm clicked, but before she could move around to her door, Walker beat her to it, holding the door open and reaching for her hand to help her onto the high running board.

As his hand gripped hers, she couldn't quite ignore the feel of his fingers—or the memories that assailed her of what those broad, strong fingers had done to her the previous evening.

Damn it.

She'd gone nearly two hours without reliving those moments. Why the hell did she have to screw up a nice afternoon and go reliving them now?

She dropped his hand and reached for her seat belt.

"You hungry?"

Sloan turned to answer and her breath caught, trapped in the dead center of her chest. Walker stood next to her, but the height of the SUV put her gaze flush with his. "Is that a good idea?"

"Why wouldn't it be?"

"You did witness my performance on the ride up here, did you not?"

He grinned broadly. "I promise, we'll make sure you get some good protein in you and Jack's got his stash of sodas. Come on, it won't feel any better on an empty stomach."

He made a damn convincing argument. "Will we still make our flight?"

"We've got three hours. I think we'll make it."

"That sounds good, then." Was that breathless voice hers? How did he manage to confuse her so badly?

She did not want this man.

Okay, she *did* want him, but she didn't want someone who had made his preferences so clear the night before.

"You all buckled in?"

She watched as he extended one long finger and reached out to stroke the top of her seat belt. He didn't even touch her—his hand stayed firmly on the part of the belt that was between her body and where it hooked to the seat—but a wave of heat stole over her that had nothing to do with the heavily padded coat she wore.

"I'm in."

"Good."

And then before she could analyze their interaction any further, he moved back and closed the door.

Sloan sighed softly as she acknowledged the sad truth. Last night, as she'd lain in bed tossing and turning, trying to fall asleep, she'd resolved to shove all her growing feelings for Walker in a nice, tightly sealed box.

With a lock and key.

She was on vacation and she was coming off an unpleasant week of family stress that had her emotions all churned up. They were two healthy adults who had spent a few stolen moments engaging in adult activities.

That was all.

It was reasonable. Logical. And something she could walk away from with her head held high.

So she'd wrapped the feelings up and put it all in that locked box, with a neat, tidy bow.

She'd held on to that airtight logic all through the flight. And during their visit to the mayor's office. And even through his invitation to dinner.

Then he'd reached out and stroked that damned seat belt.

And in a split second, like the proverbial opening of Pandora's box, all those neat explanations were blown to hell.

The muted lights of the Anchorage welcomed them as Walker escorted Sloan into the steakhouse. It was one of his favorite restaurants—he loved the dark paneling and the intimate atmosphere. The interior was inviting and cozy, despite the minus-fifteen-degree temperature outside.

"I can't quite get used to how early it gets dark here. Or actually, maybe a better comment is how it really doesn't get all that light."

"We're nearly at the height of it, but yeah, winter is a beast. There are some days that feel endless."

Today not being one of those days, Walker thought as he watched her shrug out of her coat. Her slender shoulders, wrapped in gray cashmere, gave her a soft, willowy look that made him want to reach out and pull her to him. The V at the neck of the sweater framed the slightest hint of cleavage and he found the subtle inference more erotic than something far more revealing.

"And then you have almost twenty-four hours of light."

Her words interrupted his errant thoughts and he quickly shed his own coat.

"It must be the oddest sensation."

"I've lived with it for most of my life. Except for the time I spent away during college, it's just a fact of living up here. You get used to it."

"Which is true of most things, I suppose." Sloan slid into the seat opposite him, her gaze traveling around the restaurant. "What a lovely place. I can see why you like it."

He took his menu and opened it up. "You up for some wine?"

"Absolutely. I realize we only met a few days ago, but have you yet to see me not up for some wine?"

"Fair point." He glanced through the menu, and a Bordeaux caught his attention. Closing the list, he couldn't resist a bit of prodding. "Has Avery dug into the Rothschild yet?"

"You know about that?"

"It's a badly kept secret and she only doles it out on special occasions, but yeah, I know about it."

Walker gave the sommelier their selection, then turned back to his menu.

"Is that how Roman buys her off?"

"Is that how—" He broke off as her casual question registered through his review of the porterhouse or the rib eye. "It's not buying anyone off."

She shrugged and his gaze was helplessly drawn back to those slim shoulders. "Could have fooled me."

Walker knew he should be defending his friend, but even he had to admit some of Roman's antics over the years had been a bit much. "Come on. It's not that obvious."

"Seriously?" Sloan eyed him over the rim of her menu before folding it gently and laying it over her charger plate. "Not that obvious? They've got a freaking work of art in the lobby and thousand-dollar bottles of wine in their personal wine rack. And I'm sure that only touches the surface."

"You haven't even met him."

One delicate eyebrow arched high over that electric-blue gaze. "Am I wrong?"

"No."

"I rest my case, Counselor."

She waited a few heartbeats, before adding, "I know I'm coming off as judgmental, but she deserves better."

"Avery deserves a lot of things she hasn't gotten and doesn't deserve a lot of the things she has."

Sloan held up a hand before he could say anything further. "It's not for us to discuss the details."

Their wine was poured and the waitress had taken their orders before Walker had a chance to press on her comment. Most women—heck, most people—would be chomping at the bit to gossip about someone else. Especially someone who had a history with a celebrity.

But not Sloan. She'd shut down the conversation before he could even say things he suspected she already knew.

"That's rare, you know."

She glanced up from swirling her wine. "What's rare?"

"The blessed lack of gossip."

She took a sip of the wine, her eyelids briefly dipping

as she tasted it. A small drop pearled at the corner of her mouth. The dark red caught his attention and his fingers itched to wipe it away, but before he could act on the thought she lifted her napkin and dabbed at the excess.

Eyes on her glass, he sensed she was considering something. Weighing it, the same way she had savored the flavor of the wine.

"I know what it's like to be talked about. To be the subject of gossip. I don't like it and I have no interest in doing it to someone else."

"Interesting angle. Most would feel differently. In fact, most in that position would feel they were even more entitled to gossip."

"Well, then, I guess I'm not most."

No, she certainly wasn't.

And that was what killed him in all this. She wasn't like anyone else he'd ever met and he could feel the bonds of interest wrapping ever tighter around him.

Hell, the women he normally dated wanted the most premium table and the surf and turf. She'd spent the evening defending Avery and calling him on his bullshit.

It was a heady combination of respect and camaraderie, wrapped in a sexy package he couldn't tear his eyes off.

He shouldn't be interested. Shouldn't be this fascinated with her. She wasn't a woman to toy with. Hell, she had commitment and forever stamped on her like an invisible brand.

Add to it the fact that she wasn't staying in Alaska and he owed her the courtesy of keeping his distance.

Avery's interruption the evening before was a fortunate accident. One his body had been torturing him over ever since. But it was for the best.

It was all for the best.

Sloan was surprised to find their dinner was turning out to be a far more pleasant experience than she'd have expected. In fact, the entire day was. Walker was an interesting companion. He wasn't exactly funny—his lawyerly sensibilities threaded through his personality in dry observations—but he was fun and he'd kept things interesting and their conversation light.

She also couldn't help but give him mental points for his words about Avery. There was a kindness there and a willingness to acknowledge his friend's shortcomings that she had to admire.

You could love someone and still see where they'd fallen short. And he had the decency to admit Roman's actions weren't above reproach.

And, if she were equally fair to someone she'd never met, small towns weren't the easiest places to deal with a breakup. Roman had spent an awful lot of money on gifts, not to mention giving significant thought to his selections. She'd like to give him the benefit of the doubt in thinking that he'd meant the gestures sincerely.

And why do you even care?

The sensible inner voice took her completely off guard, but so did the resounding answer.

These people had all gone about their lives very well without her and they'd do so again.

So why was she feeling so damned proprietary about the residents of Indigo, Alaska?

She'd come up here to help Grier. That was the whole point in making the trip. They still had a bit more work to do, but she'd spend a few more days helping Grier get things on track; then she'd finish out her stay and go home.

Back to her own life in Manhattan.

And if the thought depressed her, it was something to contemplate later in the privacy of her room. Right now, she had an attractive dinner companion and one of the best cuts of steak she'd ever eaten.

As she raised a bite of her steak to her mouth, she focused on their day. "So you and the mayor are poker buddies?"

Walker waved a hand in dismissal as he reached for his glass. "Actually, I'd like to know when you were the subject of gossip. Is there a skeleton or two in your closet, Ms. McKinley?"

The evident humor in his gaze eased the delivery of the question, but she couldn't help kicking herself for saying anything at all.

Of course, seeing as how she'd dug this hole for herself, she had two choices. She could either pick up a shovel and dig deeper, likely igniting even more interest, or she could give a lighthearted version of the truth.

"My mother is obsessed with getting me married off."

"Obsessed?"

"Like a paparazzi photographer on Angelina Jolie. It borders on manic."

"While I can oddly relate—and seeing as how you've met my grandmother, you know what I mean—what does that have to do with gossip?"

"I'm the town disappointment."

"Excuse me?" She had the momentary satisfaction of seeing his eyes widen at the statement, but even that wasn't enough to stave off the inevitable pain.

Do it fast, like ripping off a Band-Aid.

"I was the ugly duckling who turned out okay but never met Prince Charming. The fairy tale's incomplete."

"I can't believe you. I bet you were a cute kid. Besides, you're hardly ready for the nursing home. You'd think your mother could calm down a bit."

Walker's casual words filled her with a delicious warmth, and she was surprised at how comfortable she was baring her childhood embarrassments.

Without warning, her mental image of her mother's face morphed into the sweet visage of Sophie Montgomery. "Your grandmother nags you about marriage, but she's so damned lovely about it. How does she do it?"

"I'm not sure 'lovely' is the word I'd use to describe my grandmother's matchmaking tactics." She didn't miss the twinkle in his eyes. "But I do know it comes from a very genuine place that cares about my happiness."

"That's it!" Sloan leaned forward and clutched Walker's hand. "You've hit it."

"Hit what?"

"If I thought my mother's constant harping was about wanting me to be happy, it might be more tolerable. But it's like some sort of status symbol to her." Sloan shook her head. How had it taken her so long to realize it? "Thank you, Walker." She reached for her glass and lifted it to his.

"What are we toasting?"

"About fifteen years of emotional baggage just fell out of the cargo hold."

"I'll toast to that."

His glass had just met hers when they were interrupted by a high-pitched exclamation. "Walker? You didn't tell me you were going to be in town!"

Sloan stared up at the woman who stood next to their table. Dressed in a winter-white suit, the woman was wrapped in sophistication from head to toe. Add in the predatory gleam in her cool blue eyes and the hand draped on Walker's shoulder and she positively glowed with the unmistakable air of no-strings-attached sin.

And she was staring at Walker as if he were her next meal.

Chapter Thirteen

$\mathcal{A}$s soon as Walker saw Victoria Watson, unease began to unfurl in his gut like a bad meal. The feeling wasn't unlike a bad jury verdict or that moment before a car accident when everything around you slowed down.

It was that moment that screamed disaster.

And this was about to become one if he didn't move quickly.

"Victoria. How are you?" He stood and gave her a brief hug, then resumed his seat. The silent lack of invitation to join them didn't go unnoticed by Victoria. He turned toward Sloan and finished making introductions.

"Sloan is visiting from New York."

Victoria's laugh was brittle, bordering on the razor's edge of arrogant and cruel. "Are you, now? One of your old college chums, Walker? She looks about your age."

Ooh, that was a low blow, even for Victoria. And not all that original, either.

"Hardly. I'm an old man."

"Especially according to his grandmother," Sloan added, a merry twinkle in those baby blues.

"I've been representing a good friend of Sloan's and she's up here visiting."

"How lovely for you." Victoria's eyes glittered with the light of battle, but her insistence on standing there and continuing the conversation was in poor taste, even for her.

What had he ever seen in this woman? What he'd thought of as sophistication simply looked shallow to him now.

And rather cold.

"Are you competing in the contest, darling? The one Walker's grandmother throws every year?"

Victoria's gaze was wide-eyed, but no one could mistake the question as anything other than malicious.

"I am."

"Isn't that good for you. Travel is so enlightening. You never know what you might find." Victoria tittered lightly. "Possibly even a husband."

"Actually," Sloan interjected smoothly. "It's the centerpiece of an article I'm writing."

Victoria paused in brushing some lint off her sleeve. "Article?"

"Yes. I'm a writer."

"Really? What do you write?"

"Magazine articles, mostly. All freelance. I do everything from travel pieces, which this is, to how-to articles or the occasional celebrity piece. My interview with Johnny Depp appeared in *Vanity Fair* last month."

"I don't believe I read that one."

Walker couldn't help but notice how the wind in Victoria's sails died ever so slightly, the smug look slipping at the reference to Sloan's Hollywood connections.

"I'd be happy to give Walker a copy for you for the next time you get together. It sounds like you're old friends."

Victoria's eyes narrowed at that, but she didn't reply. And damn it, based on that response, it was obvious Sloan knew exactly what sort of friends he and Victoria really were.

So why the hell did that bother him?

He didn't owe Sloan anything. Why should he feel embarrassed that he'd once dated Victoria?

He had no real reason to apologize.

Their small talk was interrupted by the arrival of their waitress, bearing dessert menus.

"Would you care to join us for dessert?" Sloan's sugary-sweet tone and broad smile were clearly the other woman's undoing.

With a tight smile and a nod, Victoria excused herself. "I need to get back to my friends. It was nice to meet you. And lovely to see you again, Walker."

He stood and brushed his cheek to hers for a quick kiss.

And wasn't surprised when she didn't make any overtures for any future plans. Victoria Watson was one *friend* he'd likely not be seeing again.

Sloan fisted her napkin in her lap but kept her smile firmly in place as that infuriating woman walked away.

Nothing like an ex-lover to ruin a perfectly good date.

Even though this wasn't a date, she added to herself.

Definitely not. It was *not* a date. So why did she have that same sinking feeling in her stomach she'd had overhearing her mother's friends in the kitchen on Thanksgiving evening?

And why did it matter so damn much?

She liked her life. She enjoyed the varied elements that made up her daily existence. She was happy with the choices she made and the person she presented to the world each day.

So where was this coming from?

Sloan reached for her glass of wine and studied the dark, burgundy depths.

Did she really work this hard to be a good person—to live a life she was satisfied with—to be this freaking maudlin all the time?

And was she really that defined by whatever image her mother had decided she was supposed to be instead of who she wanted to be?

When did simply being Sloan McKinley become enough?

Her gaze caught on the darkened windows of the restaurant and the soft lights that framed the parking lot beyond. A light snow fell, the flakes illuminated in the streetlamps.

"She's a beautiful woman," Sloan murmured, shifting her attention back to Walker.

"Yes. I used to think so."

"I'm sorry?"

"You heard me. I used to think Victoria was quite interesting. Fairly compelling, actually. Funny how my idea of compelling seems to have changed."

When she didn't say anything, he added, "Why do you think that is?"

"I really have no idea."

Walker leaned forward, his brow furrowed as if he were troubled, puzzling through a particularly difficult problem. "Actually, I think maybe you do."

Sloan wasn't sure what it was—his facial expression, the tone of his voice or the simple fact of having all of this man's attention focused on her—but the moment spun out before them, his comment hanging between them and connecting them by the thin strands of desire and need and something else she couldn't quite define.

There was something darkly persuasive about him that wouldn't let her write Walker Montgomery off as someone she didn't need to give another thought to.

The sharp tone of his cell broke the moment.

"Excuse me." Walker snapped open the phone. "Jack? I thought you needed us back at six?"

Sloan stopped fiddling with her napkin as she watched the play of emotions across Walker's face shift. Harden.

"Do you need to leave without us?" After a pause, he added, "Okay. We're fifteen minutes away. Bye."

"What's wrong?"

"We need to leave. There's been an accident on the mountain and Jack needs to get back to Indigo with a couple of ER doctors. It's all hands on deck."

Mick held the plane as steady as he could while wind shears buffeted them like a ship at sea. Another round of animalistic cries of pain assaulted him as the two scientists in the back of the plane tried to comfort their friend.

What the hell were these guys doing up there?

He'd heard mumbled, incoherent words about re-search, but to his way of thinking, it was a suicide mission to attempt to do anything for any extended period of time on the bitch in fucking December.

She didn't tolerate it.

And the guy fighting for his life in the back of his plane was yet further proof of that simple fact.

Maggie's voice echoed in his headset—harsh and de-manding, her authority unyielding.

Damn, but it felt good to hear her voice.

She might be a pain in the ass, but the woman knew how to manage in a crisis.

"You're fifteen minutes out, Mick. Care Flight's on the ground here and ready for you."

"You cleared everyone else out of there?"

"Damn straight. Runway's all yours. How bad is he?"

Mick tuned in to the noise behind him, heard the heavy thrashing and cries, and whispered, "Not good."

"Leg's bad? Severed?"

"Yes, and the femoral's hit, too."

"How are the friends handling it?"

Mick risked a quick glance over his shoulder. The friends traveling with the guy were in bad shape, but they were managing. And most important, they'd acted immediately, which was the single biggest factor giving their friend a fighting chance.

"Holding on." With a quick glance at his instruments, he added, "Wind's a fucking bitch tonight."

"Storm's kicking up." Mick wondered if the Care Flight guys would be able to move the man to Anchorage but held his question. The cabin was too closed in to risk being overheard. "Do they have a plan B?"

"Doc Cloud's here helping them set up a unit in the lobby just in case."

Mick held the plane as steady as he could as another wind shear struck his flank, but the staggering course was enough to elicit more agonized cries from the back. "I think they're going to need it."

Maggie let out a soft sigh before switching back to all business. "All right, cowboy, bring it in. We're waiting for you."

Fighting another set of wind buffets that nearly had them shifting sideways, Mick navigated his way through dense cloud cover. With a quick flip, he turned on the mike and barked out orders. "I'm breaking about fifteen laws not asking you to buckle up, but I need you guys to get as close to him as you can. Keep the pressure on his leg and don't let up. This is going to be rough on the way down."

He heard the muttered agreements, trusted that they understood the gravity of the situation and fought the wind.

Mick knew he had a reputation as being one of Alaska's best pilots. He knew and trusted his equipment. And he knew and trusted his instincts.

As the lights of Indigo came into view, he prayed like hell he'd gotten to this guy in time.

Sloan could see the whirling sirens on the ground, lighting up the small airport in bright red and blue hues. Jack had two doctors on board to add support to a Care Flight team already on-site. No one had spoken on the flight back and the airsickness that had bothered her on the way down had seemed to fade in the face of the tension gripping all of them.

Her stomach didn't feel great, but she wasn't afraid she'd lose whatever she'd had for dinner.

Sadly, there was something far bigger to focus on.

She'd heard a murmured conversation between Jack and the doctors and had pieced together the basic facts. Three research scientists, doing something on the side of Denali. An equipment failure coupled with a fall off the side of a cliff and one of the researchers was in very bad shape.

The plane pitched hard to the right as Jack muttered an "oh shit" from the front of the cabin. Walker turned to give her a small smile as he reached for her hand.

"You okay?"

"Hanging in. I'm not nearly as bad as some others right now."

"No." Walker nodded. "I suppose not."

"It's bad out there."

"It's not great. It's probably a good thing we got out earlier than we'd planned to or we'd be spending the night in Anchorage until the storm blew through."

She squelched the image of how he most likely spent his evenings in Anchorage. It wasn't her business. How he spent his time—in the past or in the future—didn't have anything to do with her.

Even as she thought it, she knew she was lying to herself. Something she made a policy to never do. With a start, Sloan glanced down to where their fingers twined together, his large hand dwarfing hers.

Comfort.

It meant something. *He* meant something. Even if in the long run, *they* weren't to be.

And that's why the idea of how Walker Montgomery spent his free evenings in Anchorage *did* matter.

With a mental shake of her head, Sloan admonished herself to get it together. She had a home to go back to and she hadn't come up here looking for a fling with someone she'd never see again.

Walker squeezed her hand when the plane did a hard bank to the right as Jack came in for a landing. His touch reassured, calming her nerves as another panicky wave threatened to grip her.

As she squeezed back, Sloan had to acknowledge the truth.

Even if it had been her intention to simply come on this trip to support her friend, it had turned into so much more.

Because she had met Walker.

The next hour passed in a blur. The intimate moment she and Walker had shared in the cocoonlike warmth of Jack's plane came to an abrupt end as they arrived at the airport.

Walker was pulled away immediately by his grandmother, her role as mayor ensuring she'd been called the moment something happened. Although she hated the reason, Sloan was grateful for some time apart. Her resolve weakened when she was with Walker. It was time to collect herself and all the wayward thoughts that had taken up residence in her mind and wouldn't let go.

From where she stood in an out-of-the-way corner, Sloan saw Dr. Cloud assisting the Care Flight team while the doctors Jack ferried cleaned up. Whatever shortcomings she might have expected in the form of medical care in this remote place was quickly banished as she watched a highly competent team of people work to save a life.

The man who'd been brought in off of Mick's plane was being managed in a makeshift triage unit. Despite Dr Cloud's age, which she put at about seventy, he moved in tandem with the staff, stepping in where needed, moving back when someone had to take over. Every member of the medical team moved with purpose and confidence.

A medical helicopter sat on the runway, but she wondered how it would ever take off. The snow that had started in Anchorage had followed them north and what had been a pleasant winter wonderland was rapidly turning into a bad storm.

"So this is Alaska," she murmured to herself as the white flakes came down with increasing speed.

"That it is."

She turned to see Mick move in next to her, his hand pressed to the window as he stared out at the runway. "They're never taking off in this."

"But he needs help. They can't stay here."

"They can't risk going up, either."

Her gaze shot back toward the doctors as they fought to save the man's life in the middle of an airport terminal. "Does this happen often?"

"Often enough." He shrugged, the half-drunk cup of

coffee in his hand sloshing with his movements. "About every year or so. Less if we're lucky. Denali asks for a steep price from some."

She wondered at his words, especially knowing a good portion of his business was tied to landing on the mountain with tour groups, but held her tongue. It didn't take much to see the rescue had taken its toll and he was hanging on by a very thin thread. His blue eyes looked overly bright, his normally tan skin unnaturally pale.

Sloan knew there were any number of flaws with her upbringing, but perfect social skills wasn't one of them. Couple that with an innate gift for small talk and she could usually diffuse most difficult situations. "You've lived here your whole life?"

"Born and raised."

"Do you ever wonder what it's like somewhere else?"

He shrugged, but Sloan was pleased to see his hand was steadier when he did. "I get out of here from time to time. Nothing ever caught my fancy well enough not to come back."

"I've always felt that way about New York." *Had* always felt, she mentally corrected herself.

"Do you miss it?"

"Not as much as I thought I would. Besides, it's way more important to be here for Grier. New York's not going anywhere."

Mick hesitated for a moment, as if weighing his words. Before she could wonder too long at it, he rubbed a hand over the rough stubble on his face. "She'll go back once this is all settled. All this stuff with Jonas's house and all."

"I guess."

"Shame."

"What?"

Mick shook his head. "Nothing. It's nothing."

A loud shout went up before Sloan could say anything in response. She whirled in the direction of where the doctors were working, but she knew immediately what had caused the noise.

The man Mick brought off the mountain hadn't survived.

Chapter Fourteen

*I*f the night of her arrival was the height of revelry, this evening was its somber opposite. Sloan allowed her gaze to roam around the Jitters—the large coffeehouse that sat at the end of Main Street next to the Indigo Blue—overcome by a wave of sadness. She had gotten to know the residents of this quirky town and felt their collective grief as her own.

Although they were a far smaller crowd than had filled the Indigo's lobby after the town hall, there were enough people assembled to sit in a strange sort of memorial for the fallen researcher no one actually knew personally. People kept their voices low, engaged in the reassuring camaraderie of having others nearby.

Again, Sloan found herself awed by these hearty people and the life they'd built up here. In a harsh, unforgiving climate there was a close-knit community of people who cared about one another. Shared with one another. Comforted one another.

Even when the tragedy involved a total stranger.

Walker had stayed behind at the airport with his grandmother, so Sloan had gotten a ride back with Mick. He'd disappeared shortly after depositing her at the coffeehouse and she now sat in a small circle with Grier and Avery.

"Did you enjoy Anchorage, at least?" Avery reached for the foamy latte that sat on the small table between them.

"It was interesting."

"Oh?" Grier's eyebrows rose as she reached for an oversized cup full of mocha. "That's a loaded answer."

"Let's just say it was a loaded afternoon."

At the twin stares, she quickly caught them up on what had happened at dinner and the subsequent flight home.

"Victoria's got a bad reputation even up here in Indigo," Avery offered. "None of us could figure out what he saw in her."

"I have a pretty good guess," Sloan added dryly.

"Saw, Sloan. Past tense. He hasn't run with her in a long time."

"Define long."

"Months. Since well before the summer."

Sloan shook her head. "Like it matters."

"It does matter," Grier added in a show of solidarity. "You were on a date with him and the two of you were intruded upon."

"It wasn't a date."

Grier's sole response was a raised eyebrow.

"Oh, don't give me the eye." Sloan waved a hand at Grier, which her cheeky friend immediately reached out and grabbed, linking their fingers in a good, tight squeeze.

"Well, what did you go and do that for?"

And there it was again. The offer of comfort and companionship. Only this time it was the familiar comfort of more than a decade of friendship.

Hot tears pricked the backs of her eyes and Sloan dropped Grier's hand after squeezing back. On a deep breath, she continued. "So payback's only fair. If you can dole it out, so can I. I think you need to end the sex moratorium and jump Mick O'Shaughnessy's bones."

Grier's wide smile fell. "Excuse me."

"He's got it as bad for you as you do for him. All anyone needs is to get in, oh, I don't know, about a hundred feet of the two of you to see it. But tonight at the airport cemented it. That man wants you."

A sly smile lit up Avery's face. "Did he say something?"

"It was more what he didn't say. I'm telling you, Grier. You need to give up the chase and spend some time with that man."

"I'm not going there."

"Why not?" Although her friend wasn't one to casually fling herself from one man to another, Sloan really couldn't see a single flaw to her plan. Especially since she'd never seen Grier this twisted over a guy. Not even her ex-fiancé.

Grier shook her head no, but her eyes gleamed with a bright yes. "That way lies madness."

"Going without it lies the way to madness, too," Avery suggested helpfully.

Sloan clinked mugs with her. "So very true."

"I'm not sleeping with Mick."

"You might think that tone is full of conviction, Grier Thompson, but I hear the cracks."

"Some best friend you are." Grier punctuated the comment with a small pout. "You're supposed to be supporting me from making bad decisions."

Sloan wasn't sure when the devil on her shoulder had landed, but now that it had, she couldn't resist offering a not-so-innocent push. "From where I'm sitting, it's not only a good decision, it's fucking inspired. Besides, you know it would be fun. And he seems like a really great guy."

"The best. And," Avery added, "he's at the hotel right now."

"What's he doing there?" Sloan had assumed he was heading home after dropping her off.

"I sent him into the sauna to warm up before I walked over here."

"See," Sloan turned toward Grier as she kept pushing her point. "It's a great idea. And he's all alone."

"No, it's probably not a great idea." Grier's smile fell as a soft, faraway look took over her misty gray eyes. "But I'm quite sure it would be an incredible ride."

Walker deftly avoided glancing at the far corner of the terminal as he took a seat next to his grandmother. With gentle movements, he touched Sophie's arm to get her attention.

"Are you all right? There's really nothing else to be done here. We should be going. Jack left the car running so it could warm up."

"It's just terribly sad, Walker. So very, very sad. A young life lost, others which will bear the scars of this day for the rest of their lives."

He glanced out the window of the small lobby to where the snow continued to fall in heavy flakes on the landing strip, his grandmother's words ringing in his ears like alarm bells.

He knew about scars. Knew about the days that changed your life and actions you couldn't take back.

Choices you couldn't take back.

"Come on. If we wait too much longer we're going to have a hard time getting home. We probably should have left an hour ago."

"That young man's family needed to know what happened."

"You could have called them in the morning. Or from home."

She shrugged and for the first time he noticed just how her age had started to catch up with her. Although Sophie Montgomery had a wonderful spirit and a commanding presence, he had to admit she was showing the strains of her age.

And she wouldn't be with them forever.

"I wanted to make sure they could ask questions of the doctor if they had any."

"So you did what needed to be done. His family's been called, the doctors have done what they can and the sheriff's taken care of the other researchers. There's nothing else to do here."

His grandmother sighed and took the arm he offered, allowing him to walk her toward the exit. Jack had waited for them with his big SUV, which was why Walker had given Sophie the extra time she needed. Jack's Yukon might not be foolproof against a bad storm, but knowing they had a ride in the big boat had allowed them some breathing room to deal with the evening's events before the driving conditions got too bad.

What an evening.

The day replayed in his mind as they walked out into the cold night air.

Sloan.

Why couldn't he get her out of his head? It was as if she filled his thoughts until there wasn't room for anything else.

After settling his grandmother into the backseat, Walker climbed in next to her, surprised when she reached for his hand.

"Do you understand why I push you so much? About getting married and having a family?"

"Actually, I think 'harass' might be a better word. 'Harangue.' 'Badger.'"

He was surprised when his teasing words failed to elicit even a small smile. Instead, she simply squeezed his hand harder as tears spilled down her paper-thin cheeks. "I don't do it to badger you or make you mad. I do it because I hate the idea of you being alone."

She pointed toward the airport. "That young man in there. He'll never have a family. Or know the love of a spouse or the joy of children. He'll never see the future or share it with someone. Life is too short, Walker. Much too short. I miss your grandfather every day, but I had so many years. Wonderful years together. I want that for you."

His throat grew tight and he didn't know quite how to respond to her earnest pleading. He couldn't change who he was any more than he could change what had shaped him.

"It's not that easy, Grandmother. Besides, that life's not for everyone."

"And you think you're one of those not suited to marriage?"

He always had.

Ever since that day when he'd discovered the truth about his father, he'd believed that a life with a partner would eventually lead him down the same path of deceit, omission and half-truths to whomever he shared his life with.

All bathed in the lies he'd tell himself about being a good person, a good father and a good husband, albeit one who simply found an outlet elsewhere from time to time.

An image of Sloan filled his mind's eye again, first the curve of her cheek bathed in the glow from the candle between them at dinner. Then the impish spirit she showed in dealing with Victoria, never allowing the woman the upper hand, despite the awkwardness of the interruption. The strength she'd shown at the airport as they realized the extent of the tragedy.

She'd be a woman a man could share his life with and still never discover all her facets.

And that was the crux of it, really.

How did someone who'd spent their adult life focused on dodging any form of commitment let go of that conviction? That certainty?

That absolute, unshakeable belief that vows and obligations simply weren't for him.

The heat of the sauna washed over him, but Mick felt none of it. The harsh cold he'd spent most of the day in had seeped into his bones and nothing—not the bottle of Jack Daniel's Avery had thrust into his hand or the warmth of the room—could chase it away.

Neither could they chase away the cold reality of death. It had interrupted all their lives and offered a dour reminder of the severe environment they all chose to call home.

Images continued to bombard him, ones he knew he'd see for a long time to come. The researchers as he came upon them on the side of the mountain, almost delirious with panic as they tried to keep pressure on their friend's wounds. The blood that congealed in a great pool a short distance away.

He'd reacted on instinct, simply taking over and doing what had to be done. Just as he had for his mother that horrible, awful day.

And now he'd pay the price with memories that intertwined, mixing the events into a swirling morass of misery.

"Fuck."

Mick slammed the bottle to his lips, taking another long swallow, abstractly wondering when the alcohol would kick in, helping him to forget.

It was a remedy he avoided most of the time, but hell, he was only human. He figured he was entitled to a good old-fashioned bender.

Fucking-A.

"What are you doing in here, all by yourself?"

Mick's gaze collided with Grier's where she stood at the entry to the sauna, her voice hitting him a moment after the soft snick of the lock dropping into place registered.

"Trying to warm up."

"I can see that." She sauntered toward him, her cheeks a ripe shade of pink. "Mind if I have a sip?"

"You like Jack?" Surprise mingled with humor at the image of his little angel knocking back a few belts, which she proceeded to do with surprising speed.

"Not particularly," she muttered on a harsh cough. "Damn it, but that stuff never gets any better."

"So why'd you take it?"

Her mysterious gray eyes bored into him, like he was the only person on earth. The sole recipient of her focus and attention. It was heady and exhilarating and so mind-bendingly sexy that he felt the first surge of warmth finally penetrate through his somber mood.

"I believe it's called liquid courage."

Before he could even begin to process her words, the reality of what she'd come to the room for hit him at the same time as her small, curvy little body. Surprisingly strong arms wrapped around his neck and her fingers threaded through the hair at his nape, pulling him close to her.

"What are you doing?" he mumbled against her lips.

The tight grip she had on his body loosened as she pulled away. "If that's your answer I'm clearly not doing it right."

"Damn straight you're doing it right," he muttered on a growl as his hands landed on her, one on her ass and one between those narrow shoulder blades. He pulled her toward him before slamming his mouth against hers.

With a sort of raging desperation, he plundered her

mouth. His tongue met hers and they tangled in a rush of need and pent-up desire.

She was so delicate. And so damned sexy he could only thank God she'd somehow known what he needed.

Like an erotic dream, the moments played out along the razor's edge of his senses and crescendoed into the most sensual experience of his life. He drank her in, the taste of her beyond his most wild imaginings, better than his most heated fantasies.

The softness of her skin as he skimmed his fingers along her stomach before reaching to lift her thin sweater over her head.

Her luscious scent, the light sweetness of vanilla that mixed with the musk of her skin and the dry heat of the room.

The beautiful lines of her body as she arched under his touch.

His fingers trembled slightly as he undid the hook of her bra. The black lace fell away to display the heavy globes of her breasts, pink nipples high and tight in the muted light of the room.

"Oh God, you're beautiful."

"The way you're looking at me makes me feel like I could conquer the world."

Reality came crashing in at her words. This world—the one they were both firmly planted in—wasn't the time or place for this.

"Grier. Maybe we shouldn't do this." Her face fell and he quickly rushed to explain. "You're leaving soon and you deserve more than a fling and especially with what you're dealing with for your father, you just don't need this—" He broke off as she moved up into his space.

"You're wrong. I do need this. I need you." Her pupils were dark disks in the subdued light of the sauna room. He saw heat and need, pleasure and anticipation in those gorgeous gray eyes and his body responded in kind. "And you're wearing far too much."

The first smile of his day spread across his face as the vise that had gripped his chest loosened. He knew it was a fool's errand to do this—to allow himself to get even more deeply infatuated with Grier Thompson than he already was—but he'd be damned if he could stop in the face of such unerring sincerity. "I do believe you're right." He leaned in and nipped her chin before whipping the heavy flannel of his shirt and the T-shirt underneath it off in one swift gesture.

"Anyone ever tell you you've got some smooth moves, O'Shaughnessy?" She jabbed a finger in his chest as humor threaded itself through all those other emotions in her eyes.

"Never anyone as sexy as you."

"Good."

Her mouth found his again, their tongues clashing in another wave of intimacy and, he quickly found, an incredible sense of fun.

He felt the smile on her lips against his own. Felt the joy radiating from her body as she draped her half-naked form over his chest. She traced the lines of his body over and over again with a light sweep of her hands over his stomach and hips.

This was life.

The sense of fun shifted, morphed into an urgency as that great, driving need clawed its way to the surface, impatient for more.

With sudden clarity, he felt the hard wooden bench underneath his back as she straddled him.

"Wait, baby," he muttered against her mouth. Shifting them into a sitting position, he eyed the stack of white, fluffy towels on a bench on the opposite side of the room. He whispered against her neck as he reluctantly let go of her body with a breathless, "Hang on."

Mick managed two steps before the reality of his situation hit. His erection rubbed painfully against the fly of his jeans and his normally long-legged gait slowed as he crossed the small chamber. Damn, but he felt like a horny teenage boy. He couldn't stop the broad grin that spread across his face as he reached for the towels.

A loud peel of laughter registered and he turned, an armful of white cotton in his hands.

"What?"

"You look uncomfortable there, cowboy."

He couldn't stop the flush that crept up his neck. "All your fault, I might add."

"Well, then." Her voice dropped as the laughter fled, even as merry mischief rode high in her eyes. "With a compliment like that, I guess it's up to me to make it worse."

In a move reminiscent of his shirt removal, she had her jeans and panties off her hips in one smooth move.

And promptly fell forward on a quick stumble as her jeans caught in her boots.

*   *   *

Grier wasn't sure if she was mortified or delighted to have six feet two inches of solid, rangy man haul her off the floor of the sauna, cradling her in his arms. When she felt his forearm on her naked ass, Grier decided it was delight.

Definitely delight.

And then her gaze caught on her bunched jeans and panties where they had caught on her boots.

Nope. Mortification.

"Are you okay?"

When he gently settled her on the bench, a hard knot fisted in her chest. Whatever desire she'd seen in his bright blue eyes had fled to be replaced with concern. She had to get this back to light and playful. "Mick. I'm fine. Really."

"You sure?"

"Oh, I'm bringing the sexy back"—she brushed a bunch of wayward strands of hair behind her ear before she reached down to work on the fuzzy boots at her feet—"but I'm fine."

Maybe if she stayed down here long enough he'd lose interest.

Grier felt the heat of the bench against her very naked ass and realized that was likely a pipe dream, but hey, a girl could hope.

"Well, if you're sure you're okay."

And then the knot in her chest turned into a great, huge, gooey hole of need and desire and something she refused to name as he kneeled before her and gently took over removing her boots.

Without warning, an image of her ex popped into her mind. Cool, confident, all-business Jason who wouldn't even dream of having sex if she wasn't freshly showered, perfumed and in recent acquisition of a bikini wax.

Pushing at Mick's hand, she mumbled around the intrusive memory, annoyed it had somehow found its way into this tender moment. "I . . . I can do it."

He never moved, never slowed in his actions. He simply brushed her hands away. "Because you've done such a good job up to now." His hands lingered on her calf as he pulled the heavy, furry boot off, those clever fingers kneading into the flesh there.

It was the most erotic moment of her life.

Sitting there, naked before this large man as he gently massaged her calf muscles.

The next boot slid off as his hands roamed over her ankle. "Ah," he murmured as he shifted and tugged the heavy material of her jeans down over her foot. "There we go." With gentle movements, he reached for the other pant leg, sliding it fully off.

Leaning forward, his hands braced on either side of her, he whispered against her lips, "It's all better now."

She pressed her lips to his, the embarrassment fleeing on the heels of something so real—so life-affirming—she could no more stop it than she could stop the snow falling outside. "I want you."

"That's very good to hear." He pulled back from her and stood, leaning forward to toe off his own boots. "Now watch carefully. See how it's done."

A carefree giggle bubbled up her throat and Grier

threw one of the towels at him. "I know how to get my boots off."

"All evidence to the contrary."

The second boot went flying across the room, landing with a thud in the general direction of the door.

"It sure is hot in here." Mick reached for the fly of his jeans. "Better do something about that."

At the cocky grin that covered his face, she stood and moved toward him, reaching for his hands before he could fully remove his jeans. "I think I can help with that."

He reached for her, his hands settling on either side of her face, his wide palms resting on the top of each shoulder. On a soft sigh, Grier slid her hands into the waistband of his jeans, the hard length of his erection pulsing against her hand. He bent down, pressing his forehead to hers on a heavy groan.

"You kill me. I swear, you do."

In that moment, as feminine power poured through her, for the first time in months, Grier felt light and care-free. Youthful.

Happy.

As her knees touched the back of the wooden seat, Mick leaned around her and spread handfuls of the towels over the bench.

She sat, then continued with his jeans, pushing them down over his firm ass, her hands running the length of his thighs as she removed the heavy material.

When the jeans hit the ground with a soft thud, he stepped out of them, pulling her up and toward him.

"Was this what you had in mind when you walked in here?"

As she stared up into those bright blue eyes, dark with desire, Grier knew she'd never wanted anything more.

"Absolutely."

And then there were no more words as she leaned forward, her tongue on an unerring mission toward his nipple. The smooth swirl of her tongue over the flat disk had him gasping and she felt his erection where it pressed against her stomach.

"Grier." Her name came out on a strangled moan. "You really do kill me." He buried his hands in her hair, pulling her mouth to his as he plundered, over and over. She matched him with lips, tongue and teeth, using her mouth to mimic the acceptance she offered with the rest of her body.

The urgent pulse of desire rose in her, the beat growing louder and louder as they touched and tasted, offered and took. Grier sighed as his fingers traced a path through the dark curls at the apex of her thighs, his clever fingers sliding through the wet heat that was all for him. Pleasure crested hard and she screamed with the pressure, before his mouth covered hers. With a smile he caught the sound while her body clenched around him.

Without giving her a chance to catch her breath, Mick sat on the heavy swath of towels, pulling her on top of him. He positioned himself at the opening of her body, his long length pressed to her swollen flesh. Still fresh from her orgasm, she nearly cried out at the exquisite sensation as he filled her, inch by glorious inch.

"You with me, baby?" The low growl in her ear nearly had another wave of orgasm crashing through her.

"Yes." She caught his gaze, that electric blue, and leaned forward to kiss him. "Yes."

"Hang on."

Grier Thompson did just that.

And had the ride of her life.

Chapter Fifteen

"You had sex last night."

Sloan didn't mean it to sound like an accusation, but found she couldn't stop the proclamation as Grier sat down next to her in the small dining area off the Indigo's lobby.

She'd thought to avoid pancakes for the third day in a row, but one look at Grier's face had her reconsidering. Carb-loading might go a long way toward stemming the spurt of jealousy that had suddenly taken root in her belly.

"Shhh." A bright flush crept up Grier's neck.

"No one's in here. And I want some details." Sloan reached for the carafe of coffee on the middle of the table and began to pour a cup. As she set it in front of Grier, she almost fumbled the saucer as her oldest friend burst into tears.

"Oh no." The green-eyed monster fled on swift feet as she switched chairs to sit next to Grier. "What happened?"

"Everything." Grier whispered.

"Oh?" She held back any further comment and simply waited.

"Oh is right. More like oh yeah." Grier heaved a miserable sob before another wave of tears hit. "As in oh yeah it was wonderful and amazing and I orgasmed three times. And that was just the first time we had sex."

Ooo-kay, jealousy with a side of scrambled eggs was clearly on tap this morning.

Sloan weighed how to play this. Sweet and gentle or psycho bitch friend.

After a moment of appreciation for three orgasms, she opted for the latter. "So I'm supposed to feel sorry for you?"

Grier's head popped up from where she had it in her hands. "I'm crying, aren't I?"

"Based on what you've told me so far, I can't quite understand why."

"Because it was wonderful."

Sloan slammed a hand on the table. "Ergo my point. Wonderful sex and you're sitting here blubbering like a baby the morning after."

"Sloan!" The tears turned to shock, then to anger, the emotions as clear as day as they flitted across her face.

"What? You want me to pat you on the head and say 'Oh, poor baby.' Sorry, sweetheart. I'm not biting this morning. You're damn well welcome to call me petty for it, too."

"Well." Grier flopped back into her chair with a large sniffle, followed by an even louder one.

Sloan fought a smile as Grier grabbed her plate and walked over to the sideboard to get some breakfast. She didn't miss that the plate was heaping with food when Grier walked back to the table.

Unable to leave well enough alone, Sloan decided a

bit more friendly poking was in order. Besides, she was having far too much fun to stop now.

"So when did this blessed event happen? You were at the coffeehouse until around nine."

"After that." Grier's tone was prim as she took her seat and made a rather large production of opening her napkin on her lap.

"That's all I get?"

"It happened in the sauna. Well, the first part happened in the sauna. The rest happened in my hotel room."

Sloan briefly reconsidered the jealousy one last time before abandoning it to dig for the good stuff. "You really and truly got it on with Mick in the sauna?"

"Really and truly."

"I guess they don't call him a bush pilot for nothing."

"Sloan!"

She laughed at Grier's obvious offense. "So you took me up on my advice. Inspired advice, I might add. And thanks to Avery, you knew just how to find the promised land."

As if they'd conjured her, their new friend materialized in the room with a fresh carafe. "I sense details being shared and I so want in."

"Um." Grier fumbled with her napkin.

"Oh, don't go all quiet on me. I turned off the damned security camera last night, like a true friend. For that, I deserve some details."

"Cameras?" Grier squeaked.

"Yes, there are cameras. Let me guess. You thought you were the first one with the clever idea to go at it in the sauna?"

"Um, no. I just . . . well, yes, actually."

Avery patted her arm. "Don't worry. I turned them off when I sent Mick in there. Clearly it was a smart move on my part."

"Oh God," Grier moaned as she dropped her head in her hands again.

It briefly crossed Sloan's mind to wonder why Avery seemed to have all the responsibility. Where was Susan? Or some of the other hotel staff? Pulling back on the urge to say something, Sloan knew it wasn't her place to poke at it.

Yet.

Even if she did think it was curious. And really, really unfair.

"Come on. Spill it, Steamy."

"She had three orgasms," Sloan added helpfully, gratified when Avery gifted her with a broad smile and a refill on her coffee. "And that was just the first time they slept together."

"Sloan!"

"What?" Sloan shrugged as she sipped her hot coffee. "It's a detail. And the woman asked for details."

"I knew I shouldn't have told you."

"Actually, it's part of the best friend code. Orgasms require some details."

"And triple orgasms usually require the confessional," Avery added helpfully. "Lucky for you we're snowed in. I could, however, ask Father Joseph to come on down if you need to do a little confessing. I can turn off the cameras in the conference room for you if you need it."

"Avery! I'm fine. Thank you."

She shrugged her slim shoulders as she poured herself a cup of coffee and settled back in her chair. "I'm just trying to be helpful."

"Oh, you were that." Sloan laid her napkin on the side of her plate.

Whatever annoyance Grier must have felt evaporated into giggles and Sloan couldn't help laughing in return. "Three, G? Really?"

"Yup."

Sloan met Avery's gaze. "I say we dump her body out back in one of the larger snowdrifts and go jump the man. He's stranded in here somewhere and no one will find her until spring anyway. We can both be long gone by then."

"Long gone and several orgasms richer." Avery nodded. "It sounds like a good plan."

Grier grinned up at them, a faraway look filling her eyes. Sloan was pleased to see whatever sadness had accompanied her when she'd arrived had clearly moved on.

"We'll go after I finish my coffee. Give her a head start."

Sloan gasped as a napkin smacked her in the head. "You really are the biggest bitch, Sloan McKinley."

"Oh, come on. You forced my hand with the triple orgasm comment. And then rubbing it in about how that was only the first time."

Grier's grin only grew broader as she delicately wiped the corner of her mouth with her napkin. "Figured that'd get your goat."

"I'm a small enough person to admit that it most certainly did." Sloan couldn't stop her laughter from joining

Grier's as she leaned over to kiss one cherubic cheek. "It's a good thing I love you."

Avery reached over and snatched a slice of bacon off of Grier's plate. "Have I mentioned how glad I am you two came to town?"

By the time Walker dug out the snow covering his driveway and then his grandmother's, it was almost eleven. He itched to head over to the café, feigning hunger for an early lunch, but had fought the urge and went in to work instead. Things always slowed for him around this time of year, with the usual town frenzy over the bachelor competition only contributing to the slow pace of business during the holidays.

No one seemed all that inclined to start divorce proceedings at Christmas. Wills were usually a New Year's resolution, not a fun holiday activity. And property disputes were always saved for the spring and summer when pieces of land could actually be surveyed.

As he flipped through the few active files on his desk, his gaze caught on a public drunkenness charge he was handling for Denny Fitzgerald. Why the man thought he'd even try and fight the charge Walker still hadn't figured out, but he'd agreed to take on the case.

Denny wasn't a bad guy. He'd made a bad choice—managed to do so every couple of years or so—but he was a good person all in all. He helped his neighbors and always pitched in on town activities. He was the first to help someone move or take down an old tree or set up for the town Fourth of July festivities.

And he was going to be one of the bachelors in the auction.

Walker had seen him eyeing Sloan a few times—all the guys in town had their eyes on her. Hell, she was a beautiful woman who no doubt drew attention even in overcrowded Manhattan. There was no doubt she'd draw significant attention in a town with an impressive population of seven hundred and twelve.

"You look like you've been sucking on lemons."

Walker glanced up to find Myrtle poking her head into the office. "And good morning to you too, Myrtle."

"You know damn well it's almost noon, so don't sass me. And what the hell are you doing in here?"

"Working." Walker made a big show of glancing at his watch. "Which is clearly more than I can say for you this *morning*."

"It's barely eleven thirty. You're lucky I made it in at all, especially since I had to deal with Mort."

"What's wrong?" Walker immediately thought of Myrtle's angina-attack prone husband.

"That man is going to drive me to drink, I swear on all that's holy. He spent the whole damn morning bitching about the traffic on Main Street since your grandmother closed off the intersection in front of the bank. Why does she do that? I swear, it makes my husband bat-shit to deal with that."

Walker almost laughed at the idea of traffic in Indigo. Road congestion generally meant waiting one whole rotation of the town's traffic light turning from green to yellow to red and back again. Opting to ignore a subject he knew he wouldn't win, he shifted the conversation.

"We got two feet of snow yesterday. Don't tell me he was out shoveling this morning."

"I damn well know how much snow we got." Her voice softened. "And no, he wasn't. The Stark boy came over and shoveled early this morning. And don't be changing the subject. Why does your grandmother close off that damn street?"

He shook his head, barely repressing a sigh. "You know she does that every year. For one week, the street gets closed off for the competition."

"A whole week," she muttered to herself as she walked out of his office and to her desk in the front lobby. Despite the distance, he heard her continued mumbling. "For one afternoon's worth of activity."

Bored with his own company, he followed behind her. "You know that's where they set up the pail races."

"Well, why the hell does she have to set up so early?"

"So they can plow off the street every day and get it good and dry so none of our fearsome competitors slip on any ice."

"It's a pain in the ass."

Walker sighed out loud this time and wondered how Mort Driver had put up with the lovely Myrtle for damn near forty years.

"Speaking of pains in the ass," Myrtle added. "I was hoping you'd be out of my hair today. Certainly there must be things you need to take care of in town."

"You trying to get rid of me?"

The bottle-red curls on her head bobbed in the affirmative. "Yes."

"I'm trying to get some work done."

"There's nothing that needs doing. The few case files that are active are still moving along at a crawl. Get out of here and let me do my filing."

Walker glanced down at her pristine desk. "I don't see a single file on there."

"Then get out of here and let me play Spider Solitaire."

"Remind me again why I pay you?"

"Because I'm the best damn paralegal in the state. And I work and slave for you. Just because your lazy ass doesn't know how to drum up business in the dead of winter doesn't mean it's my fault. You want me to work, get me some case files to work."

Myrtle leaned down to shove her purse into a desk drawer, her mutterings continuing to float up above her like thought bubbles. He heard the word "lazy" mentioned a few more times, along with some admonition about the hazards of idle hands.

Walker caught a blaze of movement outside on the street and saw several women in heavily padded coats walk into the middle of the town square. Curious, he moved toward the windows, surprised to identify them as Sloan, Grier and Avery.

"What are you looking at?"

"Our intrepid visitors."

Myrtle moved up behind him and let out a low whistle. "Those two sure are shaking up things around here. I hear the bachelors are anxious to be bid on by one of them."

"Who says they're bidding on anyone?"

"Sloan let it slip that she was planning on bidding on several for her article."

"Several?"

"She's got four more days after next weekend. Says she plans to make good use of her time. Every man I've talked to so far sure is anxious to find out if she picks him."

"So you think she's going to bid on four guys?"

"She could bid on up to eight. Girl's got to eat lunch and dinner. Hell, make it twelve. She could throw cocktails in between lunch and dinner."

"There's no way she'll bid on twelve men. Do we even have that many signed up in the competition?"

"We've got thirty-eight at last count, two more just signed up yesterday. She could handle a third of that, no problem. Expense account," Myrtle added in a knowing voice.

"She is not bidding on twelve men."

"Theoretically, she could. It's not like she's assured of winning each and every one."

An unnatural spear of annoyance twisted and turned at this decidedly unsavory development. He reminded himself Sloan had a job to do. That was all.

So why was he suddenly fighting the insistent need to pound on a few of his friends and neighbors?

"Well, isn't that sweet?" Myrtle's voice pierced through his imagined fistfight with Denny.

"What's so sweet?"

"It looks like Bear and Tommy Sanger just started a snowball fight on the Square."

"With who?"

"With the girls. Oh, I do think I'm going to pull up my chair. Love is in the air; can't you feel it?"

"Like hell it is."

Without a second thought for his actions, Walker snatched his coat, hat and scarf off the rack near the door, shoving into the sleeves as he stomped across Main Street.

It would be a long time later before he remembered Myrtle's knowing voice as she hollered at him on the way out. "It's about damn time."

Icy snow dripped down her neck when Sloan ducked to dodge a second snowball from Tommy. He might have gotten her squarely with the first one, but she'd be damned if he got her again.

Unmarked snow crunched under her feet as she ran toward where Grier and Avery hid behind a bench to prepare their attack. The cold air pierced her lungs, the pure freshness like a drug to her senses as she wiped at the dripping snow with her mitten.

No black snow piled up in gutters as it melted, she marveled. Nope, not a bit. The Alaskan snow was pristine and as bright white as a wedding dress.

"Here. You're due." Grier plopped a huge snowball into her hands, packed as tight as a softball.

Sloan judged the distance from where they hid behind the bench to how many feet she'd have to throw the snowball to hit the guys and decided she'd have to expose herself to attack to get the type of hit she wanted.

Eyeing the distance and lining up her shot, Sloan allowed Avery to toss a few to distract them before making her move.

The moment Tommy was occupied dodging Avery's attack, she raced in Bear's direction as a diversion tactic, then swerved at the last minute.

"Take that!"

She barely had time to pump her fist in victory as the snowball hit him square on the head before Bear's booming voice rang out, followed by a heavy thud of snow. It grazed her shoulder before veering off to ground.

"Ooooh," she taunted at the man who had to be twice her size. "I've seen four-year-olds in Central Park with better aim than you."

He lunged forward with a deep belly laugh that made her think he must play the town's Santa and he almost caught her around the ankles before she dodged away. "No pitching skills and no tackling skills, either. Poor baby."

"Sloan!"

Avery motioned for her to head back to base before Bear could pick himself up. His laughter still echoed across the snow-covered lawn and Sloan couldn't contain her own. "This is fun!"

"It sure beats that black, scummy snow we get in New York."

"To be fair," Sloan added philosophically as she bent down to hard-pack another snowball, "it does start out white."

"True. It just doesn't stay that way. But up here ..." Grier put her hands on her hips as she surveyed the landscape. "Wow. It's just amazing."

Sloan stopped what she was doing and wrapped an

arm around Grier's waist, her gaze fixed on the town that spread out before them. "It's really incredible. I'm glad you asked me to come here."

"I'm so glad you came."

They were about to hug when a loud shout pulled them back.

"Oh shit," Grier muttered as she dropped her arm. "Reinforcements."

Three men walked up to Bear and Tommy. She recognized Skate and it looked like a guy she'd met the first night and another she recognized from breakfast with the bachelors. "We can take them."

Sloan had begun to pack another snowball when a low voice caught her attention. "If you think that, you've never had a snowball fight in Alaska."

She straightened and came face-to-face with Walker. She hadn't seen him since the airport and wasn't the least surprised when ribbons of desire wrapped themselves around her rib cage, making her gasp for a full breath.

Damn, but how did he manage to look like a magazine ad with a woolen cap pulled down over his head? There was nothing sexy about woolen caps.

Yet he looked like a walking billboard for the health and vigor of the great outdoors.

"You're taking our side? Won't that make you a traitor to the cause?"

"Traitor?"

"You know." An impish urge overtook her, and she stretched up to whisper in his ear. Even through the layers of padding between her coat and his, she could feel the warmth of his body. "You're selling out against the Penis Squad over there."

A loud bark of laughter greeted her. "I think the Penis Squad has more than enough dicks. Besides. I much prefer the view over here."

"Walker. Would you shut that lawyerly mouth of yours and get your hands dirty. Honest to God," Avery muttered as she smacked him on the back of the head. She thumped the wool cap he wore, then added to the insult by slamming a snowball in his hands. "Quit flirting and get to work."

"Aye, aye, Captain."

She heard the flood of insults that flew across the snow as the men booed and hissed, swore and antagonized. Walker's smile only grew as he hollered back. "And who's over here with three beautiful women?"

Five matched expressions—dropped mouths and wide eyes—greeted his logic before he launched two missiles at the center of the line.

"Direct hit. Yep"—Sloan patted him on the back—"we can use you."

She allowed herself one lingering gaze as his dark eyes took possession of hers. Heat arced between the two of them like the aurora borealis she'd watched in online videos, so intense she was surprised the air didn't turn a deep, vivid shade of red.

The urge to kiss him—to ignore the people who were rapidly filling the square and simply take what she wanted—nearly overtook her, but she resisted.

And instead slammed a snowball into his head.

Chapter Sixteen

The Great Snowball Fight of 2011 would go down as legend in Indigo. Walker glanced around the square, now filled to bursting with a good portion of the town's population, and couldn't keep the smile from his face.

He felt like a kid.

And he hadn't felt like that in a long time.

A *very* long time.

The snow on the square was alternately hard-packed and pitted from an afternoon of attacks and retreats as snowball after snowball was constructed between gloved hands. The diner had set up a coffee and hot chocolate station and he saw his grandmother along with Mary and Julia, holding court in lawn chairs not too far from there.

His gaze caught on Sloan a little farther away, where she stood in deep conversation with Grier. A heavy wool cap with a bright, sewed-on patch that read TASTY'S BAIT AND TACKLE covered her head, which he could only assume was a loan from their intrepid proprietor of any and all ice-fishing needs.

Even with the less-than-stylish headgear, he couldn't stop his groin from tightening as his gaze once again returned to Sloan. Impish mischief flooded his veins and a deep craving for hot chocolate suddenly gripped him and wouldn't let go.

"Did we determine a final score?"

Walker turned as Avery came up next to him, her cheeks bright pink with exertion and a broad smile riding her face. "It may have to be a draw. No one's giving up that last round."

"No matter. We kicked ass."

"That we did."

He wrapped an arm around her heavily padded shoulders and reached up to tug her hat off. "Tasty get to you, too?"

"He made us an offer we couldn't refuse."

"When did that happen? I was playing on your side."

"I think it was when you were nursing that cramp in your foot like a big baby."

"It was an old basketball injury that got aggravated."

"Uh-huh."

"Okay, smart-ass. So what did he give you in exchange for your modeling skills?"

"Free use of his very splendid ice fishing house for an entire Saturday."

"No shit?" He couldn't keep from being impressed. "I had no idea the old coot was so generous."

"Clearly he knows a good place to advertise when he sees it."

"That he does."

"Besides, I'm not above being a shameless shill for commerce. I could see way better in this cap than trying to see around the rim of my hood."

"Which would account for those late-game death

bombs you nailed our opponents with." Walker pulled
her close in a side-armed hug. Years of friendship made
the move as natural as breathing and he grinned when
she laid her head against his shoulder.

"You doing okay, Ave?"

"I am. I really am."

"You've changed."

"I think I have. For the better, too."

"You're enjoying Sloan and Grier?"

"It's nice to have friends without baggage, you know?
They don't know any of my history. Or any town bullshit.
They're just fun to hang out with."

He gave her shoulder another squeeze before shifting
slightly to look her in the eyes. He *did* know. "My offer
still stands. If you want it."

Avery's eyes went round in her face. "Walker. I'm not
taking your money."

"It's not taking any money. It's accepting a loan that
you can pay back at any time."

"Where would I go?"

"Wherever you want to."

She paused for a moment, whatever she was about to
say getting caught somewhere between her brain and
her mouth. Before he could jump in, she held up a hand.
"Wait. Sorry, just wait."

As her breath made steamy puffs in the air, he
watched the girl he'd known for so long fade before his
eyes. She was replaced by someone more confident and
more relaxed. Maybe the old Avery had been fading all
along and he just hadn't noticed.

Or hadn't thought to look.

But in the last week he'd finally begun to realize she wasn't the same girl he'd known since he was small. The woman who stared back at him had seen her fair share of life and it had marked her.

Made her stronger.

More interesting.

And far more valuable than she'd been given any credit for.

"When he left, I thought my life was over," Avery said in a quick rush. "And it wasn't. It took me a long time to realize that. But it wasn't over. *I* wasn't over."

"Of course you weren't."

"He left, Walker. Left to see the world. To live the big life. And he never looked back. I think that's the part that hurt most of all."

"He did look back, Ave. You know he did. All the gifts. He's not immune, you know."

"Gifts don't count as looking back. They're guilt. There's a difference."

Walker didn't entirely disagree with her, so instead of replying, he rubbed a hand over her back.

"I'd have been okay if he'd just ended it. I really would have. But the hiding. The unwillingness to remember where he came from. The abandonment. I can't forgive that."

"You don't have to."

She let out a small laugh and she bumped him with her hip. "Good. 'Cause I'm not."

He bumped her right back. "So don't."

"Come on, lover boy. I know you're only being nice standing over here talking to me."

"Nice, nothing. You're a hottie in that skullcap you're wearing."

"I'm damn hot and don't you forget that, Walker Montgomery. However"—she shoved at his shoulder, the impact just enough to turn him in the direction of Sloan and Grier—"I believe there is a certain lady over there who's managed to capture all of your attention."

"You mean the one who slammed a snowball at my head to kick off the competition?"

Avery patted him on the cheek. "You know you loved it."

Scenes from the big fight flew through his mind on a fast track, with Sloan in the center of each and every one. "She's extraordinary."

"Then what are you doing standing here talking with me? The girl next door doesn't hold a candle to extraordinary."

"Now that, my dear friend, is where you're wrong. And since it's a well-known fact I have exquisite taste, it would make me quite happy to spend the rest of my evening with several extraordinary women."

"Then lead the way."

The giggles wouldn't stop as she and Grier stood in a small circle with several opponents from their snowball fight, all with steaming mugs of hot chocolate in their hands. Sloan took a moment to reflect. Had she ever felt so relaxed? Or enjoyed herself more?

With a shake of her head, she tried for stern voice as she stared up at the massive mountain that was Bear. "There is no way you stared down a moose."

Bear stopped his impression of his showdown on Main Street the spring before—his third retelling of the event—as her words penetrated.

"I most certainly did, Miz Sloan. It was one of the scariest moments of my life, and I've had quite a few of those, if I do say so myself. I'm a big man, but those animals are huge."

She patted him on the back, the width of his shoulders further evidence of why the man was called Bear. "I'm just giving you a hard time. I believe you. Honest."

Bear let out a loud guffaw. "Nah, you don't. But that's okay. Speaking of things that are hard to believe, you two have some arms for city girls."

"We're tough broads, my friend and I." Grier moved up and wrapped an arm around him from the other side. Sloan could have sworn the man was practically glowing as his smile split his face.

"With hearts of gold, no doubt." Walker's voice floated over her, the dark, husky tones drawing her attention immediately as he and Avery walked up to join the group.

"But of course." The hard slam of attraction buffeted her like the Alaska winter wind and Sloan fought to stand through it—fought to keep her wits about her—when all she really wanted to do was wrap herself around the man and never let him go.

How did he manage to turn her upside down so easily?

The snowball fight had been a revelation. The man she'd thought of alternately as the stern, legal eagle or the sexy, committed-to-his-bachelorhood single male had showed a different side.

A *fun* side.

And she was even more infatuated than she'd been before.

Which meant only one thing. She needed to make a decision—the proverbial fish or cut bait argument.

Of course, all her hormones wanted to do was fish.

And Walker Montgomery was quite the catch.

Sloan hadn't missed the way the townswomen looked at him. The single women looked at him like he was their next meal and the married ones looked at him with the longing of youth, when their futures held endless possibilities.

"I'm getting cold," Grier interjected before turning a huge smile back on Bear, then to the broader circle of friends that surrounded them. "And I hear there are enough burgers being fried up inside the diner to feed all of us three times over."

"I'm in," Avery shouted, untangling herself from underneath Walker's arm.

Before Sloan could blink, everyone had taken off like the town square was haunted. "Was it something I said?"

"Mass quantities of beef products have a way of doing that to people."

She only shrugged, her suspicions running high that it wasn't only the lure of burgers that had people moving. Maybe it was the saucy wink Grier had tossed her as she'd herded everyone toward the warm, welcome lights of the diner.

"You're quite the snowball warrior, even if you did think my head was fair game." Walker moved into her line of vision and Sloan was instantly aware of the ugly cap she'd willingly put on her head in the heat of battle. The large patch proudly announcing her loyalty to Tasty was funny in the moment and decidedly not so now as he stared down at her with a sexy longing in his eyes.

"I had to make sure of your loyalties."

"Is that what it's called?"

She couldn't stop the nervous giggle. "I'd already taken three snowballs. You needed to catch up a bit. Ruffle that lawyerly exterior."

"Speaking of exterior." Sloan reached up to tug at the edge of material that lay over her right ear, the wool already slipping off her head when Walker's hand covered hers. Even through both their gloves, warmth slammed through her, the heat seemingly enough to melt the entire square that surrounded them.

"Oh no, leave it on."

"It's hideous."

"It's sexy."

She couldn't hold back her indelicate snort if her life depended on it. "It's awful, Walker."

His hand never moved from hers as his head dipped, his mouth moving ever closer. "It's incredibly sexy."

She tilted her head back to receive his kiss, her eyes nearly closed when an explosion of light filled the sky. "Oh my God!"

"What?" He lifted his head, his gaze darting to the diner, toward the square and then back to her, but she was already moving out of the loose circle of his arms.

She saw his confusion, but figured he was smart

enough to keep up as she moved away from the lights of the diner and toward the middle of the square to get a better look. "I don't believe it. That's really it. It's really what they look like."

His boots crunched on the snow as he followed behind her and he might have even grumbled under his breath. The masculine complaint was like music to her ears.

He *wasn't* unaffected.

The urge to fish grew another jolt stronger.

With a glance over her shoulder, she pointed toward the sky. "The northern lights. I didn't think I'd actually get to see them while I was here."

"It can be hit or miss, but the cold crisp night we're having is a perfect time to see them."

His voice was flat as it carried on the frigid night air. Was it the interrupted kiss that had him irritated? With a mental shrug, she ignored it, unable to tear her gaze away. "They're amazing."

Bright swaths of color lit up the sky, a dark iridescent red that fascinated as it drew the eye.

"They're a favorite of the tourists."

"I can see why."

He came up behind her, his breath hot on her ear as he leaned down toward her. "I know a better place to see them."

Whatever annoyance she thought she'd heard had vanished in the sensual notes of his deep voice.

"Where?"

"My backyard."

She turned quickly, shocked surprise mixing with

good old-fashioned feminine wisdom. "Oh, that's smooth, Walker Montgomery. Is this like 'come on over and see my etchings'?"

"Hardly." His arched eyebrows had mischief stamped clear through them. "Unless, of course, you *want* to see my etchings."

She lifted onto her toes and wrapped her arms around his shoulders, her lips curving in response as he moved closer. "Tell you what. Let's go look at the lights and we'll figure out the rest as we go."

As his mouth came down over hers he whispered, "What man can argue with that?"

Tension gripped his body as he and Sloan walked the short distance to his home. The distance would be the equivalent of three Manhattan blocks to her, but it felt like an endless walk.

Desire for this woman had turned to a dark, driving need that lit up his nervous system like a freaking Christmas tree. The sharp edges of it hardened his body and it was all he could do to keep from snatching her up in his arms.

"What made you pick a place so close to town? I had you pegged for the outskirts-of-town-in-a-cabin sort of guy."

"That's Mick. Man likes his space. I, on the other hand"—he led her up the freshly shoveled walk to his front door—"like being in town. It's easy to get to work and it keeps me close to my grandmother in case she needs something. Plus, I'm the town lawyer. It lends a certain Andy-Griffith-in-Mayberry comfort to folks to be that close to Main Street."

"You look out for her."

"My grandmother?" He pulled off a heavy glove to fish around in his pocket for the keys. "I do. She makes me bat-shit insane, but yeah, I look out for her."

"And your parents?"

"Gone a while now. Mom's in Seattle and my dad's in Phoenix."

"They're not married?"

He heard the surprised speculation in her voice as he unlocked the door and pushed it open. They were met with a blast of warmth. "Technically, yes. In actuality. No."

"I had no idea."

He flipped a switch to the hallway lights and forced a light note into his voice. "Most people don't. Including my grandmother, so I'd appreciate it if you kept that one to yourself."

"Of . . . of course."

The confusion in her response lanced through him. Damn it, when had the conversation turned to such an unpleasant topic? He was on the verge of a sexy encounter with Sloan and the last thing he wanted to discuss was his parents.

Her still-gloved hand came down on his arm. "Come on. Let's go see the lights."

"Are you warm enough?"

"I'm wearing about ten layers."

"It's winter in Alaska, Sloan. You have to be careful." She lifted on her toes and pressed a kiss to his cheek. "I'm warm enough. Now, come on. I presume it's that way." She pointed down the hallway toward his back door.

"Yeah."

She walked ahead on carefree feet and he held back, watching her. Whatever curiosity the subject of his parents had raised was gone as she unlocked the back door and twisted the knob. Another shocked "oh my," this one far louder than when she'd first seen the lights on the square, drifted back to him.

Unlike most of the people who lived in town and all the people who visited, he wasn't a huge fan of the aurora borealis. Shitty memories had a way of doing that to a person.

But a glance at Sloan's wide, breathless grin as she waved him on from the doorframe had him rethinking things.

Maybe it was possible to make new memories.

Memories that would erase the pain that had come before.

Jack stared out the window of the diner. The flashes of light filling the sky were a welcome diversion from Mick's sullen face. "The lights are strong tonight."

"It's the cold air. Does it every time."

"That it does."

Silence descended between them, but they'd both have to be deaf to miss the repeated peals of laughter that rang out from the far side of the diner.

"You want to get out of here?"

"Not particularly."

"She's got your dick in a twist."

Mick shot a sullen glance over his shoulder, his gaze unerringly finding Grier in the middle of a table full of men. "Clearly I'm not the only one."

"She's not doing anything. And I haven't seen her move from that seat she's sitting in."

Mick shrugged. "Doesn't matter. She's not sitting here."

"Seeing as how you look about as welcoming as a grizzly, can't say I blame her."

Waiting a beat, Jack decided to go for broke. He knew Mick's bad mood was tied to Grier, but he suspected there were still quite a few raw spots left over from the rescue on Denali as well. "You get those researchers back to Anchorage?"

"Yeah."

"Did it go okay?"

Another sullen shrug greeted him as Mick reached for his burger and took a large bite. After he swallowed, he added, "Good as can be expected."

"You doing okay?"

"What the fuck, Rafferty? You channeling my grandmother?"

"Nothing wrong with asking after a friend. I figure if you don't want to talk about it, you'd just say so. Seeing as how you're all prickly and miserable, I have to wonder if something else is wrong."

"Nothing's wrong." Mick crumpled his napkin and Jack watched as the man fought for control. The happy-go-lucky grin his friend usually sported was nowhere in evidence and tension rode high on his shoulders.

"Funny, because that's not the way I hear it."

"Oh yeah? What have you heard?"

"Grier's not giving you the time of day since you gave her the bum's rush this morning."

"I did not."

"Avery's telling a very different story."

"Shit. When did Avery become the town grapevine?"

"Since she became thick as thieves with Jonas's daughter. Besides, she only said it to me. My guess is she wants me to talk some sense into you."

Mick ran a frustrated hand through his short hair before making a fist. "What the fuck was I supposed to do?"

"Stay put and spend some quality time, man. Don't tell me you don't know better than that."

On a shake of his head and a muttered curse about the "fucking Oprah treatment," Mick took a deep breath. "It was the most mind-blowing sex of my life and at five this morning, she crawls out of bed and goes to cry in the bathroom. I can read the signs a mile away and this one screamed regret in giant letters."

Jack winced, imagining the slight. Sex gone bad was an unfortunate experience. But when it was *good* sex that ended badly, well . . .

He caught sight of Jessica where she sat between Avery and Grier, her head back and laughing at whatever joke Skate was telling.

With the force of a battering ram, the erotic images assailed him. The heavy feel of her breasts in his palms, the play of her fingers up and down his body and the unbearably hot, wet heat of her as he sank himself to the hilt.

And the sullen face staring at him across the table was a vivid reminder of what he'd done to Jessica.

How he'd made her feel afterward.

And ever since.

And wasn't that just a fucking bitch?

"Look. Thanks for the therapy session, but I'm getting out of here."

"You in for more setup tomorrow morning?"

Mick let out a snort. "Like my grandmother would let me get away with anything less."

"I'll see you then."

"Later."

Jack sat there for a long time after Mick left, nursing his coffee and thinking. The holidays always put Molly in the forefront of his mind, so it was surprising to realize that Jessica McFarland was edging out his late wife for the honor.

Had he really done that same thing to her?

Let her see his regret?

With a resigned sigh, he had to admit that he had.

"More coffee, Jack?"

"Only if you still have some of that amaretto to add to it."

"Sure thing."

"Nancy. Wait."

When the waitress turned back around, he nodded in Jessica's direction. "Send one over to Jess as well."

He saw the speculative light in Nancy's eyes—and knew his actions would be spread around town before he even got to the square in the morning—but oddly enough, he couldn't say he cared.

He sat and watched her, the crowd she'd been sitting with thinning out as people headed home for the evening. Even Skate had given up when he'd obviously realized his endless parade of jokes wasn't going to get him laid this evening.

Nancy returned with a tray and set down his cup, then moved on toward Jess's table. He saw the moment the gesture registered. The quick look of surprise that marred her features with confusion, followed by a subtle flush of pink high on her cheeks.

God, she was beautiful.

A long sweep of hair framed her face and her large, brown doe eyes shone in the florescent lights of the restaurant.

He stood and walked toward the table, his legs giving a subtle shake as he crossed the length of the room.

"Mind if I sit down?"

Those beautiful eyes widened before a small smile hinted along the edges of her mouth. "Of course not."

He nodded to Avery and Grier, who were already standing to grab their coats. Avery nodded at him as she stood. "Jack. Good evening. I'm so sorry to rush off, but Susan just IMed me and she's having fits at the hotel."

"And I figured I'd pitch in and help," Grier added on a rush.

He saw through the lies, but didn't have any interest in the polite niceties of keeping the other women there.

He had to make up for lost time.

Chapter Seventeen

*B*right swoops and swirls lit up the sky as the northern lights put on a show. Sloan sat watching from a lawn chair in Walker's backyard. Vivid color flashed in bright sweeping arcs, one more vibrant than the next, and each time streaks of red exploded before her eyes Sloan grew more and more awed.

She'd read about the aurora borealis, of course. No proper tourist guide book on Alaska would be complete without mentioning it. But to actually be fortunate enough to see it was another thing entirely.

Even the videos she'd watched online couldn't come remotely close to sitting outside in the crisp night air, taking in the real thing.

"Are you sure you're not cold?"

"Hardly." Sloan turned toward Walker, tearing her gaze away from the brightly lit sky. Despite his signals he'd rather be anywhere than staring at the lights, the concern in his voice was clear. It was that thoughtfulness—so freely given and, sadly, so rare—that had her stomach doing a quick squeeze. "This is the most incredible thing I've ever seen. And the likelihood I'll see it again is slim to none. I don't want to miss a moment."

As soon as the words were out of her mouth, she wished she could bite them back.

Stop the reality of what she hadn't said out loud.

She was leaving Alaska.

When this trip was over, she was going back to New York. Back to her life.

If Walker had a reaction to the mention of her eventual departure, he kept it to himself. "At least tell me you don't think they're a sign that aliens really exist."

She laughed at that and offered him an exaggerated eye roll. "What do you take me for, Walker Montgomery? I'll have you know this city girl can spot a scam from a mile away. Anything that has the word 'alien' tied to it is a scam and a half, no doubt about it."

He shrugged and offered her a small smile that didn't quite meet his eyes. "It was worth a shot."

Her gaze drifted back to the startling display of nature in the nighttime sky and she kept her voice casual as she asked, "You don't like the northern lights much, do you?"

"I like them just fine." She could see from the corner of her eye that he shrugged along with the simple statement, but she wasn't buying the casual nature of his response.

It was *too* casual.

Too calculated.

"Could have fooled me."

"Look, Sloan. You wanted to come out here and freeze your ass off. I'm obliging. What the hell else do you want me to say?"

"I guess I don't want you to say anything."

"Good. Because I don't have anything to say."

"Fine."

She let it go. The NO TRESPASSING sign was up, clear as day, and she had no right pushing.

It was curious, though. He'd been full of lighthearted fun all day until she'd caught sight of the lights. And with their appearance, his attitude had taken a nosedive. Even the promise of sex—one she'd given freely—hadn't taken the strain out of his voice.

"They're like the Empire State Building." His voice rang clearly in the crisp winter night.

"I'm sorry?"

"The lights. They're no big deal when you live here. Sort of like the Empire State Building is for you."

"Really? That's interesting. I actually like looking at the Empire State Building. I've even been known to go up on it from time to time. It's still one of the best places in the entire city to see the views."

"Then you're a rarity."

And that's when she heard it, loud and clear in the all the things he wasn't saying. "Oh?"

"Most people don't see what's in front of their faces. They're jaded. And they lack interest in the things that grow stale."

"That's a choice, Walker. Not everyone believes the things around them should be taken for granted."

"Maybe so. It doesn't make it any less true."

"I believe it does."

"Then you're as rare as you seem."

She stood and reached for the back of the lawn chair to fold it up.

"What are you doing?"

"It's cold. And it's time to get inside."

"We don't have to go in."

A wave of sadness filled her as she looked at his face. The stubborn set of his chin and the rich, bold red of his lips as hot puffs of air escaped with his breath were limbed in defiant lines of hurt and pain.

A pain, if she wasn't mistaken, that went as deep as they come.

He looked miserable.

"Come on." She held out her hand. "Let's go inside."

Walker took her outstretched hand, surprised at the lack of pique in her. He knew she wanted to sit and stare at the lights—and he knew he was acting like a total asshole—but here she was, her hand out to his in open invitation.

Could she really be so worldly, yet unjaded? So free of any of the usual games men and women seemed to play with each other with excruciating regularity.

She truly *was* extraordinary.

Sloan McKinley was an incredible mystery, and every facet he managed to uncover only intrigued him more.

They moved back into his house, the bright lights and warmth of his kitchen welcoming them in. He wasn't big on decorating—everyone from his grandmother to Avery to Jessica had teased him about the lack of décor in his very beige kitchen—but the image of Sloan standing in the middle of it made him finally understand.

She was light and color, brightness and warmth.

And he'd been living a life in beige and neutral tones that, while safe, wasn't all that interesting.

He'd chalked it up to a satisfying bachelor lifestyle, but was it?

Was he satisfied?

"I've hated the northern lights since the night my father told me he was cheating on my mother while we looked up at them."

She was midway through unwrapping her scarf when she froze, her bright blue eyes going round as she laid a hand on his forearm. "Oh, Walker. I'm sorry. I'm so sorry."

"Thanks. But if I'm going to do this, you can't play the sympathy card on me."

She nodded, understanding filling her gaze and he thought yet again what a revelation she was.

Most women of his acquaintance would have been hurt by his words—miffed at his harshness—but she understood.

She could see he needed space and she was secure enough to give it to him.

On a sigh, he shrugged out of his coat and gloves and took a seat at the table opposite her.

"When did it happen?"

"About fifteen years ago. I was in my early twenties, home from my senior year of college on winter break. I don't know if he thought I was old enough to hear the truth or if he was just sick of keeping the lies to himself, but he told me."

He could still picture that evening in his mind, the images so crisp and clear they could have happened the day before.

His father's jovial voice and hard slap to the back,

telling him how it was no big deal. How a man needed his space. Needed some time away from the things that had grown old and tired.

"My mother didn't know. It took another three years for that to happen. When she did find out she was so embarrassed she didn't tell a soul. She refused to admit there was anything going on. Or anything wrong with their marriage."

He got up and crossed the room, the urge to move overwhelming. He hit the fringe and hunted around for a beer. "Do you want one?"

"Sure."

With quick, efficient movements, he popped two caps and walked back to the table, handing her a bottle as he sat. On a long drag, he thought about those long, endless awkward moments when he had first come home from law school. Wondering if his mother knew. If his father's secrets were finally apparent to the woman who shared his life.

"So he kept it from her. He played the good and devoted husband. And then one day it finally all came out. I still don't know how. Maybe he was just sick of keeping secrets or she finally got wise to all his overnight trips and late-night phone calls."

"People get divorced all the time. It's sad, but it's not uncommon. You mentioned earlier that no one here knows. What do they think your parents are doing, with two separate addresses?"

"As far as anyone knows, the Montgomerys live in Seattle and are enjoying their empty nest. No marital problems and no separate addresses. My mother sends out Christmas cards like clockwork, each and every year, signed with love from both of them. And they make their annual pilgrimage once a year together to visit family. It was the one and only thing she required of him when she found out about the cheating."

"It seems like such a waste. For her especially."

"There's nothing I can say to change her mind. Nothing I can do to convince her she'd be better off divorced. I finally stopped trying."

"So this is why you're not so crazy about the annual games. Or why your grandmother's insistent view of love is such an irritant."

He took another swallow off the longneck. "She raised a man who represents the antithesis of love, commitment and devotion, yet she believes in it to the depths of her toes. It's all a game. And when the game's over, there's always a loser."

"It doesn't have to be that way, you know. Even my parents—for as crazy as my mother is—love each other. Understand each other. Are devoted to each other. It's not the same for everyone. There are people who spend their lives together. Willingly. And happily."

"And there are just as many people who live a lie."

He heard the frustration tinge her words as she continued to argue her point of view. "It's not all a lie. Our lives are not lies. And the feelings we have as part of the human experience aren't lies. Don't tell me you don't realize that."

"I think we create stories to suit ourselves at a given point in time. Just like you're doing, Sloan."

Her voice was quiet when she spoke, yet the words

slammed into him with the force of an oncoming Mack truck. "I really am sorry you feel that way. Sorry you feel there's nothing true in this world. That you feel the only thing between two people is a game to be lost."

"Oh come on, Sloan. You're leaving here in less than a week. You said so yourself. Don't tell me you've suddenly developed a love for the wilderness. You've got a very nice doorman building awaiting your return, sweetheart. If you want a quick fling up here in the wilds I'm your man, but somehow I don't see you as the type to handle the decided lack of commitment that comes with a one-night stand."

"Well, then." Sloan stood, laying her full beer bottle on the table before her. "I should probably get going."

"You probably should. Come on. I'll walk you back to the Indigo."

She rebundled herself, Tasty's hat scrunched in her hands as she kneaded the fabric with her fingers. "I'm not expecting love, Walker. Or a heap of false words. But I am expecting someone whose feelings are pure enough to acknowledge something that's real. I don't think you're in that place. I don't think you're even capable of it."

"I'll walk you back."

"Actually, I think taking in the fresh air—*alone*—will do me good. It's suddenly become rather oppressive here."

"You're not crossing the town by yourself."

"I live in a city of eight million people and I get along just fine. I think I can handle three blocks where I'll be lucky if I see a soul. Good night."

He wanted to go after her, but he knew she was right. Besides, he could watch her walk all the way to the center of town. The bright lights would illuminate each and every step she took.

Cold air wrapped around him as he stood in his doorway while the heat pressed at him from behind. He watched her take every one of those steps to the hotel. And with each footfall that took her farther away, he cursed himself every type the fool.

"Stubborn, ignorant, arrogant asshole." The words had become her litany and she repeated them over and over on her walk back to the Indigo.

It was for the best, she tried to convince herself. For the best that she didn't take this any further. She already knew having sex with Walker was going to leave a mark. She'd developed feelings for him, and taking that to more than a physical level was only going to make it harder to leave.

And leave she would.

She didn't belong here. She had a life back home. A life she enjoyed. Most of the time.

Didn't she?

And that's when it hit her like a ton of bricks. If she hadn't known Walker was still watching her from his front door, she'd have plopped down on one of the benches in the town square.

"Oh, McKinley, you are such a fucking idiot. Really and truly. Why the hell did you go and fall in love with him? Of all people, why him?"

Suddenly, Grier's tears that morning over breakfast made a hell of a lot of sense, especially as tears of her own threatened via the fist-sized lump in her throat.

She was three thousand miles from home, developing a completely inconvenient, idiotic, *emotional*, attachment for a man.

A man, she added to herself, who not only didn't believe in love, but who actively avoided anything that even remotely smacked of commitment.

Or did he?

After all, he lived in town, where the eyes of Indigo recorded his every move. All that bullshit about Mayberry and being a small-town lawyer sure smacked of commitment, didn't it?

And taking care of his grandmother and looking out for her. Oh, he played the long-suffering grandson, but he did what was right. He stood by her and helped her and looked out for her.

And if that wasn't commitment, what was it?

If she asked him, he'd probably say it was duty.

But it wasn't.

It was a choice. Walker Montgomery was clearly capable of choosing commitment.

He just wasn't capable of making it with her.

Jessica glanced around her small living room and wondered what had happened since the time she'd left this morning and this very moment.

The room looked the same. The bright red overstuffed couch with the accent pillows in vivid, vibrant primary colors still sat askew from where she'd left them last night after watching TV. The throw blanket she'd wrapped herself in was still in a heap on the floor. And the latest paperback thriller she'd been reading while the commercials were on lay facedown on the coffee table.

There was one noticeable difference, though.

Jack Rafferty sat on the middle of her couch.

She fiddled with the tassel on a throw pillow. "You helping the guys finish up in the square tomorrow?"

"Sure am." Jack stared down at the can of Coke she'd nervously heaped on him when they'd walked in.

A good hostess never lets her guests go thirsty.

Her mother's words rang in her ears and she nearly broke out in a laugh at the remembered lessons on etiquette, poise and entertaining her mother had regularly doled out. Somehow, those lessons never included what to do when one wanted to jump the visitor sitting on the opposite side of the room.

Nor did they include lessons on what to do when one had already jumped said visitor and had been given the proverbial cold shoulder ever since.

At the remembered slight—and the overly polite niceties they'd shared over the past eighteen months— some of the warm glow she'd been feeling evaporated.

She'd spent all these long months letting Jack know she was open to getting to know him better and he'd kept her at arm's length.

Worse, he'd left her feeling like the weekend they'd shared had been some cheap thing he'd like to forget.

"Mary, Julia and Sophie don't let anyone out of manual labor, do they?"

"No, not really." He offered a small, rueful smile. "Taskmasters, those three are."

"Yet they remain surprisingly lovable."

"That they do."

Jack's gaze returned to his Coke can and she wondered again what they were doing here. He'd been all warm smiles and friendly conversation at the diner. Nothing overtly sexual and damn it, she was so crazy about him, she was willing to settle for even that.

When he'd suggested they go back to her place so Nancy could close up the diner and go home, she'd been so surprised she'd agreed without a backward glance. But now that they were here, she was fast coming to think this hadn't been one of her brighter ideas.

Of course, nothing had been the same since that glorious weekend she spent with Jack all those long, long months ago. Bright ideas and her reaction to the man just didn't belong in the same sentence.

Even if—in her own defense—her skin did crawl with anticipation and excitement every time he came within her field of vision. It was like some torture designed especially for her. The damn man could make her hot and bothered from a hundred paces.

And all the son of a bitch wanted to do was have a friendly chat over a soda.

God, she was hopeless.

"Jess?"

"Hmmm? Sorry?"

"You look a million miles away."

"Just thinking."

"About?"

"Oh, nothing." She waved a hand. "Nothing important at all."

"Yeah, it's funny. Thinking."

"Oh?"

His gaze never left the can and his words were soft as he exhaled on a deep breath. "I've been thinking a lot about you."

"Oh?" Her breath caught in her throat.

Even as her hopes soared, she tried desperately to rein in her feelings. He could be thinking about any number of things, none of which had anything to do with her. Or more to the point, her unrequited feelings for him.

He lifted his gaze from the can and his fingers stilled. "Are you participating in the games this weekend?"

She shrugged, her hopes plummeting again as she mentally called herself an idiot a million times over. "Yeah. Why?"

"Would you reconsider if I asked you to?"

"Why would you want to do that? Ask me to, I mean? I compete every year."

His dark gaze never left her face. "Because I've been thinking a lot about you. And I realize I haven't been completely honest with you."

"Honest about what?"

At that he stood and moved over toward where she sat, kneeling down in front of her. His long fingers spread over her knees and she felt the heat of his touch through the heavy material of her jeans. As if branded, that simple, light touch shot sparks through her and she grew damp at her core.

With gentle movements, he pushed her knees apart and positioned himself between the cradle of her thighs. His arms came up and caged her into the chair as he moved in, his lips so close to hers she'd barely have to lean forward to kiss him.

"About how I feel about you. About the way you make me feel."

Tears welled low in her throat, almost painful as she swallowed around the lump. Was it possible?

Could he actually feel something, too?

Had all these long, lonely months of waiting actually led to something?

"How's that?"

He leaned forward and pressed a kiss against her throat. Whatever heat she'd felt from his fingertips was nothing compared to the flames that immediately consumed every part of her. "Alive," he whispered against her skin, and at that Jessica lost it. "You make me feel alive, Jess. That and so many other wonderful things."

Her arms came up around his shoulders and tugged at his hair so he'd look up at her. "Are you sure? Because I can't go through another eighteen months like the last ones."

"I'm sure."

"Really sure?"

Jack shifted and sat back on his heels, but he reached for her hands, his fingers threading through hers. "I've been so unfair to you. So fucking unfair."

The tears she fought to hold back welled up on their own volition. "Yeah. I understand why. I mean, I think I understand why. But yeah, you have."

"Ah, Jess, I'm sorry. Really sorry. I've been so torn. Between feeling like I've betrayed Molly in the worst way and feeling like I finally have hope inside me again."

She wanted to believe him so badly, but she had to see this through. Had to understand why he'd behaved as he had. "What changed your mind?"

"A lot of things. The last few days. Those guys Mick picked up on Denali. The games and all the talk about bachelorettes that hits this time of year. But it was Mick who clinched it."

"Mick?" At the thought of his rangy, devil-may-care partner, Jessica couldn't keep the smile off her face. "What in God's name did Mick have to do with this?"

"Grier's got him in a twist. And he's not sure why."

"I don't think she knows."

He waved a hand as his brows furrowed. "I really do not want to know the details. Avery was chewing my ear off earlier and the way I see it, Mick's love life is none of my business."

"I still don't see what his love life—or lack thereof—has to do with you here in my house."

"I got to thinking about how I've treated you over the last year. And how it's the last thing Molly would have wanted. For me or for you. She liked you, you know."

"Molly?"

Jess thought about the pretty, petite woman who had been Jack's wife. They'd been several years apart in school and Molly had even babysat her a few times when she'd been that awkward age of not old enough to stay by herself but almost too old to need sitting. They'd read teen magazines and *ooh*ed and *aah*ed over celebrities.

"I liked her, too. She was a wonderful person. And I can't imagine the hell you've lived with. Losing her. And before that, her getting sick."

"She loved life and it was taken from her too soon. But she wouldn't have wanted me to lose mine along with her. I'm not sure why I couldn't see it for so long, but sitting there tonight, watching those guys flirt with you in the diner. I just knew."

"Knew what?"

"Knew it was time to do something."

She squeezed his fingers, wanting to believe him. Desperate to believe they'd turned some sort of corner.

"I never meant to go after you. I hope you know that."

"What?"

She unthreaded their fingers, twisting hers before her as she tried to find the right words to explain.

"I don't horn in on my friend's husbands and even though she and I didn't know each other that well, I liked Molly, too. I wasn't one of those women waiting in the wings, hoping to land you. I hope you know that."

"I never thought that."

"Yeah, well, a lot of other people have."

"No one knows what happened between us, Jess."

"I suspect more people know than you think."

He shrugged. "Doesn't matter if they do. It doesn't concern them."

"We live in a small town, Jack. And gossip is the engine that keeps it running."

"Well, then"—he smiled up at her as he nestled closer, his fingers reaching for the bottom of her sweater—"maybe we should give them something to talk about."

Chapter Eighteen

Walker knocked on Sloan's hotel room door, his stomach in more knots than a teenage boy on his first date. He'd watched her from his front door until he saw she had safely arrived at the Indigo and had intended to go back inside and finish his beer, followed by a chaser of scotch.

It had taken exactly two more minutes to acknowledge he was the world's biggest asshole.

"What are you doing here? I didn't think the hotel let strange visitors up after ten?"

"Sloan. Come on."

Her arms folded and the mulish expression on her face let him know she wasn't only mad, she was good and mad.

An important distinction that made a difference to war generals, police officers and men who were about to grovel.

"Can I come in?"

"What's the point?"

He stood there a moment, letting her words penetrate. What *was* the point?

Either he was in or he wasn't, but he knew this parade of bad behavior wasn't fair anymore.

"Maybe I've been thinking about what you said."

"Yeah. Well, maybe I've been thinking about what you said, too. And it dawns on me"—she reached for the door to push it closed—"we're way too far apart to come to any sort of compromise."

With a quick step, he put his foot inside the doorframe. "Not so fast." She arched an eyebrow, but stopped pushing on the door. "Can I come in?"

"Be my guest."

He moved into the room and shut the door quietly behind him. Her room was exceptionally neat, with everything put in its place. Her suitcase was perched on a small stand in the corner and he couldn't find a thing lying on the floor, the bed or even peeking out of the closet. The TV blared a twenty-four-hour news station as he made his perusal of her living arrangements. "Can you turn that off? I'd like to talk to you."

She flipped the TV off with the remote and took a seat in the chair in the sitting area of the room.

Now that he had her attention the nerves whipped up again, battering his stomach with a series of dive-bombs that made him very glad he hadn't added the scotch on top of his beer.

"I owe you an apology. I was surly when you wanted to look at the lights and then I got all moody and assholeish on you."

"Assholeish?" Her lips maintained their frown, but he thought he might have made a slight dent in her armor—the light note in her voice was encouraging.

"It's a very special legal term, reserved for very special occasions. And it's an incredibly apt description of my behavior this evening."

"I see."

"Look. The whole thing with my parents is ugly and raw and just not something I share."

"Obviously."

"And looking at the lights brought it all up. Add your questions on top and, well . . ." He trailed off as the mulish expression resettled itself on her face.

Whatever inroads he'd made with the joke had evaporated. The deep blue of her eyes had gone a stormy gray.

"So it's my fault?"

"I didn't say that."

"Yeah, but if I hadn't asked you any questions . . . If I had just closed my eyes on the damn town square and kissed you and not made a big deal about the lights, none of this would have happened. Right?"

"Yeah. Well, no. I mean." He ran a hand through his hair, tugging on the ends before he took a deep breath. "Okay. Look. I'm fucking this up royally and you're not making it any easier."

"You don't deserve to have me make it any easier on you."

He stopped at that, his fingers going slack midtug on his hair. "What?"

"You're not the only one with a shock of emotions you don't know what to do with, Walker. Did you ever think about that?"

"Well . . ." As he broke off, he realized the answer *was* simple. No, he hadn't thought about it.

"I didn't come up here to meet a man and I sure as hell didn't come up here to get my groove on with one.

I came up here to help my friend who's in a tough spot."

He couldn't stop the smile that broke across his face and he'd dare any healthy, red-blooded American male to resist the same at the image of this woman getting her groove on. "What would be so bad about that?"

"About what?"

"The groove part."

"Nothing, except grooving and caring have no place together."

"They do when they're done right."

"That's not what I'm talking about here."

"So what are you talking about?"

"If I'd come up here for a fling and nothing more, I'd treat this thing between the two of us like a fling. We'd groove a bit and I'd go on my way. No harm, no foul."

A tight fist closed around his chest and he was help-less to hold back his next words. "You do that often?"

She only smiled, the broad grin a mocking reminder to him of what he'd just stepped in. "I'm not answering that. But let's just say that I'd guess I've done it far fewer times than you have. And never with a perfect stranger."

He skipped doing a quick estimate and refocused on the other thing she'd said. "And the other? About meet-ing someone and a shock of emotions?"

"Yeah. That. I'm not looking for a relationship, Walker. But damn it to hell if you don't make me see dates and picnics and all that other mushy shit that lives in a wom-an's mind and reaches up to grab her around the throat at the most inopportune times."

"Mushy shit? Is that another legal term?"

"It's a fucking pain in the ass is what it is. I see picnics and dates with you, Walker. And it pisses me off. You're supposed to be fling material and instead you look at me the way you do and you engage in snowball fights and you even think I'm sexy in the most hideous hat in the entire world. So, yeah. You make me think of mushy shit."

He moved in, unable to stop himself. Leaning down, he neatly boxed her into her chair, his hands wrapped around each of the wooden arms. "Maybe I like the fact that you think about mushy shit."

"You mean you're not ready to run for the door?"

"Not by a long shot."

"So what are we going to do about it? We want different things and we have different lives."

"We both want the same thing now." It sounded like a line. He knew it, even though he didn't mean it that way. But all he could see was Sloan. And while he couldn't see his future, he couldn't imagine anyone else in it.

Didn't that count for something?

On a soft sigh, she reached up and wrapped her arms around his neck. "I know."

Pulling her to her feet, Walker drew her against him and wrapped his arms around her slender frame. He settled his hands in the curve of her lower back and whispered in her ear, "I'm so glad we agree."

With a dark growl, he pressed his lips to hers, suddenly desperate to feel the connection between them. Her arms tightened around him and their tongues met in a fiery wash of need. Desire speared through him in hard, pulsing waves and he abstractly realized he'd need to make the most of these moments because he wasn't likely to get many more of them with Sloan.

The thought of her leaving stopped him momentarily and he pulled back to look at her. Her blue eyes were heavy lidded and she opened them slightly to peer up at him. "What?" she whispered.

"Nothing." He hesitated, almost saying more. Like how glad he was she'd come to Indigo and how he'd like her to stay. Like how his feelings for her went beyond a fling. This wasn't just a groove or a booty call or whatever adults came up with to explain scratching an itch.

She wasn't an itch.

She was *Sloan*.

And she had become everything to him.

How had she managed it? How had she gotten under his skin, forcing him to reevaluate everything he knew to be true?

Everything he *thought* he wanted.

But he held back and didn't say anything, pushing it all to the back of his mind. It was just the heat of the moment. The satisfaction of finally having her back in his arms.

Refocusing his attention on her, he dropped back into the here and now. "It's nothing."

Another searing kiss ignited between them, the soft mewls in the back of her throat so erotic it threw his already hard body into overdrive.

He pulled his mouth from her lips and kissed a path toward her throat. "Are you sure you want this?"

"Yes, Walker."

With her arms still wrapped around his neck, she took a step backward, pulling him with her. With unerring movements, she maneuvered them toward the bed, tugging him down on top of her once her knees hit the edge.

She sighed. *"Yes."*

As he followed her down, he couldn't escape the thought that everything was about to change.

Everything he thought he knew.

Everything he thought he wanted.

Everything he thought he was.

Sloan reveled in the feel of Walker's large body pressed over hers and the wanton reactions he could pull from her with the lightest touch of his fingers. Her core pulsed almost painfully where he fitted against her and she knew her panties were already damp.

With questing fingers, she ran her hands over the broad width of his shoulders, intrigued by the tight play of muscles at the backs of his arms before she moved on to explore other places. Her five-foot-eight-inch frame had ensured she never felt all that small, but Walker's large, heavy musculature had her almost feeling petite.

The sensation was heady and enticing, all at the same time.

Her explorations continued as she ran her hands along the planes of his chest, captivated by the mix of hard muscle and heat that warmed her palms.

Suddenly impatient to feel him without so many pieces of clothing, she fumbled between their tangled bodies for the snap at his waist, sighing when the rough material of his jeans gave way. She gently loosened the zipper, insanely pleased when he let out a harsh groan as her fingertips grazed his hard length.

She couldn't have stopped the exhale of breath if she'd tried. "Why, Counselor, that's quite an impressive argument you've got there."

"If you think my opening remarks are good, wait until you see me close."

"By all means, then"—she nipped at his jaw—"please state your case."

Heat and need coalesced and the laughter fled from her voice as he shifted, rolling to his back and taking her along. Straddling his hips, she shuddered as he ran his fingers under the edge of her blouse, skimming her stomach on their way to her breasts.

His large hands cupped her, his long fingers unerringly finding her nipples through the silk of her bra and Sloan arched into his touch, pressing herself forward into the swirling storm of pleasure.

"You are so beautiful." His voice was quiet—reverent—in the silence of the room as he touched her and gave her pleasure. Long, restless moments unfurled, one after the other as the dark pleasure built inside of them both.

With suddenly impatient hands, he gripped the material of her shirt and lifted it up and off, tossing it carelessly over the edge of the bed. She reached for her bra herself, anxious for the feel of his hands against her skin without the barrier of silk.

Another wave of heat ignited within her as his oh-so-clever and capable touch again took her body to new heights.

Walker.

What was this attraction between them? Where had it come from? And who would have thought she'd have to travel so very far to find it.

To find him.

Ignoring the creeping thoughts, she refocused on the man underneath her, his large body hers for the taking. She was here now and she refused to cloud her time with Walker thinking thoughts of what was to come.

Tonight was just for them. To give and take pleasure. To share.

Together.

Restless, Walker shifted them again and Sloan found herself once again on her back as he made quick work of her jeans. He ran his fingers down her legs as he dragged the heavy denim and thin panties off her in one long, smooth move. Lifting off the bed, he removed his jeans and dropped them in the small pile he'd already made with her clothes, returning again to settle himself over her.

"That was very smooth. You practice that one, Counselor?"

Walker's eyes clouded as his eyebrows slashed over those dark orbs. "You're not practice, Sloan. Or a conquest. Or like anything else I've ever experienced."

She swallowed hard around the sudden lump in her throat. "I didn't mean—"

He shifted, placed a finger against her lips. "It's okay. I just wanted you to know you're different. What's between us is different. That's all."

"Okay," she said on a soft sigh that filled the space between them.

The seriousness of the moment evaporated as his eyes took on a bright shine and a wicked grin lit the corners of his mouth. Before she could even guess his intent, he slid down her body, settling himself between her thighs.

Whatever pleasure he'd been able to pull from her body was nothing compared to the great, glorious waves that consumed her as his mouth found her core. The wet heat and long, languorous strokes of his tongue shot electric currents streaking through her in a swirling pattern so like the aurora borealis they'd watched earlier.

Just like the constantly shifting lights, she was unable to grab on to anything, couldn't hold a single thought as the pleasure drove her farther and farther up.

Closer and closer to the peak.

"Walker." She breathed his name on a sigh, her voice sounding foreign to her own ears as the moment crested over her, tearing her apart as her body went soaring.

Before she could gather herself—or even regain a moment's quiet—he ran his hand up the length of her body, then muttered something as he reached over the side of the bed for his jeans. With swift movements he fumbled with his wallet, pulling out a small packet.

She heard the quick tear of foil and wondered how she could be so far gone to have forgotten.

"Let me help you with that," she whispered against his throat. As she reached for his hands, she was oddly gratified to find his trembling and she took over, rolling the condom down the long length of him with deliberate slowness.

"Ah, Sloan. You're really trying to kill me, aren't you?"

"It's only fair seeing as I still haven't fully regained my sight," she whispered as she leaned forward and pressed a kiss to his chest.

There were no more words—nothing but whispered moans as Walker braced himself on his forearms and positioned himself between her thighs. Sloan read his intent and gripped his hips and lifted her own until he was fully sheathed inside of her.

She lost herself to the swirling waves of pleasure again as he began to move inside her. Long, smooth strokes as he pulled from her body and then filled her again. He drove her to dizzying heights, so like before yet different as the heavy shape of him pressed against her.

She wrapped her arms around his sweat-slicked shoulders and reveled in what she'd missed for so long. Reveled in the ability to make this large man so vulnerable and open to her. She delighted in the pleasure they brought each other.

The telltale signs of her impending orgasm filled her and she cried out his name. As her body tightened around him, she heard his shout, long and low, as he buried himself to the hilt. Sloan held tight to his large body as his own orgasm overtook him, the play of muscles along his back telegraphing the pleasure that swept through him.

As they both lay there spent, she acknowledged the two facts she'd kept hidden from even herself.

Walker Montgomery wasn't a fling, no matter how hard she tried to tell herself otherwise.

And leaving Alaska was going to be the hardest thing she'd ever have to do.

"Sloan?" Walker whispered toward her inert form.

"Hmmm?"

"Are you okay? You haven't moved."

She groaned as she opened one bright blue eye, then the other one. "I just had two almost back-to-back orgasms, Walker. Where do you want me to go?"

A laugh rumbled low in his chest, surprising him that he had the energy for that. "I just wanted to make sure you were okay."

"To say I'm okay would be an understatement of monstrous proportion."

Satisfaction whipped through him at her words although the sheer cavemanesque quality of the reaction caught him off guard. "You sure do know how to make a man feel good."

"Right back at ya, Slick."

He had no idea why, but her earlier words rose up to taunt him as to her estimate of how many lovers he'd had. His memories traveled over that long, twisting road of adult activities as he thought about the women he'd shared his bed with.

Bright, attractive women who were looking for the same things he was and who knew what they were getting into.

Adult activities, with adult expectations, nothing more.

So why did that thought all of a sudden leave him empty?

Especially when he looked down the barrel of his future and realized that was all that awaited him.

It's what he wanted. What he'd always wanted.

Wasn't it?

Chapter Nineteen

Sloan was up early the day of the competition, anxious to capture the thoughts and feedback of the various competitors as they ate breakfast in the Indigo Blue's dining room. She'd spent the last two days interviewing various women as they arrived in Indigo, but she wanted to capture the excitement that would inevitably drive everyone before the games started.

If her days were spent with the competitors, her nights had been spent with Walker. She'd slept at his house the last two nights, the heat between them growing more and more intense with each passing moment.

A heat that refused to be sated by the passion-filled hours.

With each encounter they shared, she couldn't escape the nagging acknowledgment that she'd be gone in less than a week.

Realistically, she knew it was for the best. What was between them was meant to stay it its own little box. A box that had no strings and no regrets attached to it. She knew she should focus on the present and not worry about the future.

So why couldn't she stop thinking about her impending departure?

And the empty nights that would follow.

She shook her head, trying to shake off the maudlin thoughts as she helped herself to a hearty breakfast off the buffet table. Scrambled eggs, bacon, hash browns and two pancakes for good measure.

"What is it about the pancakes here?" Grier's sleepy voice greeted her over her shoulder.

"They certainly seem to be a staple," Sloan agreed as she reached for the ladle of syrup.

"I swear, I can count on one hand how many times I've had pancakes in the last five years."

"And I've managed to surpass one hand in the week and a half I've been here," Sloan added with a smile. "It seems I manage to find an excuse every day. I'll chalk up today's indulgence to keeping my strength up for the competition. Besides, they're too yummy to resist."

"Speaking of yummy . . ."

Sloan shot Grier a dark look, but it bounced off that petite back where her friend stood facing the coffee urn.

"What's that supposed to mean?"

"You know exactly what it means. You've been doing the down and dirty with Counselor Yummy and yet you've not shared one single detail with me."

The sour taste of guilt rose up as Sloan took her seat. She had held out on Grier and Avery, and somewhere in the back of her mind it has niggled at her like a sore tooth.

Grier joined her at the table, a steaming mug in her hands. "I've given you your space because I know you needed it, but I'm done giving you room. What's going on?"

"Only the best sex of my life."

"That seems to be going around. Who the hell knew there were all these virile men in the middle of the winter wilderness?"

Sloan kept her tone casual as she probed Grier. Seeing as how she'd not been the most forthcoming soul, she knew it wasn't fair to ask for the same honesty in return. "You slept with Mick again?"

"I most certainly did not." Grier actually looked sort of offended.

"You don't have to look so upset about it."

"I wouldn't sleep with him again if—"

"If what?"

Sloan heard the small sigh before Grier took another sip of her coffee. "He has completely ignored me. Which makes him the last man I should sleep with ever again. Well, actually, that's Jason. Make Mick the second to last man I should ever consider sleeping with."

"He's crazy about you. Why's he staying away?"

"Umm . . . it's probably the frosty glares and don't-fuck-with-me vibes I've been giving him."

Sloan laid her fork down. "Grier. What's going on with you?"

"I really don't know, Sloan. Honestly, I don't know. It's like all these thoughts are jumbled up in my head. The broken engagement. My dad's death. And then this thing with Mick that just sort of happened."

She dropped her head on top of her folded arms. "Oh God. I want him, but I'm so *afraid* to want him."

"Have you tried talking to him about it? I think he'd listen."

"And say what?" Grier lifted her head, the storm clouds back in full force in the swirling depths of her gray eyes. "I'm sorry I approached you like a half-deranged, lunatic sex maniac. Are you interested in signing up to be my human vibrator for the duration of my stay in Indigo?"

"You don't feel that way about him. You know you don't."

"Maybe it's all I've got to give."

"I don't think you really believe that."

"Well, how else am I supposed to feel about him? He's not a guy you get serious with, Sloan, and you know it."

Sloan felt her friend's misery as if it were her own. And she understood—on a level she never expected—what Grier was saying.

"What if he is?"

The question hung there between them, shifting like fog. Sloan knew her thoughts about a relationship with Walker changed at least every other hour. She suspected Grier's on the subject of Mick weren't too far off.

Sounds from the kitchen shook them out of their musings and Sloan glanced up to see Avery coming through the swinging door with a large platter in her hands. "What are the two of you doing up so early?"

"Preparing," Sloan said.

"Commiserating," Grier said at the same time.

"Uh-oh. I likely need some coffee for this." Avery filled up a fresh mug at the coffee urn and then joined them. "What have I missed?"

"Actually, not much. Sloan was just about to give me all the juicy details on sex with Walker."

"Oooh. I'm so glad I got a head start this morning." Avery reached forward for the cream, dumping about half a mug's worth into her coffee before reaching for the sugar. "That means I've got time to sit here and idly gossip with friends. Spill it, Sloan. And use adjectives, girlfriend. The good ones."

"Amazing. Wonderful. Awesome. Mind-blowing. Oh"— she shot a look at Grier—"multiorgasmic, to boot."

"What is it with the Alaska air, Avery?" Grier asked. "Does the higher altitude do something to your clitoris or what?"

Avery almost spit out her coffee. "I'm sorry?"

"No, no." Grier waved an arm. "I'm serious. It's like something has happened to me. I mean, I like an orgasm as much as the next girl, but there's something in the air up here. They're so . . . so *easy*. And plentiful."

Avery shook her head as giggles overtook her and Sloan couldn't help but join in. "You really are a lunatic, you know."

"Yeah, a half-deranged, lunatic sex maniac."

Avery's eyebrows shot up, her expression sobering at Grier's comment. "What's this about?"

"Oh, that's the part you did miss. My avoidance of Mick as sure evidence of my deteriorating mental state."

"Or fear," Avery added. Her voice held no judgment, only an honest assessment of the situation. "You could just be afraid of what there might be between the two of you."

Whatever humor had existed between the three of them was gone and instead, Sloan was struck by the simple truth of Avery's statement.

Fear.

It had a powerful ability to weaken, delude and muddle a situation.

"Maybe you're right," Grier said softly as she looked down into her coffee.

Sloan couldn't hold back the question from the very deepest part of her conscience. *Was she afraid?*

No way.

In fact, her relationship with Walker was quite the opposite. It was empowering, even. She was a grown woman, making a choice that made her happy.

"Or maybe it's a matter of perspective. I know I, for one," Sloan added, picking up her fork again and digging into her pancakes, "have been so focused on what something with Walker can't be that I've forgotten to acknowledge what it can be."

She ignored Grier and Avery's silence, instead taking comfort in her new epiphany as she took another forkful of pancakes. She didn't have to know where things with Walker were going. And she also didn't have to spend the next three days worrying about going home.

What they'd shared meant something to both of them. She knew that. Maybe she didn't need to worry about any of it being anything more than that.

Maybe she should just enjoy what it *was*.

Sloan had almost convinced herself when a soft, barely audible gasp reached her ears, pulling her attention away from breakfast.

A deep, masculine voice that was a mix of Scotch and

sin rumbled across the length of the dining room. "I heard there was some breakfast to be found in here."

Sloan recognized him instantly.

The six-foot-four-inch athletic frame with shoulders the width of a small car. The shock of black hair that curled at base of his neck. The vivid green eyes every female in New York dreamed about.

Roman Forsyth.

Even if she hadn't known who he was, the rapidly draining color from Avery's face would have given her all the clues she needed.

"Help yourself." Avery waved a careless hand toward the buffet table.

Before any of them could say anything else, Avery stood and grabbed her coffee mug. "I'd better be getting back to the kitchen. The guests will be arriving any minute and I need to get a few more things ready."

Sloan allowed Avery her polite lie—and the breathing room she needed—and shot her a small, encouraging smile. As her friend walked across the dining room toward the swinging door of the kitchen, she didn't miss the way Avery gave Roman a wide berth.

She also didn't miss Roman's sidestep away from the coffee urn, effectively placing himself in her way. Although she couldn't hear what was said from across the room, she'd have had to be blind to miss the tension as the two of them came within close range of each other.

"That can't be good," Grier whispered.

"It doesn't appear so. She looks like a cat who's just been thrown in a tub, her back's so stiff."

Grier kept her voice low as she reached for her mug again. "I think I just figured out how Avery knows so much about the fear of falling for someone."

"I suspect you're right."

Walker stood with Mick and Roman on the far edge of the town square. The last-minute preparations for the day's events were nearly complete and the three of them had been put to work setting up the winner's area.

"It's damn good to see you." Mick slapped Roman on the back. "It's been a long time, buddy."

"Yeah." Roman rubbed his gloved hands together. "It's been a busy year."

Walker was as glad as Mick to see their friend, but he couldn't forget his conversation with Avery after the snowball fight.

Roman had abandoned them. All of them, but Avery in particular. To top it all off, the NHL star had missed a lot since his last visit to Indigo.

"I can't believe the grandmothers are still doing this thing." Roman's gaze ranged over the buzz of activity across the middle of town.

From where they stood, Walker could see Jack and Bear setting up the skeet-shooting area. The street in front of the diner had tables set up for the sandwich and beer runs. And his favorite—the mini-Iditarod—was in progress at the opposite corner of the square, with Chooch and Hooch's dogs scampering around in the snow as their owners worked on setting up their mini sleds for the event.

"Not only are they doing it," Mick added, "but they've got a record number of entrants this year."

"Wow." Roman shook his head. "It's hard to believe."

The three of them worked in silence as they finished setting up the three-tiered winner's platform. The grandmothers awarded gold, silver, and bronze, just as they did in the Olympics.

Roman sat back on his heels after finishing up his section. "Do the winners still get served at dinner?"

"Oh yes," Mick nodded as he stood up from where he'd finished hammering the last nail in his side of the platform. "First-, second- and third-place winners all get their dinner served by their favorite bachelor before the auction starts."

"Mick's served five years running now," Walker couldn't help pointing out. "Even though he refuses to enter the actual auction."

"A perennial favorite, then."

Mick tossed off a muttered, "Shut up, assholes," before bending to pick up his tools.

"So what you're really telling me is that not much has changed around here."

Walker wasn't sure why Roman's assessment chafed so much, but it did, lodging under his skin like a splinter. Glancing up from where he knelt to finish up his last few nails, he couldn't keep the edge from his voice. "I guess that all depends on your perspective."

"What's that supposed to mean?"

"Just what I said, it all depends on your perspective. And from mine, I'd say life in our town is full and exciting. Donny Sanderson's boy went off to Harvard this past fall. And Theresa McBain got a publishing deal last spring with the book coming out in a few more months."

Roman's broad grin fell a few notches, but he pressed

his point anyway. "Come on, Walker, you know what I mean. Nothing really changes. The same old things just keep on happening. Life plods along."

The splinter began to throb and Walker found he wasn't at all interested in Roman's city attitude. "And it doesn't in New York?"

"There's always something going on in New York. You know that."

"Really, Roman? Because your life hasn't changed all that much in a decade and a half, has it? You're still obsessed with a game nine months out of the year. When you're not playing, you're hanging out with hordes of women who could give a shit about you and only care about what you do for a living. And each year you trade in one luxury car for the next. Have I missed anything?"

"What the hell's wrong with you?" Breath steamed out of Roman's mouth in heavy puffs and Walker didn't miss Mick's widened gaze from where he stood behind their friend.

Regaining his feet, Walker moved closer to Roman. He knew he was picking a fight, but he still couldn't stop the words. "Nothing's wrong with me. I just think you might want to stick around and pay attention to people for more than five minutes before you start passing judgment on your friends and neighbors."

Before Roman could say anything else, Walker turned and left. With a quick holler over his shoulder, he pointed toward the diner. "I need to go lend a hand over there."

Walker still couldn't shake the anger an hour later as he filled up on breakfast at the diner. It was extraquiet with so many out on the square or over at the hotel prepping for the event and it suited his mood.

Roman's words had crawled under his skin and the more he thought about the careless insult, the more he wondered what had happened to his friend.

"Mind if I join you?"

Speak of the devil. "No."

Roman took a seat in the opposite booth and smiled up at their waitress. After ordering steak and eggs, he began dumping creamer into the coffee their waitress had left behind.

Walker continued eating his breakfast, not overly inclined to make conversation.

"I saw Avery this morning."

"Oh?"

"Yeah. I got in late last night and headed down to breakfast this morning to find her with those two women everyone's talking about. The New Yorkers."

"Sloan and Grier."

"Yep."

"So if you ate breakfast, what are you doing sitting here ordering another one?"

"I only ended up having coffee."

"Why?"

Walker glanced up when Roman didn't say anything, but it didn't take a decades-old friendship to recognize the anguish stamped on his friend's face. Deep lines crossed his forehead and his mouth was set in a grim slash.

"Roman?"

"She walked out of the room like I was the last person on earth she wanted to see."

Walker debated briefly before settling on the truth. "Well, that's basically because you are."

"It was a long time ago, Walker."

"The way you treat her makes it seem like it happened yesterday."

"I've been gone for thirteen years."

"Yeah. And you're still as guilty as the day you walked out of this town."

"It's not guilt."

Their waitress laid down Roman's breakfast, then refilled both of their coffee cups before heading off to welcome a few late stragglers for breakfast.

"So what is it?"

"It's—" Roman broke off as he sawed into his steak. "It's not guilt."

"Okay."

"Damn it, Walker."

"What do you want from me? You lay into Mick and me this morning, insulting everyone around here, and now you're lying to yourself about your own actions. I'm done making excuses for you."

"You make excuses for me? What the hell for?"

"Sure I make excuses. And so does Mick and so do your mother and grandmother. Everyone makes excuses for the great Roman Forsyth, hockey god and local legend."

"I had a chance to live my dream."

"And no one begrudged you that."

Roman slammed his napkin down on the table. "Then what the fuck is this all about?"

"It's about the way you did it, Roman. Face it—you ran away. And the expensive gifts just look like a payoff."

Roman's hand tightened on his mug, but the anger didn't make it to his voice. "I didn't run away. And the gifts are just that. Gifts."

"Look. I'm not the one you need to take this up with. Not really."

"I'm not taking it up with Avery."

"Then don't expect her to pull out the red carpet when you come to town. You can't have it both ways. Why can't you just leave her alone?"

"I don't know. *Damn it*, I really don't know."

As they both ate their breakfast, his own advice rumbled through his mind on a loop.

You can't have it both ways.

If he was honest with himself . . . wasn't that what he was looking for with Sloan? Nice and easy, with no strings attached, yet he had no fucking idea how he was going to let her go in a few days.

"She's really gotten to you?"

Walker glanced up from his eggs. "What?"

"Sloan." Before he could say anything, Roman added, "My mother is the fount of all things gossip-related; you know that."

"You just got here last night."

"She chewed my ear off until one this morning."

"We've been seeing each other." Walker shrugged in an effort to come off casual, even as the words lay flat on his tongue.

"She's a beautiful woman. I met her once before, you know."

An itch settled between his shoulder blades, but Walker ignored it. "Really?"

"Yep. She interviewed me a few years ago for an article on the Metros. She's awfully easy on the eyes."

The itch he'd managed to tamp down spread into a raging fire under his skin. "She is."

"She's got the kind of body that could make a man forget himself."

More embers flared to life, fanned by Roman's words, but he fought not to let it show. "She's as smart as she is beautiful."

"She sure is. She's the whole package. I do remember her."

Walker reached for his coffee and dragged it to his lips, the liquid shaking all the way to his mouth.

"Looks like I just got my answer."

He glanced up into that devil-may-care green gaze he'd known since he was in grade school. "What answer?"

"Seeing as how you're about to knock me out, I'd say she's gotten to you in spades."

"Fuck you."

A wry grin covered Roman's face. "Yeah. That's a popular sentiment around here when it comes to me."

"She hasn't gotten to me."

"Right."

"Damn straight I'm right."

"You know, Walker. The mighty really do fall."

"Well, I'm not one of them."

Chapter Twenty

Cold wind raced through Indigo's town square, creating a balmy two degrees for the start of the Great Bachelor Competition. Sloan took in the sight of the transformed town and could only marvel—once again—at the intrepid spirit of the residents of Indigo, Alaska.

The events were strategically placed all around the square, with bleacher seating set up at varying intervals so the majority of the town could get seats to watch. All the shops in town were open, offering places to warm up when the frosty air became too much, but from what she could tell, it was a matter of pride to avoid a warm up until after lunch.

The first event was off to an auspicious start, with twenty-nine of the thirty-two entered bachelorettes hitting their skeet target.

What was apparently a new addition this year was the entertainment during intermission.

"I'm not sure this is what people meant when they complained to the town council that they wanted something to relieve the boredom between events." Grier huddled against Sloan as they waited for round two of the skeet competition to begin. Two of the men drafted to help for the day were reloading the machines now.

"I do not believe that man has no pants on." Sloan hugged her sides while a wave of laughter bubbled up as Bear did a sort of strip tease with his coat that, oddly enough, resembled a jig.

A rather dirty jig, but a jig all the same.

"He's quite agile," Grier said in a thoughtful voice. As Bear reached under himself and dragged his pants through his legs, she added, "Surprisingly agile."

Another woman laughed nearby and Sloan turned toward her. "I was so not expecting this."

"Me either."

"You're Amanda, right?"

"Yep. Sloan, right? You're writing the article?"

"Yes. We haven't had a chance to meet yet. I'd like to talk to you when you have a few minutes."

"I'd love to."

The three of them stood there for a few more minutes, laughing at Bear's efforts to keep the town entertained between rounds of the competition.

Amanda shook her head. "He's got to be freezing."

"Somehow, with all this laughter and attention, I don't think he feels it."

Sophie called Grier's name from the judging podium and Grier slipped away to compete in round two.

A good-natured smile greeted Sloan as Amanda shifted her attention away from Bear's antics. "Did you come up here for the article?"

"Not really. It was sort of a lucky accident." Sloan quickly explained how she'd ended up in town and the article she'd pitched to the travel editor.

"It's going to be a great piece. I'm actually surprised

this competition hasn't gotten more attention. This is just the sort of thing I'd imagine the morning programs would eat up."

"Have you been here before?"

"Last year was my first year, and I swore I'd come back if my bachelorette status didn't change. Since it didn't"—Amanda lifted her hands—"here I am. Although, the striptease is a new one this year. I know I'd have remembered seeing *that* before."

Sloan admired the woman's tall, slender form and beautiful blue eyes. "You don't have a boyfriend?"

"Not for lack of trying. But no, I don't."

"I'd say coming up to Alaska in the middle of winter is an awful lot of try."

A merry twinkle lit Amanda's eyes before her gaze roamed around the crowd. "Coming up here makes it seem less lonely, somehow. Seeing other women. Makes me realize I'm not the only one. Plus, it's a lot of fun."

"Do you have your eye on any of them?" Sloan thought she might have seen Amanda talking with Skate earlier and wondered if the impression she had of the two of them was accurate.

"There are some cute ones, but I don't have any high expectations. This is the middle of Alaska."

"Where are you from?"

"Missouri. Not exactly next door."

Sloan couldn't keep her thoughts from straying to Walker and the unexpected moments she'd found up here with him. She hadn't had any expectations either and look where it had gotten her. "You never know, though. I did see you talking with Skate earlier."

A light flush crept up the woman's neck. "He's cute."

"You should bid on him."

The flush crept higher and was soon accompanied by a broad smile. "I'm planning on it."

"How did you find out about the competition?"

"It was a few years ago. I'd just survived the four holidays of the apocalypse and was feeling down. And then I read this little blurb in a magazine, got interested and checked out the Web site link that was highlighted."

"The four holidays of the apocalypse?"

Amanda laughed. "Sorry. That's what I've dubbed Thanksgiving, Christmas, New Year's and Valentine's Day. Not that they aren't wonderful at times, but each has its moments, you know."

Mary Jo's words in her mother's kitchen whispered across Sloan's memory. "What kind of moments?"

"Those ones where being single is not only a challenge, but a semipublic flogging to boot."

Sloan took a moment to revel in her own laughter and the growing kinship she felt for Amanda. The woman's sense of humor at dealing with a difficult subject was inspiring, and Sloan couldn't help but wonder if Thanksgiving wouldn't have been so bad if she had known Amanda's description for it. "I've never heard the holidays called that, but yeah, that has a surprising ring of truth to it. Just out of curiosity, which do you think is the worst?"

"New Year's. Definitely New Year's."

"Really? Not Valentine's Day?"

"Not by a long shot."

Amanda grew quiet and shifted her attention toward a loud shout that went up over near the skeet launcher.

After the sound died down, she turned back. "Speaking of shots, sorry. Here I am running my mouth off and there's a competition going on."

With dawning realization, Sloan laid a hand on the woman's arm. "I won't put it in my article, if that's what you're worried about."

Amanda took a deep breath, then shook her head. "It's sort of dumb, but if you really want to know."

"I do."

"I began to hate New Year's Eve the year I realized I was the lone horn blower."

Sloan sensed there was something there she should understand, but she just couldn't piece it together. "What's that?"

"You know those horns everyone gets at a New Year's party? The cardboard ones with the plastic blowers?"

"Yes."

"It was a few years ago. I was at this party and the clock hit midnight and we're all yelling and everyone's screaming 'Happy New Year' and blowing their horns. And then all of a sudden, I realize that I'm the only one left blowing my horn."

"Why?"

"Because everyone else is kissing." A broad smile spread across Amanda's face, but it didn't quite reach the bright blue of her eyes. "That's the moment I decided to make a change. And then a few months later I saw the article and well"—she flung up a hand—"here I am. And you know what? I'm enjoying myself. A lot. And if I bid high enough on a certain bachelor, I may enjoy myself even more."

Sophie's voice rang out over the loudspeaker, calling Amanda up as the next contestant. "I'd better get over there."

"Good luck," Sloan called after her, with Amanda's words ringing in her ears.

She did know what Amanda was talking about. Moments that struck without warning—those sharp barbs of reality—that rose up and swamped you. She'd had one on Thanksgiving, but it was hardly the first.

If she were even more honest with herself, it was those moments in her mother's kitchen that had helped sway her to Grier's plea to come to the wilds of Alaska. Admittedly, she'd likely have come to help her friend anyway, but the opportunity to escape for a while had certainly been a factor.

One single moment.

It was sometimes enough to force you out of your comfort zone and could change your life.

Or force you into something you never wanted or expected.

Wasn't that what Walker had talked about when he explained his situation with his father? In mere moments, his father had altered what Walker thought of the very foundation of his life.

"You must be planning your attack strategy?"

Walker's voice rumbled in her ear, the warmth of his breath sending delightful shivers down her spine and dragging her out of her thoughts. Shifting her attention to the man who had appeared at her side, Sloan realized right here—at this exact point in time—were a few moments she could take all for herself.

So she decided to take Amanda's advice and enjoy herself. "Wouldn't you like to know?"

A heavy gloved hand settled at the base of her spine and, despite the layers that separated them, she could feel the heat of his body. "I promise I won't tell."

She turned, shifted so that his arm came around her. "How can I be sure you can be trusted?"

His eyebrows shot up as a wicked grin lit his face. With one gloved hand, he ran a finger down her cheek. "You can spank me if I tell."

"And exactly who's getting punished, Counselor?"

"I guess we'll find out."

She heard her name ring out over the loudspeaker and reluctantly stepped back. "Wish me luck."

"I'll do you one better."

Before she could guess his intention, he pulled her close and pressed his mouth to hers. The kiss was hot and electric and she could barely breathe at the onslaught.

Embracing the moment Sloan kissed him back with everything she had kept bottled up for so long inside.

If there were unexpected moments of sadness that struck without warning, this was their antithesis.

And she was damn well going to enjoy herself.

After years of sullen acceptance of his grandmother's annual event, Walker found himself oddly enamored of the goings-on for the festival. The day was crisper than he remembered in the past and the events had a sense of good-natured fun that was pervasive.

Bear's "intermission" events were inspired, his latest striptease-cum-dance-routine—in which he chose to demonstrate how to lap dance with a moose—had infused the day with a new spirit of fun and laughter.

Or had it always been like this and he'd simply chosen to ignore it? More likely, he'd chosen to grump his way through what everyone else found so enjoyable.

"Is that a smile I see on your face? A real, honest-to-God smile?"

Walker leaned down to kiss his grandmother on the cheek. "You, Mary and Julia have simply outdone yourselves."

"It's a great day. The weather's perfect and the women are all lovely. Not a rotten apple in the bunch, as far as we can tell."

Walker would wager the contestants might feel slightly different, but overall the competition had maintained its intended air of good old-fashioned fun and games.

"Sloan's doing quite well."

He nodded as his gaze found her in the crowd, waiting her turn for the mini-Iditarod. "She is."

"She came in second in skeet and took the sandwich-making challenge hands-down."

"Yet another story that will live in Bear's memory for all eternity."

Sophie rubbed her mittened hands together. "I figured he'd be delighted when she chose to run the sandwich and beer to his recliner."

"Understatement of the century. Although, I think the main source of his delight was when she dropped into his lap and kissed his cheek."

"I'm surprised, though."

He shifted his gaze back toward her. "Surprised about what? It's a great day."

"I would have thought you'd be more upset she didn't choose *your* recliner."

Wrapping a heavy arm around her shoulders, he pulled her tight against him. "You know, Grandmother. A hands-off approach usually works far better than a sledgehammer to the head."

"I'm old, Walker. I don't have time for games."

He glanced down at her, not sure if her comments were meant to be as serious as they sounded. She had seemed slightly off since the night the climber from Denali died and he didn't know what to make of her references to age. "Don't go all maudlin on me, now."

"It's not maudlin to tell the truth."

"It most certainly is on a day you should be celebrating your role as mayor and town troublemaker with equal parts success."

She swatted at his arm, a bit of the feisty soul he knew and loved showing itself. "Well, now, that's not playing fair. You're going to make an old woman cry."

"Would you stop with the old?"

"I am, Walker. I really am."

"What in the world has prompted this?"

Those fiery sparks evaporated as his grandmother rubbed her hands together again and a few seeds of worry settled themselves in his gut. What *was* wrong with her?

And what had kicked off the sudden case of the blues, especially in the middle of her greatest triumph?

"Oh, never mind." Whatever had dogged her for a

moment evaporated as she pressed on his shoulder. "Get on over there; they're about to start the sled races. You have a bachelorette to cheer on."

"You sure you're okay?"

"Of course I'm sure."

Before he could stop her, his grandmother caught someone's eye and began waving, effectively ending their conversation.

As he headed to stand with the crowd watching the next event, he couldn't quite shake the feeling his grandmother's comments hid some deeper meaning.

Sloan buried her face in the heavy fur of the husky as she waited to participate in the mini-Iditarod race around the town square. Despite her multilayered outfit for the day, she couldn't ignore the seeping cold that worked its way into her bones as dusk crept forward to cut short their afternoon.

"Careful, Sloan. Baby him too much and he won't pull you on your sled," Chooch warned as she puttered around the bachelorettes, keeping the dogs occupied before it was their turn to take the sled.

"He's beautiful. What's his name?"

"That one's J.R."

Sloan hugged him again, rubbing her face over his head as she whispered in his ear, "You'll do right by me, won't you, baby?"

Avery sidled up after Chooch waved her over, thrusting a leash in her hands. "Take Bobby for me, would you? I need to get Sue Ellen off that sled before she knocks it over."

J.R., Bobby, Sue Ellen?

No way.

"Did they really name the dogs after bad eighties TV?"

Avery held tight to Bobby's leash as a broad grin stole over her features. "Absolutely. This would be the *Dallas* litter."

"You're kidding?"

"Oh no. Lucy, Cliff and Miss Ellie round out the bunch, but poor Cliff is usually shorthanded as Shithead."

"I'm not sure why I'm surprised. Nothing in this town is what I expected and this is yet another example. For the record, why *Dallas*?"

"Hooch's favorite TV show. He still contends who shot J.R. was the best mystery ever put forth to the American public."

"Ah yes. Great TV at its finest." Another thought hit Sloan as she babied J.R. "You said this litter. What was the last litter called?"

"That was the *Brady Bunch*."

"Of course it was."

"Marsha was the mother of this litter, actually."

Sloan started to chuckle as she and Avery hit the same singsong voice with a resounding chorus of "Marsha, Marsha, Marsha!"

Avery's shared laughter faded out and Sloan didn't need to turn around to know why.

Roman Forsyth's movie-star good looks and athlete's body towered over both she and Avery as he moved in next to them before dropping to his knees in a squat.

"You telling tales about Marsha's proclivities around town, Ave? That dog got into more trouble. Remember that time we found her getting into it with my grandmother's pug, Basil?"

"Can't say that I do."

If Sloan wasn't mistaken, the brief smile that crossed Avery's face meant she remembered exactly what fate had befallen Basil. And the denial meant she wasn't interested in jaunting down memory lane.

Sloan kept her smile firmly planted on her face but held her tongue. There was enough baggage between these two to keep a 747 grounded, and she figured Avery could do just fine without any interference.

"Chooch and Hooch never could keep that animal chained up."

She didn't miss the soft, faraway look in Roman's eyes, nor the fact his gaze was firmly lasered onto Avery. For a brief moment, a stab of envy lanced through her so hard she was glad she was holding on to the dog or she might have stumbled.

What would it be like to know someone that well? To have a bank of shared experiences that went back to the days you were still discovering who you were.

And who you were going to be.

Despite Avery's chilly reception, Sloan knew it was an act of protection. And even though it masked the hurt, it couldn't mask the history that lived between the two of them.

Shared experiences. Shared stories. Shared memories.

Pasting on her very best Scarsdale manners, Sloan

dove into some small talk. "I presume Basil lived to tell the tale, no doubt."

Roman pulled his gaze from Avery, the broad, killer grin that was his hallmark firmly back in place. "Oh yes, he was quite the stud about town. Our dear, sweet Basil was one able-bodied pug."

"Who impregnated half the town before someone finally wised up and got him to the vet for some fixing," Avery added dryly. "Some dogs never learn, do they?"

Sloan knew as well as Roman the conversation had veered firmly off of Basil the pug, but she tried diligently to keep the banter light and affable. "I'm surprised you're here, Roman. I didn't realize the Metros have off this week?"

"It's only two days, but enough time for me to sneak home for a quick visit. We're on the road. Anaheim followed by Seattle, so it was easy to get up here."

"Sneak is a fitting term, I'd say."

With a dark glance at Avery, Sloan fought for the composure drilled into her from an early age. "I'm sure your mother and grandmother are thrilled to see you."

"I'd call it a combination of thrilled and enterprising. Grandma's already talked me into taking part in the evening's festivities."

"Why, of course she has," Avery added. "She's seeing dollar signs at the auction tonight. What single, eligible woman wouldn't want to bid on the big, bad, professional hockey player?"

"Damn straight. And I told her I'd double the bid and add it to the auction proceeds."

"Ah yes, another example of buying your way into your family's good graces."

Sloan prayed for mercy as sparks flew through the air along with the verbal barbs. Belatedly, she heard her name in the distance, calling her to the starting line, and wondered if it was safe to leave these two alone. She was about to gesture Grier over to stand guard when Dr. Cloud came to the rescue, his voice carrying over her shoulder from behind them.

"Roman. What a surprise this is. Your grandmother's been looking for you."

Just as she'd been a few days earlier at the airport, Sloan was again awed by the doctor's calm demeanor and even presence. As the discussion shifted immediately to the upcoming hockey schedule, Sloan grabbed Avery by the hand.

"Come on, I need help getting J.R. over there to the starting line. Chooch was right and he's gone all limp and useless on me."

As soon as they were out of earshot, Sloan whispered around gritted teeth and a broad smile as she dragged her fluffy lump of fur toward the starting line, "What the hell was that about?"

"I can't stand being around him."

"I get that, but he was only making small talk and being nice." More than nice, Sloan wanted to add as she heaved the dog another few feet. Roman had sought them out, unprompted by an accidental meeting or forced social situation.

Which had to count for something.

"Small talk full of innuendo. I have no desire to

traipse down memory lane with him. Besides, he started it."

"With what? The man was making conversation, Avery." Although it did nothing to her friend, the exasperation in her voice must have gotten through to J.R. The dog snapped to attention at her side and began moving on his own.

"Like hell he was. That little story about Basil had a few details he left out. Like how he and I found Marsha and Basil after doing a bit of rolling around of our own out past the edge of town. We were sneaking back to my house when we caught the dogs."

Unable to come up with another reprimand at that bit of news, Sloan opted to finish out her thought. "Well, if you keep ignoring him, memory lane's the only place he has to go with the conversation."

Avery came to an abrupt stop, hauling Bobby up short with her. "What's that supposed to mean?"

"It means you two have known each other forever and it's the only thing he has to talk to you about. So either make a few new memories or figure out a way to tolerate the old ones."

"I never thought about it that way."

"Besides, didn't anyone ever tell you living well was the best revenge?"

"What's that supposed to mean?"

"It means you need to dress up for the auction tonight. Let that man know he might be the big, bad professional hockey player but you're the girl he was dumb enough to leave behind. Come on, Avery. It's fuck-up-your-ex 101."

Avery's eyes narrowed and Sloan read the suspicion from a mile away. "Oh yeah, because I'm such a tempting treat. The local girl running his mother's hotel and living in this postage stamp of a town in the middle of nowhere."

As they came within earshot of the event coordinators, Sloan lowered her voice and leaned in to Avery. "If I'm not mistaken, you've got the best legs this side of the Rockies and an ass J.Lo would die for. Why don't you get your head out of it and put both to good use?"

She didn't turn around to acknowledge what she knew was a dropped mouth to match Avery's heavy gasp, and she didn't need to.

A few minutes later, she rounded her second lap of the town square with J.R. lagging yards behind the other three competitors in her heat. When her sled trotted by Avery's still-angry face and folded arms, Sloan congratulated herself on a far sweeter victory.

If she wasn't mistaken, Cinderella was now bound and determined to head home and fix herself up for the ball. And Sloan was almost a big enough person to pity the big, bad hockey player.

Almost.

Chapter Twenty-one

"And in first place ..." Sophie's voice seemed to hang in the cold, late-afternoon air as she announced the winner of the bachelorette competition. "Amanda Truesdale."

Sloan clapped for the woman as Amanda stepped up to the podium, next to a woman from Anchorage who took second place and a newbie from Atlanta who took third. She'd already set up interviews with them for tomorrow and was satisfied at how the article was coming to life in her mind.

She also didn't miss Skate's broad smile for Amanda from where he stood in the front row and wondered if she'd be pitching part two of her article—what comes *after* the bachelorette competition—at some point in the future.

"So clearly we're not cut out for wilderness life," Grier whispered in her ear as Sloan felt a hand wind itself around her waist.

"Oh, I don't know. I like to think we kicked ass when it counted."

"When was that?"

"The snowball fight, silly."

"Ah, yes. The winter bacchanalia wherein I nursed my broken heart."

Maybe it was Amanda's hopeful attitude or watching Avery's anger-filled exchange with Roman, but Sloan found herself suddenly unwilling to coddle Grier's feelings. "It doesn't have to be broken. You know that."

The arm around her waist tightened and Sloan felt the tension radiating off Grier's petite frame as the two of them huddled in the cold. "He didn't even come out today. For any of this." After a moment of silence, Grier added, "I thought he might."

"I saw him this morning, but then he probably had to work. The airfield doesn't close down just because most of the town's engaged in this."

"Yeah, but since most of the town's engaged here, who's he ferrying anywhere?"

A long rumble hit her low in the gut and her unwillingness to coddle shifted into the full-on desire to make waves. Sloan felt for both Grier and Avery, but she couldn't quite shake Amanda's words from earlier. Or the woman's determination to make a change.

What did they have to lose?

What did any of them have to lose? You put your heart on the line, but the rewards were great. And despite everything Grier had overcome in the last six months, her friend was still scared shitless to put herself on the line.

"You and Avery really are a pair, I swear."

"What's that supposed to mean?"

"It means you've both got someone worth taking a chance on and neither of you can do it."

"I hardly think my situation is anything like Avery's."

"Okay, Grier. Than what is it like? You and Jason?"

Grier's eyes turned stormy in the dying light of late afternoon. On a large exhale, she turned on her heel and stomped off, moving through the crowd of people who were slowly milling out of the town square.

Following at a fair distance behind, Sloan let Grier stomp off, her own long-legged strides easily keeping her a few footfalls behind.

About half a block from the Indigo, Grier's voice floated back toward her. "I know you're back there."

"I know you know."

"Well, go the hell away. I don't want to talk to you."

"Sure you do."

"Sure I don't."

They stomped the rest of the way into the Indigo, through the front door and into the lobby. A fair number of people had come in here to get warm and more than half of the tables already had a crowd.

Sloan continued on, following Grier down the hall toward the elevators.

"Get the hell out of here."

Sloan shrugged her shoulders, projecting as much innocence as possible into her stance. "I'm just headed to my room."

"I don't believe you brought up his name." Grier stabbed the button for the elevator, sighing as she looked up toward the floor indicator and saw that it was at the top.

Sloan greeted the same news with a satisfied harrumph.

It was about time they discussed this and Grier could damn well stay put. "Why? You already spilled his name to Avery. And you've brought him up in a roundabout fashion more times than that. I didn't think it was that big a secret."

"It's my personal business."

"It's ancient history. And your robust and very interesting present has a man in it who's not only crazy about you but who makes Jason Shriver look like the wanker he is."

"Oh!" Grier's mouth opened into a wide *O* of shock and Sloan almost backed down at the defeated expression that etched itself in the set of her shoulders and filled her gray eyes with sorrow.

And then she thought about Mick and the way he looked at Grier—with real, honest-to-goodness longing—and she laid in harder.

"Mick O'Shaughnessy not only looks at you like you're the most beautiful woman in the world, but like you're a precious gift he's afraid to lose. He *sees* you, Grier."

"I thought you liked Jason."

"Not really. But since you did, it wasn't my place to say anything."

"You broke the girlfriend code."

"Hardly."

The elevator doors opened and Sloan waited for Grier to step through them, unwilling to risk leaving the argument unfinished if Grier opted to haul ass.

"You most certainly did. You never told me what you thought of him. Or didn't think of him, as it were."

"No, I didn't formally tell you. Because when I tried to tell you in a million other ways, you ignored each and every hint. So I sucked it up, acknowledged it was my issue and left it alone."

Grier stared at the elevator panel instead of making eye contact, but her interest was evident in the quick tilt of her head. "What didn't you like about him? You know. Now that he's not a part of my life and you can speak freely."

"He never put you first. Not once."

A small nod telegraphed her agreement before Grier leaned her head against the wall and closed her eyes. "No. He never did."

"And then he went and got sucked off by that junior associate two weeks before your wedding, making it more than obvious the only person he knew how to put first was himself."

When Grier didn't say anything, Sloan added, "You deserve someone who puts you first."

"So do you."

"Yes, I know."

The elevator hummed quietly as they climbed toward their floor, but neither of them said anything else. As the doors slid open on their floor, Sloan figured she'd made her point and walked through first. "I'll see you at the auction."

"Sloan."

Turning she looked back at Grier. "Does he really look at me that way?"

"Yes."

"Oh."

Sloan decided to go for broke. "For what it's worth, you look at him the exact same way. It'd be a shame to let something as insignificant as a broken engagement with an asshole who doesn't deserve to kiss your feet get in the way of it."

Walker snuck up the back stairs of the hotel to Sloan's floor, anxious to avoid the mob of women who'd congregated on the main floor. He hadn't seen her since the skeet shoot and was anxious to . . .

To what?

Touch her? Kiss her? Just look at her?

All of the above, he reluctantly admitted as he rounded toward the fourth-floor staircase.

Shocked and not a little winded, he dropped onto the first step to catch his breath.

Damn it, he was getting old. Time was he and the rest of the high school hockey team ran these stairs for their daily practices and he'd made all six floors and barely broke a sweat. He'd even kicked Roman's ass on the sprints.

And now?

He fisted his coat in his hands as he tried to make sense of what was happening. He'd always considered himself in good shape, but clearly he needed to get back to the gym if five floors could force him to take a seat.

Or maybe you have to acknowledge you're not still a fucking kid.

The thought snuck up on him like a snake waiting to strike and it left him as disoriented, too.

He knew he wasn't a kid anymore. He had a business and responsibilities and he was an adult. A grown up.

So why did he suddenly feel old and lonely?

And why did the thought of continuing with his devil-may-care attitude toward life and love feel like an empty choice?

Sloan.

Her name whispered across his senses, just as it had from the first moment he'd laid eyes on her. She was vibrant and fun and . . . *necessary.*

She made him think of his life in ways he never had before. For the first time, thoughts of his future involved someone else, not a faceless parade of women who came and went with the seasons.

A renewed burst of energy had him on his feet and taking the rest of the stairs two at a time until he reached her floor. With a swift knock, he hammered on her door.

And proceeded to get even more winded at the sight of her in a soft pink robe and a towel wrapped around her head. "Walker!"

He leaned against the doorjamb, hoping the move didn't let on just how weak his knees were or how badly he wanted to gulp in air. "You always open the door to strangers?"

"I figured you were Grier." She stood back to allow him to enter. "Besides, I love it when strange men knock on my door. It adds a certain sense of danger and excitement to my day."

Walker wasn't sure what it was. The uncharacteristic thoughts he'd had on the way here or the sight of her slender frame wrapped in the thin cotton or the freshly scrubbed pink on her cheeks.

All he knew was that he had to have her.

Now.

Slamming the door with his foot, he threw his coat on the floor and reached for her in a heavy rush, dragging her against him to plunder her mouth with his own.

She squeaked lightly as his mouth came down on hers, but quickly responded to his urgency in kind. Her arms wrapped around his neck and she pressed the long lines of her body to his rapidly heating one as the kiss changed.

Challenged.

Took.

For long, glorious minutes there was nothing but this responsive woman in his arms as their tongues met and plundered, retreated and acquiesced. With heightened senses, he felt everything.

The clutch of her hands at his shoulders. The rapid beat of her heart where her chest pressed against his. The rush of heat at her core where she straddled his thigh.

He fisted his hands in the soft cotton of her robe at her hips and used the pressure to pull her close, pressing his erection into the soft flesh of her stomach.

"Now, Sloan."

She lifted her lips from his, the bright blue of her eyes almost violet in the rush of passion that filled her. "Yes. Now."

They fell onto the bed in a flash of urgent need and desperate longing and he dragged on the tie at her waist, before diving into the opening. The towel she'd wrapped around her hair had fallen off somewhere along the trip to the bed and her hair rested against the pillow in half-dry ringlets, the blond a burnished gold from the damp.

Her rib cage contracted on a rush of air as his hands found her breasts, his fingers immediately fondling her nipples into tight peaks. She arched her back, pressing the fullness of her flesh into his palms and he replaced one of his hands with his mouth.

Sloan writhed underneath him as he made love to her breasts and her fingers played a restless tune across his back. With long, languorous strokes of his tongue he drew out her pleasure. Her movements grew more restless until he felt her tugging on his sweater. "I want to feel you," she moaned against his ear.

He pulled back, giving her the space to lift his sweater from around his waist and drag it up over his head. His long-sleeved T-shirt quickly followed and then she dragged her hands down his chest, gliding over his nipples.

A wave of pleasure flooded him at her touch and she immediately responded to his needs, rolling him onto his back and straddling him before pressing kisses down his throat and over his chest. Walker felt the gathering storm of pleasure build up within him as she laved his sensitized nipples with her tongue and grew desperate to finish the torturous game they played with each other.

Holding her still, he reached up and dragged off the robe, baring her naked form completely to his gaze. The impact of her hit him like a swift sucker punch to the gut, the dewy softness of her skin and the long, lean length of her nearly his undoing.

"You are so beautiful."

She looked down at him, her dark pupils dilated wide

with desire. "You make me feel beautiful." With deft movements, she shifted position to straddle his thighs and went to work on the button of his jeans. Each moment was an agony as her fingers applied pressure to his swollen cock.

He brushed her hands away with a wry smile around gritted teeth. "Why don't you let me do that?"

Good, old-fashioned feminine laughter bubbled from the long column of her throat and Walker could only marvel at the knowing look in her eyes. It was a look for the ages, one as likely to have been seen on Cleopatra's face for Mark Antony and in that moment, Walker knew.

Knew to the very depths of his soul that he was lost.

Lost to the same heat and passion and need that had driven men and women for millennia.

With swift movements, he sat up and dragged off his jeans, fumbling with the heavy material where the two of them lay tangled in each other.

As his jeans fell to the floor with a thud, Sloan resumed her position on top of him, positioning him at her hot, wet opening before plunging fully to take him inside of her.

The tight walls of her body closed around his length and Walker knew he'd been right. He was utterly lost to this woman.

As she began to move, more waves of pleasure flooded his body, pumping his blood in crazy, erratic bursts. His last coherent thought as the storm ripped through him was so simple—so life affirming—he wasn't sure why it had taken him so very long to figure it out.

Only in the losing, had he finally been found.

*　　*　　*

Sloan felt the telltale signs—the restless urge that built and built to an almost painful crescendo—but still, she drove them on, riding the glorious length of him until they were both satiated.

Until they'd both won.

On a throaty shout, she felt his body tighten under hers as a passionate cry burst from her own lips, her body giving itself up to the magic between them.

Her orgasm crested through her, in bright, glittering waves of pleasure she wanted to hold on to and never let go. It battered her with delicious sensations she'd never imagined could be so good.

On a final shout, Walker drove his body upward, nearly unseating her before wrapping his arms around her and dragging her down to his chest. They lay there for long minutes, hearts still thundering from the effort as their breathing returned to normal.

"I seriously hope these walls are soundproof," Sloan mumbled against his chest.

His throaty voice drifted over her like a warm blanket. "I don't."

"Why not?"

"Because you're mine and I don't care who the hell knows."

Sloan lifted her head from his chest. "That's very Neanderthal of you, Walker Montgomery."

"Damn right it is," he growled for added effect before dragging her up for a kiss. His hands were gentle where they held her face, while his mouth was anything but.

It was a kiss that branded and she found herself reveling in the raw, primal intensity of his actions. The heat flared between them again at the carnal mating of their tongues and in that moment, Sloan knew she was forever changed.

Like you didn't already know that.

She'd known it on some level but had resisted admitting it. Had resisted giving in to the powerful feelings Walker evoked effortlessly in her.

Desperate to keep the moment light, she resettled herself against his chest. "Is this some elaborate male ritual to keep me from bidding on Bear tonight?"

"Bear, Skate, Tommy, Chuck and all the rest of the guys. Save your money."

"My journalistic integrity requires me to be more broad-minded than one bid. Besides, what if you get snapped up by that accountant from Chicago?"

"The one with the big tits?"

She rose up at that one, slapping him on the shoulder. "You noticed?"

He wiggled his eyebrows in return before lifting his head to plant a wet, smacking kiss on her open—and outraged—mouth. "Of course I noticed. I have a penis and a pulse."

"An even bigger reason why I need to bid on several candidates. And I'm quite sure Bear has been a much bigger gentleman than you and hasn't estimated my cup size."

A long, low laugh greeted her, even as his eyes went dark with the unmistakable air of possession. "Want to make a bet?"

"Probably not."

"Smart choice."

"Will you at least clear your dance card for me?"

"Why, Mr. Montgomery. I do believe that is the sweetest thing anyone's ever said to me." Sloan waited a beat as his broad grin greeted hers before she went in for the kill. "Which makes it that much harder for me to have to tell you no."

"No?"

"The fine, upstanding bachelors of Indigo have been promising me dances all week. I'd hate to disappoint my adoring public."

"We couldn't have that, now, could we?"

"Absolutely not."

"I'm revoking your journalist's license if any of them get you off the dance floor."

"Impossible." She smiled broadly. "I don't have a license for you to revoke."

"Cheeky witch." He wrapped her in his arms for another searing kiss as he whispered against her lips, "What have you done to me?"

Instead of answering, Sloan opted to show him.

She pressed a kiss to his lips before trailing a path down his neck to his chest, marveling at the play of muscles under her lips. Her fingers brushed against the hard steel of his biceps where her hands held her weight on either side of his body and she was reminded of her thoughts from that first morning in the diner, before he'd taken her on a tour through town.

This man was rugged and tough and oh so male.

And *real*.

Even as she shared in the pleasure that built between

them, Sloan couldn't stop more memories from surfacing.

Couldn't stop the day's events from playing across the back of her mind.

Along with it, her discussions with Avery and Grier came back to her in a rush and her euphoria melted with the acknowledgment that no matter how many moments she and Walker shared, the clock was ticking and this thing between them was only temporary.

He'd made no move to discuss anything more serious with her.

And what if he did?

She'd spent so much time thinking about leaving she hadn't given thought to what she'd say if he asked her to stay. To uproot her life and move to Alaska.

Would she stay?

"Sloan?"

"Hmmm?" She glanced up after pressing a kiss to the flat planes of his stomach.

"Are you okay?"

"Of course. Why?"

"You drifted away there for a minute."

With a mental head shake, she pulled herself back to the present and the sexy man who made her want . . . so many things. "I was contemplating."

"Contemplating what, sweetheart?"

"The right path." She trailed her fingers along the underside of his cock, pleased when he grew even harder in her hand.

If it were possible, Walker's dark eyes grew darker as her meaning sunk in. With a broad smile, she resumed her efforts, her trail of kisses headed straight toward her destination.

As she replaced her hands with her lips around his straining erection, Sloan felt a shudder rack his body and heard his long, loan moan of pleasure.

Would she stay?

The question rose up again to taunt her.

To tease her.

To test her?

Walker dragged her upward on a groan before rolling her over to her back and plunging his body into hers in one long, smooth stroke.

Would she stay?

As the first throes of another orgasm gripped her, Sloan knew she had her answer.

Of course she'd stay.

She loved him.

Chapter Twenty-two

The Montgomery Meeting and Recreation Center was almost unrecognizable for the copious lengths of streamers, ribbon and soft twinkle lights that filled the outer hallway with an ethereal glow.

"The grandmothers have outdone themselves," Amanda marveled as she looked around the entryway. "It's even more beautiful than last year."

The two of them *ooh*ed and *aah*ed their way toward the registration table and Sloan was grateful for the company. She'd run into Amanda as they were both leaving the Indigo Blue and they'd walked over together, both laughing at their heavy winter boots and cocktail dresses as they'd trekked up Main Street.

Grier had sent a perky text about fifteen minutes before they were set to leave, suggesting Sloan head on over without her.

She'd immediately interpreted the subtext as "I'm not yet ready to talk to you but save me a seat." Which, in retrospect, she likely deserved for her earlier drubbing. The fact that it was absolutely warranted was really beside the point.

Sloan just hoped her friend was putting the extra time

to good use, donning a killer outfit for the evening that would have Mick O'Shaughnessy on his knees.

"I never expected it to—" Sloan broke off. There was that word again.

Expectation.

She hadn't expected anything that had happened to her on this trip, from the friendliness of the denizens of Indigo to the amount of fun she'd had to the amazing thing that had developed with Walker.

"Look like a fairy tale," Amanda finished for her.

"Exactly."

"I thought the same thing last year. And then I realized, it was only fitting for a town that prides itself on love."

Love.

And just like that, all her feelings from earlier came rushing back at her. Now that the afterglow of great sex had faded, Sloan could look at the situation more objectively.

And oh wow and holy shit on toast.

She was in love.

She was in the middle of the wilderness and she'd fallen head over heels in love with the town lawyer.

How was this possible?

"Are you okay?" Amanda's concerned expression pulled her from her reverie as they waited in line at the registration table, the loud thump of the base humming through the walls of the main auditorium.

"I really don't know."

"It's a bit overwhelming."

"You could say that."

"But come on; look at it." Amanda pointed to a long display of posters on the wall behind the registration desk. "Don't you have to have fun when this is your inspiration for the evening?"

Sloan suddenly realized Amanda was on a completely different wavelength and, in fact, had no clue what she was really thinking. Instead, she was focused on a row of the most outrageous pictures.

Whatever deep and desperate thoughts had gripped her had to be shelved under the visual assault of the posters. The men of Indigo—sans Walker and Mick—were all posed in a variety of places around town, wearing not much more than a thong and a smile.

"Oh. My."

"As you ladies can see"—Chooch gestured to the photos behind her as she took their money and gave them each a paddle with a number on it for the bidding process—"we have a fine selection of bachelors for your entertainment this evening. We encourage you to bid generously and please, for the love of God and all that's holy, *please*, make sure someone bets on Tasty. If I have to hear that man lament for another year that he didn't get bid on, I may kill myself."

"We'll do our best," Amanda added on a strangled gulp as she nodded in the direction of Tasty's photo.

"See that your best includes a bid, young lady," Chooch admonished before shifting her focus on the next woman to come up to the table.

"Did you see that photo?" Sloan demanded as soon as they were out of earshot of Chooch.

"See it? I think it's slightly illegal. And ewww, I'm never taking a man ice fishing if that's what it does to his body parts."

Sloan repressed a shudder, sorry the older man had gone bidless last time. She didn't mind adding him to her list, but God help her if he wanted to take her ice fishing.

They moved into the main auditorium and Sloan forgot all about Tasty and his love of the great outdoors as her breath caught at the sight. If the outer room was amazing, the large auditorium put it to shame.

"Someone told me they've been working in here for the better part of a week."

"It's amazing." Everywhere Sloan looked, something awe-inspiring captured her attention.

"Speaking of amazing, I want to go check out the auction table."

"Make sure you get your bid in early?"

"More like I want to see who may be my competition," Amanda said on a wink. "See you later."

Sloan headed the opposite direction, intrigued by the series of ice sculptures that ran the length of the far wall. As she got closer, she saw they all depicted scenes from famous love stories.

Cinderella looked over her shoulder as she ran from the prince down a flight of stairs, her shoe nestled in his outstretched hand.

Sleeping Beauty lay in slumber as a handsome man leaned over to her, his mouth inches from hers.

Juliet stretched over a balcony railing with Romeo down below.

Several more complemented them in an incredible

display of some of the greatest love stories of all time. Sloan moved down the line of sculptures, enthralled with each and every one of them, when her attention was again diverted by a large arbor that stood at the far end of the auditorium.

It was the most beautiful, fragrant arch, constructed of hundreds and hundreds of roses, all woven into the metal latticework, just waiting for someone to stand under it.

Or for a couple to stand under it.

Sloan reached for one of the petals, the texture baby soft under her fingertips. On a whispered sigh, she murmured to herself, "How did they manage this? It's the middle of winter."

"We fly them in. The roses," Mary O'Shaughnessy commented. Sloan turned around, slightly embarrassed to be caught talking to herself, to greet Mick's grandmother, her small frame resplendent in a bright silver gown covered in sequins. "Well, I say *we*. My grandson does all the work. He even did a run for me today at the last minute."

"That's why he missed the competition," Sloan murmured before she could hold back the words.

Mary's sharp gaze narrowed at the comment. "Yes, he did. You noticed?"

"No, ma'am, I can't say that I did. But someone else I know certainly noticed."

The sharp blue of Mary's eyes—a perfect match in shade to her grandson's—widened in what Sloan couldn't help but think of as pleasure. "Would that someone happen to be your dear friend?"

"Why, yes it is." Sloan leaned in with a conspiratorial whisper. "If it makes you feel any better, I told her what a royal idiot she's being."

A long, low sigh escaped from Mary on her next breath. "My grandson hasn't been all that clever himself, truth be told."

"You think they'll figure it out?"

"I sure as hell hope so. I've never seen that boy so turned out over anything except an airplane."

Sloan couldn't hold back the laughter. "Maybe we'll keep that comparison to ourselves."

"That's probably wise, my dear."

"It's beautiful in here. Surely you, Julia and Sophie didn't do all this?"

A light blush suffused Mary's features and a delighted smile spread through the wrinkles of her cheeks. "We look forward to it all year long. And while we need more help than we used to, we've got a hand in most everything you see."

"You all really love this, don't you?"

"We'd love it more if it got us granddaughters-in-law."

A loud laugh rumbled up before Sloan could stop it. "I have to say, that's what I like about all of you. You're so subtle."

Mary waved a hand. "Subtlety's for the young, my girl. I'm an old woman and I need to make every minute count."

Before she could say anything else, Mary was flagged down by what appeared to be one of the caterers—one of the kids from the high school—and tottered off on her high heels to deal with it.

As she continued her walk around the room, snapping photos of whatever caught her attention, Mary's words kept echoing in her head.

I need to make every minute count.

She'd done that up here in Alaska. After marking time for what felt like forever, for the first time she was finally *living*.

And suddenly, the thought of going back home was simply stifling.

Grier stepped off the elevator and silence greeted her from the direction of the lobby.

The festivities must already be getting underway.

Even though the only people allowed into the auction were the bachelors, the bachelorettes and those helping out, the doors would open later, allowing anyone else who wanted to attend the postauction dance to show up.

Grier suspected the entire town was home getting gussied up.

Which was exactly what she needed for what she wanted to do.

It was a calculated risk as she might see someone on the street, but it was a risk she was willing to take. Besides, if she missed the entire auction, Sloan would come back to find her.

Which was small and petty of her, but damn it, she wasn't nine. She didn't need a talking to. And she certainly didn't need her past thrown in her face.

Even if Sloan had suffered through each and every degrading moment of that past right by her side.

Nope. She had to do this and it was time to make her move.

She'd thought about it for the last few weeks and any way she looked at it, she came to the same conclusion. The law was taking far too long.

With Sloan's words ringing in her ears like the after-effects of a rock concert, Grier moved out of the elevator and heard the light swish of the doors closing behind her like a punctuation mark.

She *deserved* to be first.

And since someone *had* put her first, it was time to make her move.

The lobby was so quiet she could hear the whispered murmurs of conversation floating from the office behind the check-in desk. She was convinced they could hear her pounding heart all the way back there, but no one came out—or even noticed her—as she walked out of the hotel.

Cold air whipped around her as she made her way down Main Street, crossing over several streets before she came to the intersection she needed.

Spruce.

Her father had lived on Spruce Street.

She counted the houses although it was unnecessary. The front of the house she was looking for was emblazoned in her memory from the first time she'd looked up at it a month ago.

Her father had lived here.

An imagined presence in her life until six weeks ago, he was now tangible.

He had had a life here.

And a family.

And only in death had he thought to include her in any of it.

Grier stopped in front of the house. It was a small A-frame with bright blue shutters and a curving walkway that led up to the front door.

A home.

The tears started without warning, leaving cold tracks on her cheeks that only added to the bite from the night wind.

Stomping her way through the snow up the unshoveled walkway, she reached the door and shook her boots off on the small mat in front of the door. Digging out the key she'd pilfered from Walker's desk the day before, she inserted it into the lock. With trembling hands, she turned the key.

Grier felt the tumblers give way and reached for the door handle.

And promptly screamed as one hand came down on her shoulder while another slammed over the hand she had on the doorknob.

"What the hell are you doing?"

"Me?" she screamed as she whirled around on Mick. "What the fuck are you doing sneaking up on a woman in the dark?"

"I think it's a different story when that woman is about to commit a felony," he shot back at her.

"It can't be more than a misdemeanor," she volleyed back, her racing heart shifting from the adrenaline of fear to the heavy thud of desire. Damn it, did the man bathe in pheromones?

"Who gives a fuck, Grier? It's illegal. Especially since you're not allowed to be here. And I suspect that key's not yours either."

She didn't miss the fact that he'd moved one hand on the doorframe, right next to her head. She also didn't miss how his blue eyes blazed in the ambient light that reflected from the street—the porch lights from other houses and one lone streetlamp at the end of Spruce. "Um. Well."

"Why are you here?" He reached up to brush the cold tears from her face, running the tip of his finger first across one cheek, then across the other. A shiver ran the length of her spine as need flared to life in her belly.

"You really don't know?" she whispered.

As he finished wiping the tears away, a small smile crossed his face that she couldn't help but hope was a grudging look of respect. "You actually stole the key?"

"I *borrowed* it. I was going to put it back."

"After what? After traipsing through Jonas's house when you're not supposed to be anywhere near it?"

Conviction gave her voice strength as she tried to convince him. "It's my father's house. And he willed it to me. I wanted to see the inside."

"So ask Walker to get you a tour."

"I have asked and this place is locked up tight thanks to the injunction Kate got before I was able to get up here. Besides, I figured tonight was the perfect night to do it. Everyone's attention is elsewhere and I can get in and out unnoticed." She slammed her hands on her hips as a new thought assailed her. "Speaking of which, what are you doing here and what are you doing sneaking up on me?"

"I saw you leave the hotel and I followed you."

"You could have told me you were following me."

The slight grin morphed to decidedly cocky and Grier felt her heart simply turn over.

"And miss out on watching your cute ass, Little Miss Felony?"

"That is entirely inappropriate."

Mick leaned in, his lips a hairsbreadth from her ear. "And entirely true."

"Mick—" She broke off, completely unsure of what to say. Half of her wanted to run as fast and as far as her legs would carry her.

And the other half wanted to turn toward him, press her lips to his, wrap her arms around him and never let go.

"Why did you leave?"

"Technically, you left and I cried."

"Grier. You know what I mean."

"Come on, Mick. You know what this is. Let's not pretend it's something more. Or that it can be something more." The words burned on her tongue as she said them, because she knew the truth.

Knew that what was between them was more. *A lot more*.

"Why can't it?" He leaned in and she felt her resistance take another hit as the urge to agree with him nearly knocked the breath out of her.

"You live in Alaska."

"People live lots of places. It doesn't stop them from being together."

"My life is a raging mess right now. Even my own sister"—her breath hitched on the word—"doesn't want anything to do with me."

"She'll come around."

Just like her father had? Sure, it was easy to "come around" after you were dead. No messy emotions that way. No need for explanations.

"No, Mick, she won't."

"Grier." Her name fell easily from his lips and she knew—knew with everything she was—that this man would love her in ways beyond her wildest imaginings.

So why couldn't she let him?

Before she could decide, he took the matter out of her hands. On a heavy sigh, he closed the distance, leaned in and touched his lips to hers, using his free hand to wrap tight around her shoulders and pull her close.

Growling against her lips, he whispered in a ragged voice, "God, woman, what you do to me."

Lost to him, she lifted her face to his and drank him in.

It had been less than a week since they were together, but as his lips ravaged hers, Grier had to admit it felt like a lifetime.

The kiss went on and on like an erotic dream she never wanted to wake up from.

Who knew just kissing could be so incredibly wonderful?

His lips slid over hers as his tongue pressed along the

seam. With long, lazy strokes that made her feel they had all the time in the world his tongue mated with hers. Despite the patient assault, he kept raising the stakes, driving them both toward something more.

Wanting more. Taking more. *Needing* more.

What was she doing?

Breaking into the home of her late father. Making out on his front porch with a man who lived a world away from her. Risking her heart when she had no business doing so.

Ever.

On a breathless cry, Grier broke away.

"Oh God, Mick. God." She wiped at her swollen lips, the hot prick of tears again threatening behind her eyes and tightening her throat. "I'm sorry. I'm so sorry. But I can't do this."

The confusion in his gaze gave her the opening she needed to put distance between them.

And the moment she had enough distance not to give in and let him wrap her up in his arms, she ran.

Walker chaffed at the ridiculous rules the grandmothers had instituted for the bachelor auction. Obviously, he'd been a fool to think they'd let him ride roughshod over their event, but this was taking things too far.

When he'd complained about it, he got a sweet pat on the cheek from his grandmother and a hearty, "You've had all day to check out the bachelorettes. It's their turn to do some ogling."

He'd refrained from bitching about the fact that there was only one bachelorette he was interested in seeing—

he couldn't quite bring himself to so readily admit defeat to Sophie Montgomery.

Even if he was so far gone there was little hope for him.

He knew he'd been falling since the moment he'd laid eyes on her at the town hall, but their postcompetition romp had sealed it. He couldn't deny it any longer.

He was in love with Sloan McKinley.

And it was nothing like what he'd expected.

"Tommy and Chuck are organizing a jail break." Roman's voice intruded on his musings and he turned to stare at his old friend.

"You all right?"

"Yeah. Sure." Walker took a long pull on his beer. "Why wouldn't I be?"

"I don't know. You had this faraway look in your eyes. The sort of look guys get when they've taken a hard check that lands them on their head on the ice."

"I don't see a rink."

"Figure of speech, buddy."

"Whatever. I'm fine."

Walker glanced around the room. He, Roman and the rest of the bachelors had been closeted in a small meeting room in the back of the auditorium, hidden from view of the bachelorettes.

At least they had beer, mini-hot dog hors d'oeuvres wrapped in puff pastry and a big-screen TV broadcasting football.

"The grandmothers think of everything," Roman said around a mouthful of food. "They are seasoned women of the world who understand that cocktail weenies really do tame the restless beast."

"You have a point."

"Of course, I suspect that's also what the cow thinks when they load him into the chute and take him to slaughter."

"Cheerful thought." And one he'd have shared a mere two weeks ago.

Before everything had changed.

And if he didn't do something about it soon, Sloan was going to keep her plans to head home at midweek and he'd never see her again.

"Fuck it," Walker muttered, setting his beer on the counter that held their appetizer feast. He'd wasted enough time by not admitting the truth to Sloan.

"Where are you going?" Roman had another beer in his hand, already extended in his direction.

Unable to keep the broad grin from splitting his face, he waved off the fresh drink. "Climbing into the chute, buddy."

Without waiting for an answer, Walker ducked out of the room, grateful his grandmother at least had enough sense not to violate fire codes and actually lock them all in the room.

On swift feet, he took the long way around the make-shift stage that had been set up at the far end of the auditorium. Following the path of glowing twinkle lights around the edge of the room, he nearly barreled into his grandmother.

"Grandma!" He grasped her arms while he held both of them upright. "What are you doing back here?"

"I'm hanging out behind the scenes a bit."

"But back here?"

What *was* she doing back here? This was even too far out of the way for the bachelors to wait to take their turns onstage.

"Are you okay?"

He spotted a set of folding chairs propped against the wall, reached for one and quickly opened it, then turned back to her. Careful to keep his hand on her arm, he drew her toward the chair. "Come on and sit down here for a minute."

Once he got her settled, she reached for him. "Get a seat for yourself."

"I'm fine. Do you want anything? I can get you some water."

"No, no. Just grab a seat my dear."

Reaching for her hand, he sat there with her, waiting to get her whatever she needed. His impression from earlier in the day—that something really was wrong—rose up to haunt him again.

"Grandmother? Are you feeling sick?"

"No, no, dear." She patted his arm. "Nothing like that."

As they sat there in silence, mingled sounds swirled around them from the other side of the stage. The women were doing their level best to outshout each other and, when added to the booming loudspeaker, the room was operating at a dull roar.

"I'm glad you're not sick, but are you going to tell me what's gotten into you all of a sudden? It's the crowning moment of your day and you look like the sky's falling."

"Aren't I entitled to a sad moment now and again?"

"Of course. But what's gotten in to you today? You look forward to this all year."

"The same thing Mary and Julia are sad about."

Walker prayed for patience as he took in the clearly miserable set of his grandmother's face. Even her shoulders were visibly slumped through the bright fabric of her evening gown. "All three of you are upset? Did something happen?"

"Only that our grandsons have finally found love and they're all too blind to see it."

He nearly fell off the chair as he took in her words.

How did she know?

And Mick and Roman, too?

"Grandmother. What are you talking about?"

"You and Sloan. Mick and Grier. And Roman and Avery, although those two are so damned stubborn Julia knows she'll be well and gone before those two figure themselves out. If they ever do. And now those women are going to go home and we're far too afraid you're going to let them. And well, as I said, Julia's got a whole other set of worries about Roman."

It was the same thought he'd had as he stomped out of the bachelor cave. And as much as he wanted to reassure his grandmother, he had to speak to Sloan first.

She had a right to know. Even if his grandmother had been waiting for this moment since the day he came into the world, the woman he loved deserved to hear the news first.

He had to get to Sloan.

"Look—"

She held up a hand to cut him off. "If you could only understand where we're coming from. Where *I'm* coming from."

What had gotten in to her? "Grandmother. If you'd just wait a bit."

"I don't have time to wait, Walker." She gripped his arm again. "We all see it happening and I just can't keep quiet on this."

"Look. For the record, I could give a rat's ass about Mary and Julia and Mick and Roman. I'm talking to you. And while I appreciate your concern, I'm a grown man. And I need you to trust that I know what I'm doing."

"But it's all slipping away. Don't you see that?"

Walker was about to protest when her next words stopped him cold.

"It's just like your father."

Ice filled his veins, running cold fingers down his spine before settling low in his gut. "What about my father?"

"Don't let him stand in the way of your happiness. That woman is the answer. She's what you've been searching for, Walker."

"What about my father?"

"I know all of it, Walker." At what must have been an incredulous stare, she added, "I've known for a very long time."

This wasn't possible.

It just was *not* possible.

He'd been so careful. Had carried the secret for so fucking long. How could she possibly know?

"But how?"

"He's my son. And I love him, no matter how awful his behavior. And you of all people know there are no secrets in this town."

"But they've kept it from you. They didn't want to upset you."

"Then your father shouldn't have taken up with every light skirt he could find in Anchorage, Fairbanks and Juneau and every small town in between."

Walker fought the urge to drop his head into his hands as he tried desperately to process his grandmother's words through the shouting and merriment echoing toward him from the other side of the stage.

Everything he thought he knew was yet again turned on its ear.

He'd lived with the lies for so long—and the very person he'd thought to protect had known all along. She'd known he was keeping a secret from her and she'd never said anything.

Was anything real?

Anything at all?

Chapter Twenty-three

Sloan glanced around the now crowded dance floor and tried to stem her confusion. Most of the town was gathered in the ballroom, dancing and having a great time, but she couldn't get into any of it.

Where was Walker?

She'd sat through the entire auction, not surprised as bachelor after bachelor came up with no sign of him. With all the fuss Sophie, Julia and Mary had made about getting two of the three grandsons on the auction block, she had every expectation they'd go last.

But the auction had been over for thirty minutes and Walker was nowhere to be found.

She didn't want to be clingy. She would *not* be clingy. She hated clingy.

But where was he?

Catching sight of Roman, she made eye contact and waved him over, surprised at how quickly he extricated himself from the woman he was in conversation with. He leaned in and pressed his lips to her cheek in a gallant kiss. "I could kiss your feet right now. Thank you."

"It looks like the viper from Chicago was giving you a run for your money."

"You're not kidding. That woman could give a whole parking lot full of rink bunnies a run for their money."

"Ewww." Sloan held up a hand.

"I'm just kidding. I'm not nearly as indiscriminate as the tabloids would have you believe. I have absolutely no idea how a parking lot of women would behave."

She couldn't resist his infectious smile and despite her anxiousness at finding out where Walker had gone, also couldn't resist a small dig on Avery's behalf. "Self-diagnosis, Doctor?"

"Self-preservation, more like it."

Her gaze roamed the room on the off chance she had somehow missed Walker and wouldn't have to lower herself to asking after him.

And when another head count around the room turned up no sign of him, she bit the bullet. "Have you seen Walker?"

"Yeah. It's been a while, though. He was backstage for the auction and then ended up leaving as we were waiting."

"He just left?"

"Yeah. Said something about a bull chute."

"I'm sorry?"

The grin got even wider. "Sorry. Inside joke."

"Okay. Well, if he was there before, do you know where he headed off to?"

"Come to think of it, no."

"If you see him, let him know I headed back to the hotel."

"Will do."

Sloan had already turned to walk away when Roman

stopped her with a tap on the shoulder. Turning back to face him, she was intrigued by the lines furrowing his brow and the tight set of his mouth. "Can I tell you something?"

"Of course."

"It's not one-sided."

Sloan ran through the appropriate responses, from playing dumb to genuine outrage on behalf of her friend. In the end, she settled for simple. "Oh?"

"It's not. I mean, it's more me than her, but it's not all me." He ran a hand through his hair, no evidence of the carefree smile he'd just sported anywhere near his face. "Look. After a while, it's hard to keep coming back when all you get is your past thrown in your face. That's all I wanted to say."

She knew what it was to have your past haunt you repeatedly and for the first time, she actually felt a small measure of sympathy for Roman Forsyth. "That's the first thing you've said that makes me think you're sort of human instead of some hockey god."

The smile was back in full force. "Well, I'm a hockey god, too."

"How could I forget?"

She turned around to leave and realized she had one more thing to say. "You know, sometimes the only way to forget your past is to change your future."

"Yeah. But you have to want to change."

On a shrug, she had to admit he had a point. "I guess you're right. Still, I remain forever amazed that it's often the easiest answers that are the hardest."

Five minutes later she entered the Indigo's lobby

wrapped again in her fuzzy boots, her strappy heels dangling from her hand, her own words ringing in her ears.

Simple answers, hard decisions.

That fit her situation with Walker to a T. And maybe it was time to level with him and *tell* him that.

If she could find him.

Mingled voices rumbled through the lobby as she moved toward the elevators. It looked like a few bachelor/bachelorette combinations were on their way to getting to know each other better. She'd seen several heated glances during the bidding and had high hopes for all of them that things would work out.

And wouldn't that be a lovely ending to her story.

She caught sight of another bachelor in a tuxedo and Sloan imagined what Walker would have looked like had he made it up on the auction stage. She'd had it on good authority from Avery that he was wearing a tux and she had no doubt the man would look damn fine in black and white.

So where was he?

Stabbing the CALL button, she had to admonish herself.

Oh, who was she kidding?

The man looked damn fine all the time, regardless of the attire. Or lack thereof, she couldn't help adding to herself, as the cat-n-cream smile spread across her face.

Stepping from the elevator, she dug into her purse for her keycard and dipped the plastic into the reader. The door swung open and she immediately caught sight of a large form, sprawled on the bed in the muted light coming from a blaring TV. A moment of panic assailed her before recognition dawned.

"Walker?"

A heavy groan reached her from the direction of the bed.

The initial shock of fear evaporated as a different sort of fear replaced it.

What was wrong with him?

And what was he doing in her room? Groaning from the bed?

"Walker. What's wrong?" The stench of liquor hit her halfway across the room and the reality of why he was sprawled on the bed and not at the auction hit her. Is this what he'd been doing?

Getting drunk in her room?

"What is the matter with you?"

He rolled onto his back. "About four glasses of whiskey, I think."

She snapped on a light and saw him wince from the sudden brightness. "Why?"

"I was trying to forget. But fuck it all, it didn't work. Maybe I should have more, but it's like each glass makes it easier to think. Easier to feel."

He still wore his heavy parka and she tugged on his arm to pull him to a sitting position. Slipping off the heavy coat, she managed to get him out of one arm before he flopped back against the pillows.

She was right about the tux, at least. Underneath the heavy winter coat, he was dressed head to toe in black and white and the jacket tangled around his back and shoulder. Dragging on the lapel, she tried to pull up the material to fit to his frame.

"Come on. Help me here, would you?"

Recognizing a losing battle with the sleeve, she pushed at him, trying to force him to roll to the side she'd already removed from the coat when his hand snaked out and wrapped around her stomach. A loud ripping noise rent the air as the force of his movement stretched the ill-fitted tuxedo coat. "Hey, baby."

"Don't hey, baby me. You're drunk and semi–passed out and I want to know why. You didn't even come out for the auction, which you promised your grandmother you'd do."

"I did, too."

"So how'd you end up here?" With another push she managed to dislodge him so that he rolled enough to let her grab the other sleeve and pull the coat free.

He sighed loudly and pulled up the now shredded sleeve. "That's good. It's hot in here."

"I'd imagine so based on the layers of clothing you're wearing." She tossed the parka over one of the chairs in the sitting area and reached for a bottle of water, unscrewing the cap. "Here. Drink this."

He struggled up again and gulped down half the bottle. The bowtie was untied at his throat and damn, if the hanging ends of the tie didn't look like a fantasy straight out of a men's magazine.

Forcing her hormones in line, she switched her gaze on the depleting water bottle. She kept watch on him as he drank and didn't miss the unfocused gaze or the slight swaying of his shoulders as he gulped down the water. "That's good."

"Finish it up and I'll get you another one."

She headed for the small dressing area outside the

bathroom where the maid service restocked everything and grabbed another water. His eyes were less glazed as she handed him the second bottle and she was pleased to see he looked steadier.

"Now. You want to tell me why you're up here in my room getting drunk instead of down at the auction and dance with the rest of the town?"

"You can thank my grandmother for that."

"Walker. Come on and cut the riddles. What happened?"

"According to my grandmother, I'm in love. But I'm too fuckwit stupid to do anything about it because of my father. Or he's the fuckwit." Walker rubbed his forehead. "I'm a bit fuzzy on that. But it's all because of him that I can't seem to close the deal on love, and my grandmother's known all along and she's sad and miserable and she lied to me."

Sloan wasn't sure what to make of his impassioned speech and she couldn't quite bring herself to ask him if he was actually in love with her so she focused on the last part.

"What do you mean she lied to you?"

"She's known about my father. All along, basically. She's known the truth."

"Maybe she was trying to protect you."

"Or him. Or, hell, I don't know."

"Does it really matter?" Her voice was quiet as she tried to puzzle through what he must be feeling. Tried to justify his drunken behavior by reminding herself he'd received a large emotional blow. He was struggling to come to grips with it even as her own heart was breaking as they casually discussed what was between them.

Or not between them.

His dark eyebrows narrowed over his slightly unfocused brown gaze. "Does what matter?"

"Your father. Your grandmother. Any of what's come before?"

"Of course it matters." The angry notes of his voice floated over her, but they were noticeably less slurred than when she'd first walked in.

"But why? Can you explain that to me? Because honestly, I really don't see how it affects you. Or what's between us."

"There's nothing between us."

She leaped off the bed at that, whirling on him and his callous words. "You can honestly sit there, look me in the eye and tell me you believe that?"

With a wave of his hand, he gestured her back to the bed. "I didn't mean it the way it came out."

"Okay. So explain it to me."

"I meant . . ." His voice faltered as he stopped and gathered himself. "Aww, Sloan. Come on. Don't look at me like that. What I meant is that you and I have had a wonderful time, but you don't live here."

"If this is you digging out of a hole, you need to find another shovel."

"What? It's not like you'd consider staying, right?"

The tables turned so swiftly she had to stop herself from the reply that sprang to her lips, unbidden.

Yes. Always and forever. As long as you want me.

"I'm not playing this game with you. And you haven't answered my question. I want to know why you think your father's infidelity has anything to do with you."

"It doesn't have anything to do with me. Not directly. But at the same time it's all about me. About how I was raised and what he passed on to me."

Sloan threw up her hands, not sure if she was dealing with the residual effects of the whiskey or the residual effects of almost two decades of hurt.

Or both.

"That's bullshit, Walker. It's all about what you choose to make of your life."

"And what if I hurt you? Like he hurt my mother."

"You wouldn't do that."

"I never thought he would, either. But he did. And does. Every day he lives a lie."

She had no idea how to handle his resistance. No clue how to make him see reason. So she did the only thing she *did* know how to do.

"I can't speak for you, Walker. I don't know what drives you or what experiences you've lived through that have brought you to today. I can guess and I can piece things together, but I really don't know. All I know is what's inside of me."

And in that moment, she saw *it*. It flared to life in the depths of his gaze as he leaned forward slightly and reached for her hand. It was a tiny spark, but it gave her the smallest moment of hope there may actually be something real between them. It was buried deep and he was fighting it, but it was there.

She'd bet her future on it.

He pressed his lips to the back of her hand. "There's so much inside of you. So much good. So much that's wonderful."

"Then why are you fighting it?"

"Because I can't change who I am. And what if all the love in the world can't fix that?"

"Oh, Walker." She tugged her hand from his grip and stood to cross the room. "Do you want to know about change? When I came up here I was a different person. I saw the world in a different way and I had expectations about people that I no longer have."

Sloan paused for a moment and knew if she was ever going to go for broke, this was the moment.

"I had expectations about myself I no longer have."

When he didn't say anything, she pressed on. "I've been here less than two weeks and I can feel the changes. The change in me and the changes I've chosen to make. Or would make if you weren't such a—" she broke off, looking for his word.

"—a fuckwit," he supplied helpfully.

"Yes. A fuckwit."

"I'm not worth it."

The sad part was that Walker Montgomery was the most worth it man she'd ever met. He was beyond worth it to her. Flaws and all.

"I can't fix that for you. You have to find it yourself. But suffice it to say, I don't agree with you."

She reached for her discarded purse and coat where she'd dropped them on the way in.

"Where are you going?"

"You can sleep off your drunken stupor here. I'll go sleep in Avery's room."

"Sloan—" He broke off and didn't say anything more.

She moved across the room and the longing in his

voice caught her at the knees when he spoke next. "What do you want?"

Unbidden, she remembered her first impression of Amanda earlier that day. The bright, vibrant woman with the ready smile and an ocean of hope in her heart.

She used to be that way and somewhere along the journey she'd lost it. Now she could admit she had lost the hope and the belief that went with it that somewhere there was someone special out there for her.

It was time to get it back.

"I want love, Walker. I want someone who puts me first and who I can do the same for. I want someone who wants to be with me for a lifetime, sharing all its ups and downs. I want someone who will take the risk to be with me."

"It's not that simple, Sloan."

"Actually it is. I want to stop blowing my horn on New Year's Eve."

At his thoroughly puzzled expression, she stepped forward, reached up and laid her lips against his. He lifted his hands to pull her close, but she backed away before he could wrap his arms around her.

"I want to start each year with a kiss and I want to spend each and every day of each and every one of those years kissing the man I love. I'm sorry that man won't be you."

It was long moments later, after Avery had opened her door and gestured her toward the spare room.

After Sloan had dressed in an old pair of thermal pajamas and snuggled down in Avery's spare room bed.

After the lights were off and each passing minute

took her farther and farther away from Walker that Sloan finally allowed the tears to fall.

Walker abstractly heard one of the studs from his tuxedo hit the hardwood floor, but couldn't muster up enough interest to look for it.

How could he have been so stupid?

Struggling to sit up on his couch, he took stock of the previous evening. A quick catalog of his raging headache and increasingly uncomfortable feet where they were still poured into dress shoes offered a few clues.

But it was the knowledge that he'd let Sloan walk out that confirmed what an ass he'd been.

Toeing off the shoes, he padded in his socks to the kitchen to start coffee and figure out a game plan. He might have spent half of his thirty-six years acting like a noncommittal jerk when it came to women, but it didn't take a two-by-four to the head—or a wicked hangover—to convince him of the truth.

In all his adult life, he'd never met a woman like Sloan.

As the smell of coffee reached him, offering the promise of relief, he started to hatch a plan.

He might not deserve Sloan McKinley, but he'd be damned if he'd let that fact stand in his way.

Sloan focused on making all the arrangements to leave Indigo ahead of schedule. She had phone numbers for everyone she'd met and could finish up whatever interviews weren't yet complete. But it was time to go home.

In exactly one hour, Jack Rafferty would be waiting

for her in the lobby of the Indigo Blue to fly her to Anchorage.

Grier and Avery had understood her decision fully as they spent all day Sunday commiserating and lying around Avery's room watching bad TV. Beyond the two of them, no one else needed to know of her change in plans.

She'd send fruit baskets to Mary, Julia and Sophie with a nice apology as to how she needed to get home. And if they read between the lines and recognized her actions for what they were—escape—well, so be it.

The town was quiet as she trudged down Main Street, the day gloomy and dreary and full of the winter doldrums.

An exact match for her mood.

The lights of the diner beckoned, a warm beacon in that unique twilight that was late morning in Alaska. She briefly contemplated pancakes, but ultimately passed on the idea when she realized there were enough people in the diner that she'd be forced to make conversation. So she trudged on, walking determinedly toward her destination.

As she got closer to it, Sloan tried to consider the love monument at the edge of town with some degree of objectivity.

It was a large statue—nothing more, nothing less.

And yet it *was* more.

It was a symbol. A symbol for a belief and for a way of life. A symbol that said there were some things in life that simply meant more.

Were worth more.

That there were some things that were worth fighting for.

Kneeling down at the base of the monument, she pulled the ugly hat out of her pocket that she wore the day of the snowball fight. The first day she and Walker had made love.

The ugly hat and its corresponding label—TASTY'S BAIT AND TACKLE—brought a soft smile to her face as she ran her hands over the embroidery.

And with it the memory that in this god-awful ugly hat, Walker had thought she was beautiful.

Folding it so that the embroidery was visible, she laid the hat in front of the monument, below the inscription that had spoken to her from the first moment she'd read it.

For those we aren't allowed to keep.

Standing, she turned around and walked back down Main Street toward the waiting lights of the Indigo Blue.

Myrtle greeted Walker as he let himself into the office. "'Bout time you got in."

"It's eight o'clock, Myrtle. You're never here this early."

"I'm here today. And I expect my boss to beat me to work."

Unwilling to be baited by her incessant logic and endless harping, he walked into his office and slammed the door. It was rude and uncalled for, but if she didn't already know why he was in a foul mood, it was only a matter of time.

The town grapevine was no doubt already ablaze

about a bachelor and bachelorette who were not present at Saturday-night's auction.

At a light knock on the door he hollered out a surly, "What!"

"Here's some coffee for you." Myrtle held out a steaming mug of dark, black coffee. "I made it just the way you like it. With about four teaspoons of sugar."

"Thanks."

She walked over with her hand extended and he had the insane urge to check and see if the contents on his desk had rearranged themselves at the spawn of Satan's sudden act of kindness.

"You're welcome."

She marched back to the doorway, her expression thoughtful. As she pulled the door closed behind her, she turned to offer one last comment. "Rumor has it Sloan McKinley's chartered a flight with Jack that leaves in about an hour. You can sit there and wallow or you can do something about it."

Sloan was leaving?

For as horrible as Saturday evening was, he had been sure he could figure a way out of this.

Could find a way to make things right between them.

He just needed some time with her. And a plan to make her listen to reason.

"That can't be possible. Jack would have told me."

Myrtle shrugged. "Facts are facts."

"Is that supposed to be some sort of advice?" Walker bit out the words.

"If I'm giving advice, you'll know it. Like now. I suggest you either get your head out of your ass and do something about stopping that plane from leaving or shut the fuck up and let the most wonderful thing that's ever happened to you walk out of your life."

He choked on his mouthful of coffee as her last words registered.

"Nod once if you understand me."

He nodded once.

Sloan clicked off her cell phone with shaking hands. Her editor had loved the notes she'd e-mailed and was anxiously awaiting the final piece. They even had a name all picked out for it—The Bachelor Game—and they were already brainstorming titles for her next article due in a few weeks.

And then Serena had hit her with the really big news.

If she wanted it, there was an editorial job waiting for her, managing one of the travel magazine's sections both in print and in all their various digital formats. In addition to her overall ownership of the section, they were willing to send her around the world for articles and they'd offered a very generous salary to boot.

The brass ring.

She'd been reaching for it for so long—working with determination and diligence—it was so strange to think that it had finally arrived.

So why did it feel far emptier than she'd ever imagined?

Sloan collapsed back on the bed and eyed her suitcases sitting near the door. Her heavy down coat lay on top and the sight brought a well of tears she couldn't hold back.

Had it really been no more than a week ago when she bought that coat in Sandy's store?

How had everything she'd known—the very foundation of her life—changed so quickly?

A knock on the door pulled her from her misery and she swiped at the tears. What had happened to that resolution she'd made to herself? The one that convinced her to leave Walker.

To be hopeful and happy and ready to embrace what the world had to offer?

"In the new year," she promised herself on a whisper as she moved to open the door. "In the new year."

"I need your help." Walker burst into his grandmother's office and barely caught the door from slamming on its hinges.

"What's wrong?" Sophie stared up from behind her desk, worry lining her eyes and weighing on her like a heavy blanket.

"It's Sloan. She's leaving."

"I know."

Walker ran a hand through his hair and tugged hard on the ends. "If you know, why didn't you tell me instead of Myrtle?"

"I'm done interfering."

"Well, it's terrible timing. I need you to do it one more time."

"What's gotten into you?"

"Love, Grandmother. It's smacked me upside the head and it won't let me go."

The worry seemed to lift from her shoulders as she

stood to her full height behind the desk. "What can I do?"

"Sloan, I'm sorry but we need to make a little detour."

"Oh, okay." Sloan looked up from where she was organizing the airline tickets she'd printed off in the Indigo's business center. Her eyes were still wet from crying with Avery and Grier as she hugged them good-bye and a few extra minutes to pull herself together was likely a good thing.

"Don't worry. I'll get you to Anchorage in plenty of time."

She offered Jack a small smile. "I'm not worried."

He started up the truck and pulled onto Main Street, driving through the center of town. Sloan kept her attention diverted, fumbling in her tote bag for her phone to keep busy. She didn't want to look out the windows for fear of seeing Walker.

"This will only take a minute."

She never looked up from her phone. "Take whatever time you need."

Walker held the banner in his hands, the heavy vinyl rolled up tight. He'd seen it in his grandmother's office and had suddenly known exactly what he needed to do.

Crossing the small space between the sidewalk and the monument, he pulled a length of rope out of his pocket to secure the banner. As he crunched on the snow, his attention caught on something wedged against the monument.

Setting the banner down, he started to reach out and

realized it was someone's hat. He almost left it where it lay before his gaze caught on the embroidery on the front.

TASTY'S BAIT AND TACKLE

And he knew.

Sloan had left it there.

Reaching down, he noticed where she'd placed the hat. Just beneath the inscription that had made her cry.

For those we aren't allowed to keep.

Like the flip of a switch, Walker saw his entire life illuminated. He blinked a few times, slightly disoriented, but with each passing second, things came into clearer focus.

He'd been the worst kind of idiot.

But if he were lucky, the woman he loved would forgive him anyway.

With renewed purpose, he unrolled the banner.

"Here. Let me help you with that." Bear walked up, his arm extended to grab the side Walker was unrolling.

"Thanks, man."

"I'll help you tie it down." Skate walked up behind Bear and offered a hand.

As Walker looked up, he saw the rest of the townsfolk walking toward them, his grandmother right in front, leading the charge. When she got close enough to stand beside him, he leaned down to give her a hug and whispered in her ear, "What is this?"

"A grand gesture, my darling. If you're going to eat crow, you might as well eat a very public portion."

Walker crushed his grandmother to him in a bear hug and knew then and there that everything he needed to know about how to love someone had come from the extraordinary woman in his arms.

Everything.

"Sloan?"

"Yes, Jack?"

"Um, it looks like Main Street's blocked."

"What?" Sloan reluctantly pulled her gaze from her phone and was surprised to see what appeared to be the entire town gathered on the street. "Is that the monument?"

"Yep."

"What's everyone doing here?"

"I don't know. Let's go check."

"Jack. Wait—"

Before she could stop him, he was out of the car and heading for her side to open her door.

"Oh, I don't think we need to—"

"Come on. Let's go find out what it is. I hope it's not one of the grandmothers."

At the idea something could be wrong with Sophie, Mary or Julia, Sloan took his hand as he helped her out of his truck.

Please no, she prayed as they worked their way through the crowd. *No, no, no*.

The crowd parted, which was odd, but she didn't pay a whole lot of attention in her rush to get to the front.

And that's when she saw it.

And him.

Walker stood under the monument, twisting her ugly hat in his hands as a heavy banner hung behind him.

Nearly all the words were scratched out in black marker with new ones written above it to take their place.

WALKER MONTGOMERY ~~INDIGO WELCOMES~~ LOVES ~~ALL OUR FUN-LOVING BACHELORETTES~~. SLOAN MCKINLEY, ~~WE'RE HAPPY TO HAVE~~ WILL YOU BE MINE FOREVER?

She froze in place as she seemed to lose control of her limbs.

"Walker?" She couldn't stop looking from his face to the words behind him.

"It's all I had on short notice."

Sloan stared up at him, her red-rimmed eyes dewy and wet.

Several things ran through his head as he looked at her and Walker wanted to give voice to them all, but no words came out.

All he could do was drink her in. And then he realized there were only a precious few words that mattered.

"I love you, Sloan."

Tears filled her eyes, but he kept on.

"I love you. I know I've been the worst kind of asshole and I don't blame you if you never want to see me again, but . . . even if you don't want to see me ever again, I'm not giving you a choice. I want to be with you. In New York. In Indigo. Somewhere in between. I really don't care where. As long as we're together."

"Walker."

"We're not giving you a choice either, Miz Sloan," Bear chimed in before she could say anything else.

A resounding chorus of "no way's" echoed Bear's words.

Walker saw his grandmother move forward to stand next to him and watched as she laid her hand on Sloan's arm. "As mayor of this town, I'd like to formally address my constituents' plea."

"You would?" Sloan couldn't seem to hold the smile back any longer.

"Yes, dear, I would. You're one of us now. And we don't like to let go of our own. You belong here in Indigo."

"Well, then. How can I resist?" Sloan moved into his arms and stepped up on her tiptoes, wrapping her arms around his neck. His hands immediately went to her hips, drawing her even closer, the feeling of finally having her in his grasp the last proof he needed to know he was really home.

"Walker. You can spend the rest of our lives making everything up to me. But for now"—she pressed her lips to his—"shut up and kiss me."

He didn't need to be told twice.

Epilogue

Walker reveled in how good it felt to have Sloan in his arms as they lay curled on her overstuffed couch. They'd been in New York for the holidays and he'd willingly made the rounds through Westchester with her to visit family and friends.

But he'd put his foot down for New Year's Eve.

This night was all theirs.

They'd run through hundreds of ideas for how to ring in the new year, and had ultimately settled on eating Chinese food and watching TV in her living room.

Walker couldn't remember when he'd enjoyed a New Year's Eve more.

He leaned down and pressed a kiss to her neck, pleased at the way she arched into him. The moments they'd spent together—getting to know each other, learning each other's intricacies—were more precious to him than he'd ever thought possible.

"Walker," she whispered as she snuggled down against him.

"Hmmm?"

"What's in that bag?"

"What?" He glanced down at her, confused as to what she was talking about.

"The bag. The plastic one over there that you set down on the counter this morning after you picked up bagels."

As his eyes alighted on the bag, he couldn't believe he'd forgotten. "Hang on. I'll show you."

He disentangled himself from her, but not before possessing her mouth in a searing kiss. The dark cherry flavor of the wine they'd enjoyed with dinner mingled with a taste that was exclusively Sloan and he knew he'd never get enough of her. Abstractly, he wondered why he'd ever worried about it.

Crossing the room, he reached for the bag and came back to kneel in front of her.

"I was thinking about something you said. Before you left my sorry ass in your hotel room." He reached into the bag and pulled out a package of New Year's Eve party horns.

"The horns." Her bright blue eyes widened in understanding as a small smile played around the edges of her mouth.

"I almost forgot them and here it is about ready to hit midnight."

Ripping open the package, he handed her one horn before grabbing one of his own. Together, they watched the seconds drop on the clock as the new year drew closer.

"Ten! Nine! Eight!" They counted off the seconds, hands entwined, and in that moment he knew he'd never looked more forward to the start of a new year.

"Three! Two! One!" they shouted in unison.

As the screams of happy revelers and bleating horns

echoed from the TV, their horns fell discarded to the ground.

Walker wrapped his arms around Sloan and sealed the new year—and their love—with a kiss. A variety of emotions burst in his chest as their mouths met.

Promise and passion.

Unity and forgiveness.

Commitment and consideration.

And underneath it all there was love.

It was the taste of forever. And Walker couldn't wait to get started.

Ready for another visit to Indigo, Alaska?
Read on for a peek at the next book in
the Alaskan Nights series,

Come Fly with Me

Available from Signet Eclipse
in November 2012.

*G*rier Thompson lined up the champagne flutes in neat, even rows. Her CPA's heart gloried in the precise organization and order to be found in the small attention to detail. By her calculation, it would take about three and a half bottles of bubbly to fill all the flutes to properly ring in the new year.

The sounds of her mother's annual New Year's Eve bash swelled from the other side of the swinging kitchen door as she poured glass after glass, but the happy laughter only pushed her further into her own gloomy thoughts. She'd believed coming home to New York for the holidays would be just the thing to shake her out of the doldrums, but unlike her accurate champagne estimate, she'd sorely miscalculated this trip.

Without warning, images of the previous New Year's Eve assailed her. She'd attended the same party and smiled and laughed with all the people she'd known for years, a bright diamond sparkling on her left hand and a smart, handsome fiancé by her side.

God, so much had changed in the ensuing twelve months.

The fiancé she'd looked forward to marrying was no longer a part of her life.

The firm she'd excelled at had abandoned her without so much as a good-bye.

And the father who'd ignored her for her entire life had come calling in the form of a contested inheritance in the far-flung reaches of Alaska.

"And now you've got an annoying case of self-pity to boot," she mumbled to herself as she reached for a glass. "Which is about as appealing as an infection."

"What did you say, darling?" The door swung open to reveal her mother's oldest and dearest friend, Monica, as she floated into the kitchen, a surprisingly bright swath of feathers adorning the crown of her head. "I heard you talking to someone about a rather unpleasant matter."

Grier almost choked on her sip of champagne as she glanced quickly around the kitchen looking for inspiration. "Oh, it's nothing." Her eyes alighted on one of the bottles. "Just muttering about that last cork. What a *beast* it was."

"Of course, darling." Monica's bright blue gaze was sharp and radiated understanding, but she said nothing more as she reached for a large tray stacked on the far counter. "I thought you could use some help with the champagne. The natives are getting restless out there."

Grier glanced at the clock and saw she had less than ten minutes to go until the new year.

Monica handed Grier one of the two trays set aside

for this specific purpose and busied herself arranging glasses. "Your mother said your friend, Sloan, was up in Alaska with you."

An image of her best friend bundled head to toe in a quilted coat made Grier smile. "It was nice to have her there for a few weeks."

"And she's getting married, too?" Monica's voice was casual, but Grier couldn't quite put her finger on something that hovered beneath the question. "To the town lawyer, right?"

"Yes, to Walker Montgomery."

"Isn't he your lawyer, too?"

Grier busied herself with her own tray, forcing Monica to ask the questions. "He is."

"How's that all going? You know your mother; she doesn't say much. I swear, since she's been rattling on about this party for a month, there just hasn't been room to talk about anything else. I've never been so glad to ring in a new year."

Do I ever know my mother, Grier thought to herself. Patrice Thompson was a piece of work. One of New York's most well-established blue bloods—"Patty-cakes" to all who knew and loved her—she wouldn't deign to discuss anything that delved beneath the surface. Or caused pain. Or even remotely indicated she and her daughter had a family secret.

"It's moving slowly."

Monica's smile was gentle when she spoke. "A side product of all that cold weather?"

The champagne flutes sat in tidy rows on her tray but Grier still fiddled with them to make the rows perfect.

"More like a half sister who doesn't want me there and who's contesting the will."

"Grier." Monica's concerned tone boiled over to something unmistakably protective as she pulled her into a hug. "I had no idea."

Grier couldn't ignore the warmth—or the comfort—that hit her even through the cool sequins of Monica's dress. "Of course not. It's not like Mom to share that sort of thing."

"Your mother is reserved, darling. You know that."

It was an oft-repeated phrase throughout her childhood and Grier couldn't help but hear it as a cop-out. *Reserved* was an excuse, a way of interacting with people that allowed a person to skip over the hard parts of life with a stoic demeanor and an unwillingness to acknowledge that anything was wrong.

A loud *ding* broke the moment as the buzzer on her phone went off. She and Monica turned at the same time to look at where it lay on the counter.

Suddenly Grier was swamped by a wave of pleasure as she read the text that had appeared on the smooth screen.

WISHING YOU A HAPPY NEW YEAR. WHEN YOU GET BACK TO INDIGO WE NEED TO PICK UP WHERE WE LEFT OFF. I'M NOT WALKING AWAY, GRIER.

A sly smile lit Monica's face and Grier knew she'd seen the message. "That's a rather bold way to wish someone a happy new year."

Grier reached for the phone and turned it facedown on the counter. "It's nothing."

Monica's smile only grew broader. "You sure about that? Because that sounds like unfinished business to me. And I've found in my lengthy observations of the males of our species, unfinished business is a rather enjoyable pastime."

"It's really nothing."

"Actually, my dear," Monica reached over and ran a hand down her back, "that blush riding high on your cheeks suggests otherwise. But I won't press you any further. I also understand the need to keep a secret or two."

When Grier didn't say anything, Monica added, "It also seems like a rather lovely way to start a new year. Text messages full of promise and, if I'm not mistaken, perhaps passion and determination."

With that, Monica picked up her tray of champagne and headed through the swinging doors and into the party. Grier reached for the phone, intent on putting it in her pocket before grabbing the tray, but she couldn't resist one more glance at the message.

I'M NOT WALKING AWAY.

Mick.

On a soft sigh, Grier followed Monica's path through the swinging doors. She couldn't quite muster up the same degree of revelry as the other partygoers, but she had to admit that her spirits were higher than when she'd walked into the kitchen to pour the champagne.

After the year she'd had, she'd barely thought herself capable of feeling anything. Yet just the thought of him—all six foot, two inches of rugged Alaskan male—

made her body quiver as anticipation hummed in her veins.

He was the one thing she missed from her stay in Indigo, and even after time away and the distance, her powerful response to him had her body growing warm and her breath catching in her chest.

A loud burst of laughter interrupted her thoughts as she lifted her champagne flute to match the other party-goers.

If she touched the phone in her pocket as the entire room screamed, "Happy New Year," well, that would be her little secret. Maybe it was time Grier Thompson, New York blue blood, acted on a bit of her reckless Alaskan roots.